Wings and Shadows
Dominika Pindor

2

To my parents. This book wouldn't be here without your credit cards.

Chapter One

I had never found the sight of blood appealing. Especially when said blood was trickling out of a wounded kitten. Horseface was dangling the furry creature above the riverbank by the scruff of its neck. The pocket knife she had used to cut into its flesh was resting on the grass, staining it red. Crimson red, like her lips, which spread into a grin that revealed an array of crooked, yellow teeth. It was the grin of a psychopath, the type you would see frequently worn by murderers on the day their mugshot was taken.

And that's exactly what Horseface was—a psychopathic killer.

From what I'd heard, she'd been prowling the streets for a little over two years. She was only eighteen—a mere teenager—and yet… she looked at least ten years older. No, that was an understatement; the girl looked close to forty. The excessive consumption of drugs and lack of hygiene were to blame.

One of the two girls standing beside her was blond. Her hair was matted in numerous places and hung over her head like a drape, making her look like a background character from one of those zombie movies you could find on sale in shabby corner stores. She was recording the scene on a worn-down cellphone, but from the way her hands shook, I doubted she was getting any clear scenes. Her name was Dania Gardner. At least, that's what the rumors told.

The other girl, a tall brunette with enough acne to conceal nearly all her facial features, spat a series of slurs at the animal. I wasn't sure why she did it. To make the video more entertaining? Maybe she just wanted to participate somehow, since her friends were doing all the work—Horseface drowning the cat, the blonde recording. I found it sickening regardless.

The blonde was careful to avoid showing any of their faces as she recorded. She focused strictly on the animal, and I knew the video would end up on the Internet after they were finished.

"What a sick way to go viral," Huma whispered, her bottom lip trembling. We were hiding behind one of the nearby trees watching the scene unfold.

"Out of all the days you could have forgotten your phone, *this* is when you forget?!" I hissed in exasperation, my eyes frantically scanning the area for any nearby adults. Huma and I certainly weren't a match for the three trolls by the river—who knew what they had armed themselves with? Leaving wasn't a solution either; they would see us in the clearing, and stories of Horseface's encounters with teens our age were far from pleasant.

The "Oakwood Park" sign glared at me from the corner of my vision as I swallowed down the bile that had risen up my throat. I wished we'd never come here. The park was only two blocks away from Huma's house, but we would have to walk across the river in order to get there. And Horseface was right next to the bridge.

I heard Huma gasp as they pulled the barely twitching body out of the water. Once she could confirm the blonde was still recording, Horseface dug the tips of her boot into the kitten's spine. Her act put the animal out of its misery, and a part of me was glad. At last, its suffering was over.

Laughter erupted throughout their group as the blonde finished filming with a close-up of the corpse, and they kicked the furry body back into the river. It was instantly taken by the current. Huma tugged at my sleeve, motioning towards the clearing—now was a perfect opportunity to run. I nodded. My eyes looked around one last time to make sure it was safe to escape.

And then my heart dropped.

Horseface was staring at us, a smirk slowly replacing the ugly look of triumph that had previously marred her face. She elbowed the brunette in the side and pointed at Huma, whose face had turned a paler shade of brown.

"Hey," she called, flicking her tongue. It had been cut into two halves, just like a lizard's. "You're that famous surgeon's daughter, eh? Khatri? Take that rag off your head. I wanna see your hair."

Huma's hands reached up protectively over her hijab and she took a step back. Her mouth contorted as she swallowed. Horseface began walking towards us, the blonde girl once again pulling out the phone to record.

"I've been wanting to get my hands on her," the brunette snarled. "Put my pa' four hundred grand in debt, that little..."

"Grab her," Horseface said.

I couldn't recall the last time Huma had been so scared. Hell, I couldn't recall the last time she had cried. Something inside of me stirred. Something that made my hands tremble. My feet took a step forward, shielding Huma, and I pierced Horseface with my gaze. I wasn't in control of my actions anymore. It was as if anger and fear had fought a battle inside of me, the former wanting me to defend my best friend, the latter wanting me to run.

And as luck would have it, anger had won.

My arms glided forward on instinct, as if they were being guided by a supernatural force. They stretched before me like they were attached to a set of strings, like I was a marionette being pulled by an inexperienced handler. My fingers were twitching. Not slightly, but violently, as if they were going to break off at any moment. There was a stream of electricity coursing through my body, pouring into and pooling up in my hands, like rivers into an ocean. I felt it seeping the warmth from my legs, my gut, my neck, leaving the rest of my body cold. I wanted it to stop. I *needed* it to stop. But it was far too late. Anger had taken control of my body and wouldn't subside until… until I allowed it to do what it wanted. My fists closed, my fingernails grinding into my skin. When they opened, they were aimed at Horceface's body.

7

I remember the moment when it hit her—she screamed, thrashed around for a moment or two, and collapsed unconscious to the ground, the weight of her body crushing the pile of sticks that had lain beneath her feet. I stumbled backward, breathing heavily. Huma, on the other hand, stood motionless, the edges of her hijab blowing in the wind as she stared at Horseface and her friends. They were staring back at us, frozen in place, their eyes wide with fear.

Taking advantage of the situation, I grabbed Huma's hand and ran.

* * *

My mother's apartment building was made of light-brown brick and located on the corner of Clark Street. The lobby had no furniture except for three worn-down chairs and a wobbly newspaper stand, and was usually empty, except for a few smokers that sometimes hung out near the exit. They were the reason the hallways always stank of cigarette smoke, but it wasn't like anyone cared. Most of the people on our floor were drug addicts anyway, so why should they have? I was glad my mother wasn't one of them.

Our apartment was small—only six hundred and fifty feet, according to the landlord—and had three rooms: two bedrooms and one bathroom. I had been ashamed of this at thirteen, maybe even fourteen, but this year I had more important matters on my mind.

Like rendering a girl unconscious without touching her.

"Answer my question, Lucianne," Huma said. She was lying on my bed, clearly uncomfortable with the number of springs that stuck out from beneath the mattress. If it had been a normal day, perhaps we'd have gone to her house, a red-brick mansion situated on Wellington, a street filled with similar red-brick mansions. Unfortunately for us, this was not a normal day. We didn't want to be heard. Huma's siblings—all three of them—were extremely nosy, and if any of them heard our conversation, they would undoubtedly tell their parents.

"I don't know," I responded. She seemed terribly eager to talk about it, now that the initial shock had worn off the both of us. "Look, if I knew how I did it, don't you think I would have told you by now?"

"True," she sighed. "I just wish there was an explanation. Whatever you did... that wasn't normal. I still get chills every time I think about it."

I shook my foot, which had fallen asleep, and grimaced at the unpleasant sensation.

"It definitely wasn't normal," I agreed, glancing down at my hands. My fingernails had been bitten to stubs.

"Should we tell someone about it?"

"No," I said quickly. "That's dangerous. Haven't you read books about situations like this? About kids with weird powers like mine? The government takes them. They will kidnap me, Huma, they will kidnap me and put me through tests, and nobody in the world will know about it. They'll find a way to cover it up. I'll become an *experiment*, an *animal*. Neither of us should say anything to anyone about what happened today. Ever."

"Sorry," she said quietly. "I won't tell anyone. Promise."

"Good. Let's not talk about it anymore. Please. It's giving me a headache."

We devoted the next five minutes to staring at the wall – the same light blue wall that remembered the days of my father. Some of the paint had long since been scraped away, and patches of stickers covered a few sections of it. I had stopped trying to rip them off long ago; every time I did, a chunk of the wall would peel away as well.

Huma glided her manicured finger across my run-down dresser, a crease forming between her eyebrows. Then, she reached into her pocket.

"Your mom's birthday is tomorrow, right?" she asked, and the subject change made me relieved. She pulled a white envelope from one of her blazer's pockets. "My mom got her a gift."

"Can I see it?"

She nodded as I took the envelope from her hands. The front read:

Happy birthday Estelle! Enjoy the gift.
- the Khatri family

I peeked inside, not surprised to see several hundred-dollar bills staring back. I gave Huma a thin smile as I pushed it back towards her.

"Haven't we had this conversation before? My mother and I don't need monetary assistance. She won't accept it. Never. We're doing fine." I had recently gotten a job at one of the fast-food restaurants down the street, so our financial situation wasn't that bad. As long as I continued working, we had no reason to worry.

Huma smiled at me. "But this isn't monetary assistance," she said. "It's a birthday gift."

"Monetary assistance *disguised* as a birthday gift," I corrected her, but couldn't help cracking a smile at the faces she was making.

Huma shrugged. "It's a birthday gift," she said. "And the mall downtown has really cute clothes. See?" she pointed to her blazer, which made her look like a model fresh off the runway. "We can go shopping sometime, with our moms. I know a lot of great stores."

I rolled my eyes. "If your goal is to make me look wealthier than I am, don't bother. The whole school knows I'm poor. Plus, I'm pretty content with everything I already have. My wardrobe is fine, same goes for my furniture. And you know how my mom feels about taking money from others."

"And you know how *my* mother feels about me not delivering her gifts." She folded her arms and leaned backwards, causing another loud creak to echo through the room.

She knew I would cave in eventually. The worsening headache was partially to blame.

"Alright," I said, far too tired to start an argument. "You can give her the 'gift,' as long as I don't have to take part in it. Deal?"

"Deal."

That settled it.

* * *

My mother found the envelope in the morning, tucked beneath the wooden fruit stand on our kitchen counter. On any other school day, she would have already been at work, and I likely wouldn't have seen her again until seven in the evening. But today was different. Today, my mother was sick. I assumed she had caught a cold from one of her fellow workers; her voice was hoarse and raspy, and a dry cough would constantly interrupt her speaking. Nonetheless, she had still chosen to wake up early in the morning with one purpose: making me breakfast.

"Tell Mrs. Khatri we don't need her money," she said once I was done eating, pressing the envelope into my hand. Like every morning, she proceeded to examine my face. As her calloused thumb brushed over my cheek, I tried to examine hers as well, but it was difficult. Her once-beautiful green eyes had lost their shine. The bags underneath them were a result of the twelve-hour shifts she worked at the factory, and her thin brown hair, the opposite of my ginger mane, was growing greyer with each day. It wasn't just because she was sick. Her worsening condition wasn't something that could be cured.

My mother's aging was inevitable, I knew, but it didn't stop the feeling of heaviness from settling over my chest.

I shut the door and walked out of the house, swallowing the lump that had grown in my throat. The envelope was left inside. I didn't have the heart to give it back.

* * *

When Huma ran up to my locker at school, she was panting.

"We have a concert next week and Mr. Hunt asked me to stay after school to practice my solo, so we won't be able to walk home together," she explained. Walking home together was something both of our mothers had agreed would keep us safe, and we had done it for as long as I could remember. "I swear, if I could change the schedule I would, but—"

"Don't worry about it," I said. "Focus on your solo; I'll be fine."

"I'll ask my dad to drive you home. He says fifteen-year-old girls shouldn't be walking home by themselves."

"No need," I replied quickly. I had always found Mr. Khatri unsettling. I didn't even know where he worked—just that it involved the government. "It's only a couple blocks away, and I won't be alone," I assured her. That part was true. Kindred High had over two thousand students, and those without cars were bound to walk.

"You sure?"

"Of course."

"Oh, and about yesterday—" She stopped mid-sentence, likely remembering our conversation from last night. "We can talk about it later, right?"

"Right," I said half-heartedly. My mind was stuck on the image of Horseface thrashing on the ground. No matter what I tried, it didn't go away.

The rest of the school day passed in a blur. My brain wouldn't stop replaying yesterday's incident, distracting me from my work. What had happened? I'd felt anger numerous times before. None as intense, of course, but anger, nonetheless. Why had this time been different? Was it the fact that the anger was directed at someone threatening my best friend? I didn't know.

What I did know, was that I was dangerous. My *power* was dangerous. And if I didn't learn how to control it, people would get hurt. The thought of that happening was enough to send chills down my spine.

12

When the bell rang, signaling the start of the final period, one of my fingers was bleeding. The white crescent of the fingernail was nonexistent.

"Lucianne Allaire?" Mrs. Sod, my global studies teacher, was taking attendance. She was a short woman with dimples and light brown hair that had always slightly resembled a bird's nest. Huma said she was lazy. I just assumed she had kids.

"Present," I said.

Since the names were being listed in alphabetical order, I had plenty of time to drowse off before Mrs. Sod was finished. But I knew that drowsing off would cause Horseface's scream to echo through my head again, and though the sound was pleasant at first, I was growing pretty damn tired of it. And it certainly wasn't helping my headache, which was still as bad as it had been yesterday.

Mrs. Sod began passing out papers. They were the results of a test we had taken two weeks ago, and I was surprised she had finished grading them that early. It normally took her a month.

"Very good job, Lucianne," she said, handing me mine. She didn't bother turning it over so the red numbers would face my desk. I had gotten a hundred. "Like always."

"Thank you, ma'am," I said, sliding the sheet of paper into my folder. I had used the same one for three years. By now, it was ripped in two places, but I had managed to keep it in pretty good condition. It wasn't bad enough to throw away.

Despite my hardest attempts, I couldn't prevent my brain from shutting off mid-class. It made my headache even worse, and I was beyond joyful at the harsh ring of the final bell.

Since a large portion of the students at Kindred High participated in extracurricular activities at this time of the year (it was late September), the school grounds seemed exceptionally empty. Not to say there weren't a lot of students on the blacktop. A group of boys were playing basketball by the hoops, and several others were milling around, watching the game. Clusters of kids were heading down the road I normally took to my apartment building, so I followed them.

When I turned onto Welling Ave, the crowds began to disperse, and by the time I reached Scott Street, I was alone. At the intersection, I pressed the greasy button on the traffic light pole and leaned against it as I waited for the red circle to turn green.

"I don't mean to bother you, dear, but could you assist me with these? It'll only take a moment."

The voice came from an old woman, who had seemingly appeared out of thin air. She was short, perhaps five feet at most, and stood wearily hunched over her walker. The overflowing bags of groceries she had been referring to were draped over the rails, making the thin pieces of metal strain underneath their weight. I recognized her as Mrs. Riley, my mother's old college professor. We had met a few times when I was younger, but I doubted she remembered.

"Sure. How can I help?" I couldn't bring myself to say no. Aside from the large mole on her cheek, she looked just like my grandmother.

"Carry these," she said, pointing to the three fullest bags, each of which was filled with at least half a dozen cans. I picked them up and she grinned. "Thank you, dear." The *dear* came out sounding like *deah*. Then she coughed, covering her mouth with one papery hand.

"Are you alright ma'am?"

Mrs. Riley chuckled. "Me? Oh no, can't say I am."

I raised my eyebrows, expecting her to elaborate. She didn't. We continued walking, heading towards the assortment of worn-down, brown apartment complexes where I lived. The street was empty, except for a few vehicles parked along the sidewalk—six cars, all different shades of black, and several white trucks.

"Where are we heading?" I finally asked, curious to find out how much longer I would have to carry the bags, which were growing heavier by the minute.

14

"Over there, dear." She paused to lift a wrinkled finger and pointed it towards one of the shorter buildings in a nearby alley. "Distance won't bother you?"

There was a broken wine bottle on the sidewalk, and I had to pause to step over it. "I'm fine, ma'am. No worries."

"You know," the woman said, unwilling to lapse into silence, "you look just like my Lillian."

"Hm?"

"My granddaughter. She has red hair as well; it's the most beautiful color, if you ask me."

"I appreciate the compliment ma'am. I was never too fond of it myself," I said. My hair color was one of the only things kids in middle school would laugh about. I recalled the moment—sometime in seventh grade—when I had asked out a boy I liked. His rejection still echoed through my head every time someone brought up my hair color.

We rounded the corner and walked into the alley. It wasn't a pleasant place. A swarm of flies hovered above one of the dumpsters, which was backed up against the wall a few feet to our left. That explained the nauseous stench.

"Hope you don't mind the smell," Mrs. Riley apologized.

I couldn't reply; the odor was making me dizzy. To my surprise, it seemed to have no effect on her at all. I suppose that's what happened when you spent your entire life in such a place. The wheels of her walker rattled on the uneven ground, and a single tomato fell out of a grocery bag. I bent down to pick it up, although my own bags were threatening to spill.

"Ma'am, how much longer do we have to walk? These bags are getting awfully heavy."

She paused for a moment before answering. "We're almost there," she told me. I glanced up from the ground and realized we were nearing the short brown building she had pointed out a few minutes before. Of course. I had known our destination all along. The question had been unnecessary. I smiled to myself, hoping to ease the strange feeling that was flaring inside my gut.

There were three doors on this side of the building. The one in the center was the main entrance that likely led to the upper apartments. The others were doors to the ground floor apartments—14 and 15. We stopped at 15. The woman left her walker, climbed up the single step, and began fumbling for the keys. Her hands were visibly trembling.

Arthritis, I thought, remembering one of the lessons Huma's mother—a doctor—had taught me. The poor woman had arthritis.

"You can put the groceries down, dear. I will take them inside once- oh!" she exclaimed. Her keys fell to the asphalt, startling a rat that had begun sneaking in our direction. I picked them up and handed them to her. "Thank you dear. Thank you so much," she said. The woman coughed again. "Leave the bags on the ground. I'll take them inside once I open the door."

"Got it," I said and did as she asked. The keys jiggled in the lock, and the door finally swung open.

"Thank you," the woman said again, a warm smile spreading across her face. "Would you like me to call a taxi cab for you? An Uber, perhaps?"

"No ma'am, I'll be fine," I replied, glancing at the bags. Would she be able to carry them in by herself? She would have to unless she was going to call someone to do it for her. I decided not to pry; her business wasn't mine. I turned around to go…

And then I stopped dead in my tracks.

A large black SUV stood in the center of the road. It was positioned sideways, creating a barrier between the alley and the main road.

More importantly, cutting off my way out.

Chapter Two

Two shots rang out—both muffled—and Mrs. Riley fell to the ground with a dull thud, the groceries spilling over the cobblestone floor.

Dead.

The SUV's door was open, revealing the tall, burly man that had mindlessly killed my companion. He stepped out of the truck and walked towards me, fixing his small beady eyes on my face. In one hand, he was holding a handkerchief. In the other was his gun, which, from the looks of it, had a silencer.

For a moment, I stood still, my eyes glued to the weapon.

Then I lunged towards an opening near the side of the truck, my heart hammering in my throat, hoping it would be quick enough to catch him off-guard.

My feeble attempt at self-preservation came too late.

In one swift move, the man thrust his arm in my direction, snatching a bundle of my hair. A loud yelp flew out of my mouth as he pulled me up against him. Grunting, he pressed a foul-smelling handkerchief to my mouth, not letting go of my hair.

My mind made the connection instantly. *Knock-out drug.* I held my breath, kicking and punching anything my limbs could touch. One of my arms collided with something solid, and I heard him hiss in pain. I was about to do it again when a sharp pain suddenly tore through my muscle. He was twisting my arm—the one I had hit him with.

A bit too late, I realized I wouldn't be able to escape a man who had a couple hundred pounds to his advantage. My mind frantically searched for a solution, but the gas on the handkerchief was clouding my thoughts. Something was there, at the back of my mind, but the only thing I could feel was myself slowly losing consciousness.

Then it appeared, bright as day, and I felt stupid for not having seen it sooner. *Scream.* I should have screamed. Someone nearby, on the main street, would have heard it. I cursed myself and my idiocy. My eyes were struggling to keep open. A part of my brain had already succumbed to the lulling darkness, and I knew my time was running out. I inhaled, praying my consciousness would last long enough to let the scream out of my lungs.

It came out muffled, most of it drowned out by the folds of the handkerchief. It was too late. Spots danced across my vision, the darkness coming at me in tendrils, tendrils which were wrapping around my body, squeezing out the remaining air out of my lungs. It was as if their sole purpose was to engulf me. And with the heavy material pressed against my mouth, there was nothing I could do to stop them.

I allowed myself to be consumed by darkness.

* * *

The steady roar of an air conditioner slowly brought me to my senses. My whole body ached. As I tried lifting my arm to prop myself onto an elbow, I realized someone had strapped me down.

"She's awake," a man standing next to me grunted to his comrade. He was short and beefy, breathing heavily as if he had just returned from a marathon. The man next to him was the opposite—tall and wiry, with a headful of brown curls. He was fidgeting nervously with a small round device he held in his hand. They both wore identical black shirts, with the same design embedded on the right breast pocket—a white outline of a bird's head.

"Where's Stellinger?" the latter asked. His gaze slowly traveled up my immobilized body, his fingers never leaving the white device. He turned away the second our eyes met.

"I think he went to the bathr-"

A door behind me banged shut before he could finish the word. Echoing footsteps quickly hurried in my direction.

"Is she…?"

18

The new voice was interrupted by the wiry man, who seemed eager to give a full report on my well-being.

"Awake? Yes. Woke up approximately five minutes ago. Seems a bit groggy. I can't be certain if the effects have all worn off, but I'm sure-"

"Enough." He impatiently waved an arm in his direction. "I'll have a look myself." He leaned over my table, his long beard brushing against my bare arm. He looked no more than forty but given the number of gray specks in his otherwise jet-black hair, no less than thirty. A huge vein bulged in the center of his forehead, his mouth pressed into a thin line. I stared at him as intimidatingly as I could, but it seemed to have no effect. He glared back, his face taking on an expression of sheer disgust.

"Sir?" the wiry man piped, nervously looking between me and the monster leaning over the table. At his voice, Stellinger straightened and calmly walked towards the center of the brightly lit room, making sure to stay within my field of view. He cleared his throat.

"Name and age," he boomed in a thick voice, his small, beady eyes fixed on me. I remained silent, pressing my lips into a thin line.

"Lucianne Allaire," I replied, noticing the thick black cane he was swinging around. "Fifteen." I didn't want to think of what would happen to me if I didn't comply. Judging by the look on his face, it wouldn't be good.

Stellinger lifted his brows in amusement, turning towards the wiry man, who was holding a notepad. "Compliant. I like the compliant ones."

"Yes, sir," the wiry man replied. "So do I."

Stellinger snatched the notepad from the man's hand, squinting at something in the middle of the page.

"Why's the ability not listed?" he barked, his cold voice making me shudder.

"We…," the wiry man hesitated before continuing. "We don't know her ability."

Stellinger snarled. "O'Connor, if you've brought me another human girl-"

"No, no!" O'Connor protested, throwing his bony hands into the air as if surrendering. "She's one of them; I checked her back! Same mark as the others."

"Then why the hell is her ability not listed?!" Stellinger's face was turning an ugly shade of red.

"She's….she's like nothing we've seen before," O'Connor bit his bottom lip hesitantly. Stellinger opened his mouth, but O'Connor continued before he could get out another angry remark. "I think she makes people…. Faint. With her hands."

Stellinger shook his head in disbelief but didn't respond to O'Connor's words.

"Take her to the chambers. We leave at noon," he ordered towards a hallway out of which two guards emerged, dressed in bulletproof combat uniforms. They unstrapped me, holding me down so I wouldn't escape as Stellinger strolled over to my table. He was holding the thick, black cane.

"Alright, sweetheart. As much as I like your compliance, we can't take the risk of your escape," he said.

Then he brought the cane down on my shin.

The force of its impact sliced open my skin, and for a moment, I was aware of nothing but my howl piercing through the room. That, and the fact that my lower leg was on fire.

The tears came by themselves. There was nothing I could have done to stop them. The rivers of salt poured down my face, blurring my vision, but I still caught a glimpse of Stellinger walking out of the room, leaving the guards to haul the bleeding, crying mess of a girl into a cell.

Pain was the only thing on my mind when I slumped to the cold stone floor.

I couldn't tell how much time I spent cradling my burning foot, but after what seemed like forever, I finally gathered up the will to look around my temporary residence. I knew that when he had hurt me, he had done so to prevent me from escaping. That meant two things: I wasn't the first victim, and someone before me had already escaped.

Escape was possible.

I studied my surroundings, searching for a possible exit. The walls were caked with dirt, an occasional smear of blood crossing the stone's surface. Same with the floor, except the blood appeared in much larger quantities. It was clear that I wasn't the only victim whose shin Stellinger had smashed open.

My stomach churned.

What had happened to the other victims? The thought pried at my brain. If escape failed, I would share their fate.

I had to escape.

My eyes wandered to the only source of light in the cell—a window, through which I could see the full moon.

Groaning, I dragged myself towards it. My trembling hand reached towards one of the iron bars and grasped it, helping me regain my balance. I looked around. The four pieces of metal had specks of dried blood on them. My hand had been placed on the only bar that seemed remotely clean. Now, it too had blood on it. Fresh.

I tested their stability. No matter how much I pulled, they wouldn't budge. Stable. Beyond the bars was an assortment of tall, seemingly endless pine trees. A forest. We were in the middle of a forest.

The bars wouldn't budge.

The cell was made of stone.

There would be no escape.

Each blink that followed that realization felt like sandpaper scratching across my eyeballs. I knew tears were coming, and I knew I wouldn't be able to stop them. They rolled down my cheeks as they had just done over fifty minutes ago.

I couldn't remember the last time I had cried this much.

You're going to dehydrate, my brain reminded me, my parched throat in agreement. It did nothing to lessen the streams of tears flowing from my eyes.

I dropped to the floor, hissing as my wounded foot scraped the rough stone. Although a fresh round of tears made its appearance, I managed to drag myself to the other side of the room. There, I curled up into a ball, pressing myself into the second farthest corner from the window. It was all I could do to protect myself from the wind.

For the first time in seven months, I cried myself to sleep.

The cracking of stone startled me from my slumber. I took a shaky breath and studied the room, trying to locate the sound.

It was coming from outside.

From behind the wall.

The noise increased, and I saw something poke through the wall of stone to my left. I touched it. A twig.

How did this get here?

Another twig poked through the wall, this time of my right. I tried to squeeze myself further into the corner as the twig to my left began to weave itself back into the wall.

This has to be a dream.

My eyes widened as a section of the wall crumbled away, revealing the stump of a tree that hadn't been there a few hours ago. I knew because the closest trees had been at least twenty feet away.

Things went quickly from there.

Pieces of the wall crumbled from both sides and I saw half a dozen trees, moving at the speed of an average human, each swinging their branches to remove the rest of the brick.

It didn't take long for the final piece to be crushed into fragments. In its place stood a tall, cloaked figure, its face hidden by the hood of the black material.

I bit my tongue to keep from screaming. According to most movies, cloaked figures were usually criminals or assassins. I wanted neither.

"You can come out," said the figure. It was the voice of a teenage boy, who seemed extremely bored for someone who had just destroyed the wall of a cell.

Noticing that his words had no impact, he walked over towards me in calm, even strides. I stared at him, not daring to move as he knelt down next to me. To my surprise, he began scrutinizing my shin.

"Disgusting bastards," he muttered as he reached into his cloak. "I have a kit right beyond that tree line. Take this for now." He threw a bandage in my direction and waited for me to move.

Who are you? I opened my mouth to ask but it came out as a weak croak.

"My apologies," he said. "You must be terribly thirsty. Here." He reached into his cloak again, this time taking out a bottle of water.

My parched throat was begging me to take it, to drink up the whole thing without a second thought. But what if the water was drugged? What if it was poisoned? I didn't want to risk it.

"You don't trust me, do you?" the boy asked, as if he could read my mind. "Watch."

He uncorked the water bottle and thrust back his head, pouring one third of it into his throat and giving me a glimpse of the silky blond hair beneath his cloak.

"See? Safe to drink."

I nodded eagerly, and when he handed it to me again, I gobbled down the water in an instant.

"Great. Now let's get out of here," he said. He stood up and began walking towards the forest.

"Wait!" I tried to call out. It still came out as a croak. I cleared my throat, and my next words were clearer. "I still need to put on the bandage."

"Don't worry about the bandage; I can carry you. We need to get out of here *now*." His voice was urgent.

I nodded in agreement. Getting out of here was our greatest priority. My imprisoners were bound to return at any moment.

"Okay," I said. "Please try not to hurt my foot."

He picked me up and threw me over his shoulder, and my palm touched something large and hard on his back. I pulled it away.

"Try to hang on tight," he said.

That was the only warning I got.

I clung onto his cloak as the ground whizzed past my face, praying he wouldn't slam my dangling foot into a tree. Miraculously, he didn't.

The clearing was closer than I anticipated—only a couple dozen feet behind the tree line. He placed me on the grass next to a bush, and I noticed that he was breathing heavily. Running with a weight on your shoulder, even across such a short distance, must have been incredibly difficult.

For the first time, the hood of his cloak was off. I took that as an opportunity to examine his face. He had sharp features, with silky gold hair that fell in waves over his forehead, shining in the moonlight. His hands were placed on his knees, and he seemed to be closely examining the grass.

"Let me know when you're done staring so we can get going."

I raised my eyebrows. He had said it so casually, as if people staring at him was a normal occurrence.

"You're very observant," I noted.

He smirked, turning his head to face me. "I know."

My hand brushed over a rock in the grass, and its bumpy surface aroused a question that had been resting at the back of my mind. "If you don't mind me asking, what are you carrying in that backpack underneath your cloak?" I asked, pointing to the bulge underneath the cloth.

He laughed. "Backpack? Why, that's probably the most ridiculous thing anyone's said to me." He threw off his cloak. "I have wings."

Chapter Three

He was on top of me the second I opened my mouth, pressing his hand firmly against my lips.

"Are you stupid?" he hissed. "They'll hear your scream."

I peeled away his palm. "Scream? I'm not going to scream!" My mouth had opened to let out a gasp, one of surprise and awe. I wasn't stupid enough to scream. Not with my kidnappers nearby.

"Oh." He seemed surprised. "Sorry."

He walked back towards his cloak, and I stared at the gargantuan wings that sprouted from his back. The feathers were milky white, a shade that nicely contrasted with the blackness of his jeans. The wings were about as long as his arms. I wondered how he had managed to hide them beneath the cloak. He reached into his pocket, took out a small bag of smooth, purple stones, and began laying them out on the grass.

"What are you doing?" I asked, pointing to the circular formation of stones he had assembled.

He paused as he looked up at me, studying my expression. "Making a portal," his response was brief.

I raised my eyebrows. "A portal? A portal for interdimensional travel?"

"Uh-uh."

"Who are you?"

The question seemed to take him by surprise. He paused what he was doing and extended his hand. "Mathias Boone. Soratia's most talented phytokinetic."

I let his hand fall to the ground, refusing to shake it. "You're *who's* most talented *what*?"

"Soratia's most talented phytokinetic," he repeated, his smile fading as he noticed my lack of comprehension. "I manipulate plants," he explained.

"No, the first part. Who's Soratia?"

He laughed, as if my question was a stupid one to ask. "Soratia's not a person. It's the place I'm building a portal to. It's where we're from."

"I'm from Minnesota," I said. What did he mean?

He glanced back in the direction of my cell, and his face instantly regained the stoic seriousness from moments before. "I'll explain later," he said. "Distractions only slow down the process."

He knelt back down and continued working on the stones, making sure they were all connected. When he was satisfied with the results, he took out a thin stick and began touching each of the stones. Every stone he touched began to emit a light orange glow.

"What are you doing now?" I began scooting towards him, but he held up his hand, as if to say, *Not yet.*

"Preparing the portal. Please don't distract me."

I obeyed, fixing my gaze on the stones. There were ten of them, each one the same size, the same circular shape, and the same faint color. Once they were all glowing, he touched the ground in the center.

I gasped. The grass in the middle had been replaced by a glimmering, orange surface that rippled like water in a lake. I scooted forward again, making sure to hold my bad foot into the air.

"Is it safe?" I asked Mathias.

"Does disintegrating into trillions of particles *sound* safe?"

I stared at him, feeling my eyes widen.

"Kidding. The chances of that happening are minuscule."

"Oh," I said. I glanced behind me. Nobody had emerged from behind the tree line, but they would eventually. I would have to take the portal. There was no other option, except potentially waiting for my kidnappers to find me stranded in the woods. I shuddered at the thought.

"So you're coming?" he asked as he gestured towards the glowing surface. I nodded. "Wonderful. Now… can I trust you to go in after me or would you like to go first?"

"I'd like to go first," I replied after briefly deliberating. Going first may have been risky, but it certainly helped cease my paranoia—what if the portal disappeared with him? Then I would be left alone in the woods with an injured ankle… something that was bound to end badly.

"That's quite bold of you," he complimented as he helped ease me onto the edge of the portal. My feet plunged into the thick, orange warmth. *Like warm slime*, I thought, not bothering to consider the ridiculousness of that statement. It reminded me so much of the soft, slippery matter Huma and I had made when we were younger.

My eyes were focused on the bright, swirling colors of the substance my companion was slowly easing me into. A million questions swarmed through my head, but there wouldn't be enough time to ask all of them.

"Does it hurt?" I blurted suddenly, grasping for his forearm.

"No," he replied, slowly prying my fingers away from his skin. "It's a strange sensation, but it doesn't hurt."

My boldness faded away the moment my legs disappeared beneath the surface, replaced by a dark, gripping fear.

"I'm scared," I admitted. My heart thudded as my chest became submerged.

"Don't be." His voice was soothing, but it did nothing to calm my nerves. "There's nothing to be afraid of."

He dropped me.

I couldn't scream. I couldn't do anything, as I fell at the speed of a hundred miles an hour, my insides ready to burst out of my body. My eyes squeezed shut as a thousand needles pierced my skin, penetrating through the layers of clothing, creating a sensation so unpleasant, I would have done anything at that moment to make it stop. There was no wind in my hair.

It felt like one of those nightmares in which you begin falling, falling into an endless oblivion of darkness, a darkness that never ceases, a darkness that swallows you—

My journey came to an abrupt stop.

I was slowly floating downwards, gently descending towards whatever lay below. At last, I could feel wind swishing past my ankles. My good foot touched the ground (I had remembered to keep the other one in the air), and then I found myself sitting on what seemed to be very well-maintained grass. And yet, I kept my eyes closed, still afraid of what I would find outside the safety of my eyelids.

That is, until I remembered Mathias.

I jumped away from the warmth of the portal, my eyes instantly fluttering open. I was sitting under a canopy of green leaves, the sunlight peeking through the branches. It was an exact replica of the forest we had just left, but the atmosphere was different. Calmer. And it was daytime. As for Mathias, he was elegantly floating down from the portal, which was located about five feet into the air—so low he had to stoop down to walk away from it.

He saw me and smiled, folding his wings as he sat down next to me. "That wasn't so bad, was it?" he said, his eyes lighting up with excitement. Meanwhile, I was struggling to keep myself from vomiting all over him.

"Bad? *Bad?* You lied to me! You *promised* it wouldn't—"

"No," he cut me off, shaking his head. "I said it wouldn't hurt you. And that you'll eventually get used to it. Both are true."

"If you expect me to go into that thing again—"

He held up his hand. "I don't expect you to do anything. You don't have to go through a portal again. Portals are a luxury," he said. He stood up and reached for one of the stones. The moment he pulled it away, the others collapsed to the ground.

I wasn't sure I had heard that right. "A *luxury*?" I repeated. How could such vile objects be considered luxurious?

"Precisely. They're extremely expensive, so unless you're filthy rich or have an exceptionally useful ability, I doubt you'll be going through one again." He shrugged.

"And you are…?" I motioned for him to go on.

"The latter," he replied briefly. Then he changed the subject. "How's your foot?"

"Same as it was a few minutes ago," I answered as I pointed to my ankle, which had scabbed over and was caked with dirt. The pain had subsided a bit, but I knew I wouldn't be able to stand, much less walk, by myself. Mathias bent down to look at it, a crease of concern forming between his eyebrows as he did.

"What's wrong?" I asked, my own heartbeat starting to accelerate when his lips pressed into a thin line.

"That's going to be an infection," he said, hovering his finger over the clear liquid oozing from underneath the scab. "We're going to the infirmary."

Chapter Four

The infirmary turned out to be a small square building, situated at the verge of the trees just beyond the clearing. It was a cozy place, with a fireplace in the waiting room and several plump chairs to sit on. A short lady stood at the desk, fervently typing something on a device. When we entered the room, she spread out her wings in a welcoming manner, a huge smile plastered across her face.

"Hello, Mr. Boone," she greeted him, brushing back her short auburn hair. "Lovely to meet you, miss. I'm Mrs. Hearn."

She led us down a corridor and into a room, where she ordered Mathias to place me down on the bed. The room was small but pleasant, the walls covered with friendly drawings of strange creatures and winged humans. Mrs. Hearn took out a sheet of paper and bent down to examine my ankle.

"How is it?" I asked as she wrote something on the paper.

"Nothing too serious, dear. Just a minor infection." She left the room in a hurry, her heels clicking on the marble floor. A minute later, another lady came into the room, dressed in an expensive-looking red suit that matched the color of her wings. Her blond hair was neatly tied in a high ponytail.

"You're the one with the wound infection, correct?"

"I think so," I replied.

Her introduction was short. "I'm Dr. Girble."

I watched in astonishment as she spat onto the tip of her pointer finger and moved it toward my foot. Naturally, I jerked it back.

"What are you doing?" I said, pointing at her finger, which was dripping with saliva.

A look of annoyance crossed over her face.

"Healing your wound," she replied coolly, before glancing at Mathias. "Hold her down, will you?"

Mathias obeyed, closing his hands around my leg as she placed her wet finger on my ankle. A strange tingling sensation washed over my foot. It vanished seconds later. Dr. Girble left the room without another word, shaking her head and muttering something indecipherable under her breath. I doubted it was anything good.

"Better?" asked Mathias, watching my reaction. All traces of my wound were gone—even the dried blood had been cleaned by the doctor's spit. I moved it around, overcome by a sudden desire to run up to the doctor and thank her. I could finally *walk*.

"Much better," I said, deciding that I would thank the doctor another time. It wasn't like she was too fond of me, anyway. "What do we do now?"

"We head to the palace. It's a couple blocks from here," he replied. He stood up, straightening his jacket, and helped me off the bed. We walked outside and into the city.

Soratia was situated at the bottom of a large valley, the town in the center. Most of the buildings were made of brick and cobble, the architecture similar to the one I had seen in my mother's childhood photos from France. Perhaps most of the builders had come from Europe.

"What's over there?" I asked Mathias, pointing to the top of the valley. I wondered why the founders of this place had chosen such low grounds.

His eyes flicked to where I was pointing. "Nobody knows, aside from maybe the royals. Entry is prohibited to all citizens."

"Why?"

He shrugged. "I don't know."

Looking into the sky, past the hovering houses and flying silhouettes, there were two suns, one on each side of the sky. Most of the people walking along the street had wings, and there seemed to be no cellphones, or other similar technology

32

in sight. Mathias led me past the colorful shops, inside of which I could see numerous strange accessories and items. The clothes on display had half of their backs cut out—for wings, I supposed. Two trees stood outside the entrance to one of the shops, and I spotted a girl pluck one leaf off and pop it into her mouth. I looked away.

The palace was in the center of the city, surrounded by a golden fence and neatly trimmed hedges. We walked up to the main gates, where several guards were stationed, and Mathias took out a yellow card. His identification. One of the guards, a tall burly man in a purple suit, grabbed it and pressed it against the lock. It worked like a key.

The gates swung open, revealing a paved road that led up to the residence ahead. The palace seemed to be made entirely of marble, the roof, and tips of towers gilded with gold. We headed up the road and then up the marble stairs, where a doorman—a short bald man with a thick mustache and large sunglasses—was standing. He bowed and opened the door, inviting us into the room behind it.

Large was an understatement.

The room was massive, with a black double staircase that spiraled to the floor above, a crystal chandelier hanging from the ceiling, which was twenty feet above. A large instrument was positioned in the center of the stairs, slightly resembling a grand piano. My jaw fell open at the sight. Huma may have been rich, but *this* was something else.

"Like it?" Mathias's voice echoed as he spread out his arms and flew into the air, touching the golden chandelier with the tips of his fingers. "This is where I live."

My eyes widened even more. "As in… you're one of the royals?"

He laughed, shaking his head. "Oh, I wish. I work for Sorina, and that comes with the advantage of living in her palace."

"Ah. Lucky you."

"You're quite lucky as well, considering you'll be staying here for tonight." He shrugged his shoulders and began walking towards the stairs. I, on the other hand, was rooted to the ground.

"I'm staying in the palace?" I breathed out. "Me?"

He turned around to face me. "It doesn't happen with every newcomer, but since you spent some time with the Qroes, Sorina believes you might have some valuable information. Hence, you'll be staying at the palace for tonight."

"Crows? Like the birds?"

"Qroes. Q-R-O-E-S. It's what your kidnappers call themselves," he said. "I'm not sure why they spell it the way they do. Maybe the ones we questioned were illiterate." He glanced at the wall. "They all wear the same symbol. A crow's head, outlined in white. You probably noticed that, though."

"Yeah," I said softly, grimacing as the memories of that night returned.

We walked up the stairs and down one of the hallways, which had doors numbered 101-120. We stopped at 106. The door was dark oak and carved into it were the letters "SOR."

"It's Sorina's office," Mathias said. A golden knocker with the face of a bird was attached to the center. "Go ahead." He motioned for me to use it. My hand hesitated in mid-air for a moment, before I reached towards the handle and knocked.

"Come in," a voice sang.

Chapter Five

The woman sitting at the desk was young, perhaps twenty-five at most. Her blue hair was combed back, and she had silky black wings that folded when she stood up to greet us. She wore a long-sleeved blue dress that looked like it had come straight out of a Renaissance painting. It matched the color of her hair.

The room was gargantuan – nearly three times as large as my bedroom – and was lined with bookshelves. It must have contained more books than my local library. A large window covered the back wall, its curtains open to reveal the courtyard beyond it. Several paintings hung on the walls, and looking at the faces, I could tell they belonged to the royal family. The blue hair and royal garments made it obvious.

"Your majesty," Mathias bowed, and I did the same, making sure to cross my ankles. If my childhood TV shows taught me anything, it was that girls cross their ankles when they bow.

"Mathias." Her voice was rich and velvety, the opposite of Dr. Girble's. "You never fail to impress me." Her eyes wandered over to me and she smiled. "It is a pleasure to finally meet you, Lucianne."

I swallowed. "You too, but… how do you know my name?"

"Your father spoke of you quite often. You look just like him." She spoke of him fondly, like one would speak of an old childhood friend.

My mind went back to what Mathias had told me by the portal: *"Soratia's not a person,"* he had said. *"It's the place I'm building a portal to. It's where we're from."*

Where *we're* from.

He had promised to explain things later, but that wouldn't be necessary. I had already put the pieces together.

My father was a part of this hybrid race. And me, being his daughter, meant I was one of them too.

Hundreds of new questions bubbled up to my lips. "Could I- could I meet him? When? Where is he? Does he live in the palace too?"

Sorina noticed my excitement and her smile disappeared, replaced by a solemn expression. "I'm sorry. I should have clarified this sooner. Your father is no longer with us, Lucianne."

My mouth fell open, the last traces of excitement vanishing from my eyes. "You mean he's...?"

"Dead," Mathias's grim voice answered my question. "He died during an ambush on one of the Qroes' bases. The area he was in burned to the ground. The Qroes set fire to it after evacuating most of their people via an underground tunnel."

"Oh," I whispered. The room seemed colder, somehow less welcoming than it had been when we'd entered. My father had never been a part of my life, but he still managed to linger at the back of my mind throughout childhood. Like a shadow, slinking in and out of my thoughts every time someone mentioned the word *dad*. He had always been a touchy topic for Mother, which caused me to never bring up the topic at home. Still, I couldn't help but long for the day I would meet him.

It was clear that would never happen. The queen's words had shattered the remnants of my hopes, leaving me with an uncomfortable emptiness.

Sorina took notice of my discomfort. She cleared her throat and changed the subject, eager to move on from the topic of death. "Speaking of the Qroes," she began, "what exactly did you see when you were taken into their base?"

"Uh," I began, "I'm not sure where it was exactly but—"

"It was in North Minnesota," Sorina cut me off. "The location doesn't matter; I know where it was. I'd like to know about the events that took place while you were inside…

particularly regarding anything useful you might have heard. Names and appearances are useful too."

"Ah," I said. My mind reeled back to the events of the night before as I frantically searched for something useful. The memories of that awful evening had already begun to fade from my memory, something I was extremely grateful for. But I understood how important this was. I forced myself to try to remember the names of the men, and almost immediately, one popped into my mind. "I think one of them was called Stellinger."

"That would be Alfred Stellinger, one of the Qroes we've been keeping an eye on. We believe he might have been in contact with their leader. Anyone else?"

I bit my lip. "There was a thin man with curly brown hair named O'Connor, if that helps."

"No," Sorina shook her head. "He must be one of the new ones. I've never heard of him." She sat in silence for a bit, resting her chin on the bottom of her palm. "Perhaps you heard them talk about... a boss? A leader?" She glanced up at me, her eyes hungry for information.

"Stellinger mentioned something about leaving at noon before he... before he hurt me. I don't think he said anything about a boss."

"Not really helpful." She shook her head again in disappointment. "See, we're trying to find their prime location, along with the individual that leads their organization. That is, before they find a way to get to ours," she sighed.

"I'm confused," I said uncertainly, not knowing whether this would be an appropriate question to ask.

"Elaborate."

"These people, the Qroes, they're human, aren't they? If they're human, and they don't have the abilities your people do, why should you be afraid? I don't think they pose much of a threat to your society, which is clearly stronger—"

"That's where you're wrong," Sorina cut me off, holding up her palm. "The Qroes have both human and Soratian members. The latter are not there by will. They have developed technology far more advanced than ours, so advanced in fact that they are fully capable of taking the abilities of Soratians and giving them to themselves. They have armed themselves with weapons even my finest men are unable to replicate. Once they have captured enough of us, they will be just as powerful, if not more." Then she muttered, "Lord forbid they steal the Griffin."

I sucked in my breath. That was a lot of information to take in. Instead of commenting on anything she said about the Qroes, I decided to ask another question. "Who's the Griffin?"

I guessed it was a nickname for someone significant. Someone that wanted their identity to remain hidden.

Sorina's eyes dropped to one of the devices on her desk, a small, white square with several blinking numbers. A clock. "It is late," she said, completely ignoring my question. She turned to Mathias. "Take her to 115 and notify Cornelia. The room should be fitting for tonight." Her head swiveled back towards me, and she said soothingly, "Given your current state, I understand you may not be comfortable sharing too much right away. We will continue this conversation another day. You will rest in the palace for now, and tomorrow you'll be transferred to the dorms. I expect your companion to explain the details."

With that, she led us out of the room, shutting the door behind us. Our conversation had ended because of my question... I was certain. We walked in silence down the hallway, our feet thudding on the soft carpet. I decided not to ask about it again.

A pot of flowers stood next to the door of 115, richly decorated with designs. Mathias handed me the keys, which I thrust into the doorknob, wanting more than anything else to rest.

The room wasn't as large as Sorina's office, but still impressive in size. A queen bed with silky teal covers stood in the center, a crystal chandelier hanging over it. The room had a wooden floor and, like the office, had a large window that covered the back wall, leading to a balcony. The curtains surrounding the window matched the covers, and an expensive armchair sat in the corner.

Mathias smiled, noticing my reaction, and proceeded to show me around the room. The door to the left was the closet, he explained, which had been filled with beautiful garments for my use. The door on the right led to the bathroom, which had been appropriately equipped as well.

"And finally," he said in the voice of a show host that is about to introduce something huge, "we have the makeup area with an assortment of foundations and lipsticks and all that other face stuff you might want to use," he said. The reaction he had been expecting must have been different because he seemed incredibly surprised at the expression my face was portraying. "What's wrong?"

"Nothing. Everything is perfect. I just never had time to learn how to do it," I replied. The most I could do was wing my eyeliner, and that was only because Huma had let me use hers for homecoming. My mother had never used makeup and didn't allow me to use it either.

It's bad for your skin, she'd say. *You're a pretty girl, Luce. You don't need it. Spend your money on something else.* Thinking of her felt like I was shooting another hole through my chest. At this point, my body seemed to be riddled with them. Hundreds of tiny wounds on the verge of healing, like cuts that had just begun to scab. But they never healed. Not entirely. Because every time I thought of an event, a memory that had caused one of those holes, the wound would open. And the pain would be brand-new, as if it had never started scabbing in the first place.

He raised his eyebrows. "You're one of the first girls I've heard say that. They say it works like magic—an hour of work, and you look like a goddess. You'd be pretty enough to snag all the guys."

"Appealing to society's beauty standards is not one of my concerns. But hey, maybe if I have enough time, I'll learn how to do it. Maybe I could even find someone to teach me."

"I'm certain you will," he said. "Breakfast is tomorrow at six. Don't worry about getting ready on time; that's Cornelia's job. If you need anything, use that bell on the nightstand – it will notify one of the maids. I'll be next door, in 116. Have a nice rest, Lucianne."

"You too," I called out after him.

He lingered at the door, before finally turning around one last time. "You know, you're the first newcomer I've seen to remain so collected throughout their first day. How do you keep such a calm composure?"

His question didn't surprise me, for I had wondered it myself. "Oh, I bet it's just the adrenaline," I said. "The shock will come sooner or later. It always does." I smiled politely and watched as he closed the door, waiting for his footsteps to echo down the hallway. Drifting off to sleep was easy. The nightmares, however, were not.

Chapter Six

I found myself back inside of the cool room, the metallic table still standing in the center. This time, however, I wasn't the one strapped to it. The girl was shaking, either from fear or from the cold, a strand of charcoal hair swishing across her face. Over the rattle of the air conditioner, I could hear the faint whimpers she made as her wrists strained against the plastic constraints.

The door opened and a man in a black suit came through, followed by two accomplices. I immediately recognized him as the man that had slashed open my shin, but three or four years younger. The black cane in his hand nearly stopped my heart as I realized what I was about to witness.

Alfred Stellinger's mouth spread into a wide grin.

"Is this the one from Soratia?" he asked, clapping his hands as the burly middle-aged man in a greasy shirt nodded. The girl's panic-filled gray eyes stared up at him. Her lips began to tremble. Stellinger brought up his cane and slid it along the side of her cheekbone, stopping beneath her throat. He lowered his voice. "Where is it?"

The girl stiffened at his question, before responding with one of her own. "Where is what?" she asked. Her voice was high pitched but even, her Adam's apple bobbing as she swallowed.

Stellinger's cane pressed further into her skin, causing another whimper. "Don't play stupid. Where is the Griffin?"

"I don't know," the girl croaked, the tip of the cane clearly crushing her windpipes. Stellinger looked over at his other accomplice, a rat-faced youngster that stood hunched over next to the burly man. He was focused on the girl's face, constantly clenching and unclenching his left fist. He seemed extremely tired.

Stellinger tapped his foot impatiently before snapping his fingers. "Well?"

An expression of guilt crossed over the youngster's face as he answered, "She's lying." Before she could react, Stellinger's palm collided with the girl's cheek, causing her head to swivel around and hit the other side of the table. She gasped, the palm-shaped mark reddening her skin.

Stellinger waited a bit before continuing his interrogation. "You're a very pretty girl, Atiana. Don't make this difficult for yourself." His attempt at sounding empathetic was feeble, for I could still see the vein bulging from his forehead.

"I'm not-" She paused to cough. "I'm not betraying my family." She stared at Stellinger, all traces of fear gone from her eyes. She held the look of someone who had accepted their fate. Stellinger unholstered his gun. I stood rooted to the floor, unable to move or close my eyes.

Please get me out of here, I begged, knowing what was about to happen. *Please.*

"Very well," Stellinger said. The gun was pressed against Atiana's temple.

Nonononono.

He pulled the trigger.

Chapter Seven

When I awoke, people were rushing into my bedroom, the light was on, and a brown-skinned woman was kneeling by my side, pressing a wet washcloth against my forehead. My throat felt raw from screaming.

"Are you alright?" the woman asked, gently dabbing the washcloth around my eyes. I shook my head.

No, I wasn't alright. The girl's screams (or maybe my own) were still echoing throughout my head.

I recognized Mathias's voice as he came up behind the woman, his forehead creased with worry. "Cornelia, why is she on the floor? What happened?"

The woman didn't glance up at him as she continued dabbing me with the cool washcloth. "She must have fallen off her bed during a nightmare. It's a common side effect of interdimensional travel."

She placed the washcloth back into the bowl as I glanced around the bedroom. A cluster of people surrounded me, all keeping a distance of at least five feet—something that wouldn't have been possible back in my apartment. I propped myself onto my elbows, but Cornelia's firm hand pushed me back onto the carpet. "Don't move," she said. "It will only give you a headache."

"What time is it?" I asked. Considering that someone had turned the lights on, I doubted it was daytime.

"Nearly three in the morning," responded Mathias, briefly glancing at his wrist. His hair was still damp from showering, and the moisture had made it curl slightly at the tips. He was wearing a large, wrinkled T-shirt (with two large cuts in the back to make space for his wings), striped pajama bottoms, and a pair of fluffy blue slippers that contrasted nicely with the bottoms. For the first time, I noticed a thin scar crossing his left eyebrow. Still, he looked extraordinarily good for someone who had just risen from bed.

Despite Cornelia's complaints, I sat up. "Four in the morning?"

"You made quite a noise," said Mathias. "Nearly woke up the entire floor."

Humiliation heated my cheeks, and I fixed my gaze on the floor. "Sorry."

"Don't worry about it," Mathias said. "Tell us about the dream in the morning. Sorina will want to know."

"Nightmare," I corrected him.

He gave me a small smile and retreated from the room, leaving the door open so others could trickle out behind him. I watched them go until I was alone with Cornelia. She was a slim woman, with black hair tied back in a loose braid. She seemed to be no more than twenty, and just like myself, human. Or half-human since that's what everyone seemed to be around here.

"Can you stand? We need to get you back into bed, and I don't think I'll be able to lift you," she told me. She bent down, offering me her hand. I took it.

"Thanks," I said. Despite the nightmare, my eyes began to droop the moment the silky covers fell over my body. And just like that, I fell back asleep.

Chapter Eight

Post-interdimensional-travel nightmares may have been common, but that didn't stop them from wanting to hear about mine. *Them* applied to Mathias and Sorina, who called me into her office first thing in the morning. My stomach rumbling with hunger, I trudged to 206. Two maids accompanied me on my journey—both plump, middle-aged, and wingless. Human.

"Good morning, Lucianne," Sorina greeted me as I entered the room. She was wearing another dress, this time a purple one. "I'm sorry to hear that your first night here wasn't a pleasant experience." She was sitting at her desk, filling out a sheet of paper.

"That's alright," I said lightly. A loud growl escaped my stomach. I pressed my hand against it to try to cover up the noise.

"Oh, I apologize," Sorina said, and I felt my face heating up in embarrassment. "How do you feel about discussing this over breakfast?"

She stood up, placing the half-filled sheet of paper into a drawer. I gave her a thumbs-up, which answered her question, and she motioned for me to follow her into the corridor.

A maid was scurrying down the hall with a laundry cart when we left. She briefly paused to give Sorina a bow. Wingless, just like Cornelia and other members of the housekeeping staff. I had yet to see a wingless person in a position of power, which bothered me, considering that I was one myself.

I tried to mimic Sorina's graceful descent as we walked down the curved staircase but ended up tripping at the last step. Sorina's face swiveled around at the dull thud of my body hitting the quartz floor. My face once again turned red as a nearby maid rushed to help me up.

"I'm sorry, Your Highness," I whispered. The stairs had been wide, much wider than the ones that led up to Mom's apartment back in Minnesota, which made the whole incident much more humiliating.

You're just disoriented, I told myself. And nervous. Aside from the gnawing hunger, my stomach was full of butterflies.

We headed left, into a bright corridor filled with paintings. That led to what I thought was the living room, which had five white armchairs assembled around a clear coffee table. It also had a fireplace, and I was surprised to see the fire burning inside of it in such warm temperatures. An arch on the back wall connected to the dining room, where two dozen chairs stood around a long, polished table. Two were occupied—one by a short girl in a flowery dress, and the other by an older boy in a turtleneck. They were both bent over plates of food, and neither took notice of me and Sorina as we entered the room.

"Sit," mouthed Sorina, gesturing towards the chairs.

"Okay," I mouthed back, grabbing the one closest to me. The chair made a scraping noise as it moved, and the girl perked up, finally noticing me.

"Hi Rina. Who's that?" she looked at Sorina, inclining her head towards me. She resembled a much younger version of Sorina, except for her wings, which were a lighter shade – dark grey instead of black.

Sorina ignored her and turned to me. "Lucianne, these are my siblings. Sonia and Sofian."

"So it's a family tradition," I said. Then I tensed up, unsure of whether that remark would get me in trouble. These people were powerful, and I didn't want to get on their bad side.

"I'm not sure I follow." Her eyes were curious, which I took as a good sign.

"Your names," I explained. "They all start with 'So.'"

Sorina cracked a smile. "Oh yes, it's a tradition. Not one that I'm particularly fond of, to be honest."

"Oh," I muttered. I began examining the contents of my plate, which had been placed down by a man in a white uniform – the cook. Everything on it—from the bagel and cream cheese to the chopped pieces of a bell pepper—reminded me of the breakfast my mother would make us on Sundays, the only day she wasn't working. The thought of my mother sitting alone at our table, probably wondering where I was, sent a sharp pang through my chest.

When I looked up, Sonia was staring at me. I stared back, daring her to lower her eyes. She didn't. We were still staring at each other when two new pairs of footsteps walked into the room.

"Good morning Lucianne."

I lifted my head at the familiar voice. Mathias was standing near the head of the table, leaning against a pillar. Another man stood next to him. He was dressed in a red suit, which reminded me of Dr. Girble's. Unlike Dr. Girble, however, he had no wings and wore round, thick-framed glasses that kept sliding down his nose.

"Hello Mathias," I greeted the blond boy with a wave before turning to his companion. "Good morning...uh..." I trailed off, realizing I didn't know the doctor's name.

"Beckett," the man responded. He had a crisp, clear voice. "Dr. Beckett. I assume you're Ms. Allaire?"

I nodded. "Yes sir. Pleasure to meet you."

"Likewise. Her Highness requested my presence, so I hope you won't mind."

"No sir, I don't mind."

He grinned, displaying a row of pearly white teeth. "Very well. Let's eat."

Chapter Nine

Once Sonia and Sofian had been escorted out of the room (due to Sorina's request), and the mahogany doors were shut (also due to Sorina's request), we began to eat. I watched Sorina place an elaborately decorated napkin on her lap, and I did the same with my own. As I bit into the crisp bagel, a maid entered the room to pour me tea. It smelled faintly of lavender. The scent reminded me of the flower field by Huma's summer house, which brought along a pang of home-longing.

After the maid left, making sure to shut the door behind her, Mathias looked at Sorina and raised his eyebrows. She nodded, dabbing the corner of her mouth with the napkin.

He cleared his throat. "Do you remember what the queen told you yesterday, regarding your residence at the palace?"

I did. "Something about being transferred to dorms, right?"

He nodded. "You'll be staying another night."

"Oh," I murmured. I wasn't surprised. Not since Sorina had called me into her office. "It has to do with the dream I had, doesn't it?"

All of them nodded, their faces remaining neutral. Sorina spoke. "We think it might have something to do with your ability. You said you remember the dream vividly. Could you tell us about it?"

I told them everything. All of the details, from the way the men questioned the girl, to the sound of the gunshot as the bullet drilled into her head. I told them about Stellinger and his accomplice, the rat-faced youngster that was a human lie-detector. Both his ability and hesitation could only mean one thing: he was a half-blood.

"Her name was Atiana," I said. Mathias and Sorina looked at each other, a conversation passing between them in a matter of seconds.

"Atiana who? What was her last name?" Sorina's voice, although steady, was quite obviously tinged with alarm. "What was her last name?" she repeated, louder. As if I didn't hear her the first time.

"I don't know," I responded, feeling more useless than ever. Why could I never answer people's questions?

"What did she look like?"

I recalled the girl's appearance. "Black hair, tan complexion, and uh..." I paused. Had her eyes been green or blue? Or a mix of the two? I couldn't remember. Her face was already beginning to fade from my memory. "I'm pretty sure she had light eyes, but I can't think of the color. Oh, and she was skinny."

"Green," Mathias's voice was dull. "Atiana had green eyes."

I stared at him. Both he and Sorina knew the girl. But how?

"Pardon the interruption, but does anyone know the last resident of room 115?" Dr. Beckett, who had remained silent for most of our conversation, finally spoke. "Before Ms. Allaire, that is."

"It was unoccupied for quite some time. A few years actually." Sorina's hand flew up to her mouth. "You can't possibly think-"

Dr. Beckett smiled. "Oh, but I do. In fact, it's just what I expected."

I raised my eyebrows, but nobody paid attention to my confusion. They were all focused on the doctor, whose eyes were shining with the brilliance of a detective.

"But she's a pain manipulator." Sorina's voice was skeptical. I didn't know what the doctor was suggesting, but the Queen was right. I could clearly remember Horseface as she thrashed on the ground just a few days prior to my kidnapping. She had been in pain, all right. And I had been the one that caused it.

"She's both."

Sorina stood up from the table. "Dr. Beckett, will you please accompany me outside? I'd like to speak with you in private."

"Certainly."

I watched as they walked out of the room, Dr. Beckett nearly tripping over the threshold.

Mathias, whose hair had fallen over his eyes, was mindlessly rolling over his bagel. His eyebrows were pinched together, and although I hadn't known him for long, I could tell he was thinking. Probably about something important. I didn't want to distract him, but he was the only person in the room who knew what Sorina and Beckett had discussed. And so I asked.

"Um, Mathias?"

He looked up. "Hm?"

"What are they talking about? Me being '*both,*' I mean."

He paused for a moment, as if deciding whether or not he should tell me. The bagel was placed on the table. "They think you're a Multi," he said at last.

That only added to my questions.

"And... what is that?" I tried to be as polite as possible, but it was getting difficult. Couldn't he see I was confused?

"The word is pretty self-explanatory." He glanced up at me, his eyebrows still pinched together, clearly annoyed by my talking. Then, by whatever miracle, his expression seemed to soften. "Sorry... was that harsh?"

"Eh. I've heard worse," I replied honestly. "Don't apologize. Just tell me what they meant," I said and gestured towards the closed door through which the grown-ups had exited.

"A Multi is what we call someone with multiple abilities. They're quite rare amongst Soratians, and even rarer among half-bloods. Most Multis have two abilities. We've had a couple exceptions of course, but they're nearly impossible to find. You were lucky to be born with two."

A few days ago, the thought of having a power would have seemed impossible. It was one of the things kids would daydream about. Had someone told me that I, a poor girl from suburban Minnesota had a *magical power*, I would have never believed it. But sitting here, in another dimension, across from a guy with wings, had changed that mindset. Nothing surprised me anymore.

I recalled his reaction to Atiana's name. He undoubtedly knew her well. After all, he could perfectly remember the color of her eyes.

"Were you and Atiana close?"

The pain in his eyes answered my question. He smiled grimly. "My girlfriend."

"Oh," I said. I didn't know what else to say. *I'm sorry for your loss?* That phrase was not only bland but also incredibly overused. How many times had I heard it after the death of my grandfather? Hundreds. I had grown sick of it, and I was certain he had too. Because words wouldn't change anything.

We sat in silence, none of us daring to speak.

The click of the doorknob saved us from spending the next hour in such an awkward atmosphere. Dr. Beckett stayed by the doorway, while Sorina came into the room. She walked like someone with a purpose, just like a New York businesswoman.

"Sorry for the wait," she said. "Dr. Beckett and I would like to run some tests on you."

"Tests?" I repeated. The word had negative connotations. Tests were something scientists ran on guinea pigs. And said guinea pigs tended to die.

Sorina saw my expression and laughed. "Don't worry, it won't hurt. Follow me."

Without being given much of a choice, I stood up and walked after her. At the doorway, I turned my head towards the table, but Mathias just shook his head. He wasn't coming this time.

"So… what exactly are these tests?" I asked, trying to keep up with her fast pace. Dr. Beckett had gone ahead of us, and I could still see his head bobbing in the distance.

"Here, it's just a quick health check-up. Then you'll be escorted to the academy for your PT. All newcomers have to take it," she responded. We went through thick glass doors and entered another hallway. This one was lit with fluorescent ceiling panels and reminded me of the hospital I used to go to when I was younger.

"What's a PT?" I asked.

"A Placement Test. I believe you're familiar with the procedure. After all, you took one to qualify for that selective enrollment high school of yours," she said. Once again, I was shocked by how casually she said this. What else did these people know about me? "Of course," she continued, "this one will be slightly different. Your intellect won't be the only thing we test."

I nodded.

We came to a stop before a door that read "**Doc B**" in big bold letters. Sorina pressed her thumb onto a black screen by the door's handle. *Beep.* It flashed red, and Sorina frowned. She wiped her thumb on the material of her pants and tried again. This time the screen turned green and the lock clicked.

Dr. Beckett's office was different from Sorina's. His desk – made of white wood – was backed up against a corner, whereas Sorina's had stood in the center. The walls, instead of being filled by bookshelves, had posters of smiling children. The one nearest to me portrayed two young girls (one with wings, the other without) perched on top of a fence.

"Your Highness," Dr. Beckett bowed, placing an arm behind his back. "Please follow me," he said. He led us towards the back of the room and into a short corridor with only one door, which made me wonder why they had a corridor in the first place.

The room we entered was half the size of the bedroom I had slept in and was filled with all sorts of machinery. On the right side of the room, stood a white rack with an assortment of gadgets and remotes. The left side of the room contained dozens of screens, all attached to the wall with colorful wires, which in turn led to the huge transparent cylinder in the center of the room. Out of all the screens in the room, the back wall had the largest; it was currently displaying white static.

Dr. Beckett picked up a remote and pressed a button. The glass walls of the cylinder slid open, creating an entrance. "Stand inside. Go on, it doesn't hurt," he said to me, beckoning towards the opening with his free hand. I obeyed (did I have another choice?) and stood in the center awaiting further instructions.

The glass walls slid shut.

"Good. Good. You're doing very well," Dr. Beckett said. "Place your feet on the red marks… there. Good. Now just lift your arms so they're parallel to your shoulders… yes! Just like that." He pressed another button, and the static stopped, replaced by a loading screen. Then came a three-dimensional image of my body, so detailed I could see the movement of my intestines. I watched as he zoomed into my liver, which was flashing bright green, and jotted something down in his notepad. He continued doing this for nearly every body part, until he turned off the screen.

The walls slid open, and I lowered my arms, which had gone slightly numb.

"How are you feeling?" the doctor asked.

"Good," I responded. Aside from the fading numbness in my arms, I felt the same. "Your technology is quite advanced," I added, jutting my chin towards the blank screen. "Although, I don't really see the point in it. Your saliva alone is enough to heal all sorts of wounds."

Dr. Beckett smiled. "I'm the one who made all of it. Spent a good twenty years constructing the scan. Nobody else in this town possesses such high intelligence. As for your other claim, medical knowledge always has its benefits. We aren't capable of seeing inside the body. The scan does that for us."

Before I could respond, Sorina's firm hand gripped my upper arm. "Thank you, Dr. Beckett. I hope you don't mind us leaving so early; Ms. Allaire has her PT scheduled for twelve."

Dr. Beckett said he didn't mind, bowed, and wished me luck on the test. Sorina ushered me out the door.

"Now," she said, "you must remember: this test is not to be taken lightly. It will determine your academic placement for the remainder of the school year, and I doubt you want to land yourself in a class full of ten-year-olds."

I nodded. I didn't understand what she meant, not exactly, but by the way she was talking, I could tell this test was important. And I certainly didn't want to "land myself" in a class of fifth graders.

"Wait here," she said. We were standing by the front door of the palace. It was open, and I could see several guards stationed at the golden gates. "Your escort should arrive shortly."

"Okay." I wasn't fazed by the fact that she was leaving me. She was the Queen, after all. Queens had their own duties to attend.

She began to walk away, then stopped. Her head swiveled around briefly, and she mouthed two last words: *Good luck.*

Chapter Ten

The escort turned out to be a slim woman, dressed in a pretty red dress that complemented her black hair. When she saw me, she let out a girly squeal, clasping her hands over her chest.

"You must be Lucianne. That's such a pretty name!"

The sudden compliment took me by surprise. "Oh, uh, thank you, ma'am."

"Call me Irene," she said, extending a hand in my direction. I shook it. "I'm sure we'll become friends." She grinned.

I gave her a small smile in return.

"The weather is absolutely *beautiful* today, don't you think?"

"Sure," I replied. The woman seemed to be very talkative, and I decided to use it to my advantage. "Could you tell me more about the Placement Test? I'll be taking it today."

"Oh, I know you'll be taking it. I'm your escort." She giggled. "Don't be scared. I'm sure you'll do great."

"I'm not scared," I said, not failing to notice that she had completely ignored my question. We were heading to the side of the palace, towards an assortment of carriages.

"Of course you're not! You're a brave girl." The grin on her face was starting to get on my nerves. Why was she treating me like a child?

We stopped in front of one of the carriages. Two large snake-like creatures were standing near the rear, their eyes fixed on the palace. They were both a dark shade of blue. Each of them had two arms that looked just like a lizard's—long and scaly, with four razor-sharp claws at the bottom. Their heads looked just like a chameleon's. I knew because my old science teacher had one as a pet. A thick rope was tied around their chests, binding them to the carriage.

"Feslins," Irene said. "Such useful creatures! Very easy to discipline." She reached out towards one of the feslins to touch its scaly neck. It flinched. Irene smacked her lips in distaste and strutted to the carriage, throwing open the door.

"How far are we going?" I asked.

"To the academy," she said briefly, as if she expected me to know where that was. "They know where they're supposed to go."

No more than fifteen seconds later, the floor began to vibrate, and I could see the feslins moving towards the front gate. I leaned back against the velvety seat and shut my eyes. Maybe Irene wouldn't talk if she thought I was asleep.

The ride lasted less than two minutes. My escort's face lit up when we stepped out of the carriage.

"Majestic, isn't it?" she enthused. She was looking at the academy, which was made up of two rectangular buildings, connected by the modern shell-like structure in the center. Ribbed vaults surrounded the exterior, and the front of every building had an arch. Aside from the shell, it looked like the type of structure you would see in a textbook on gothic architecture.

The shell's opening was made of glass, and I could see silhouettes moving around inside. The buildings were about as large as several apartment complexes, and had huge, marble wings sprouting from the back of each, towering over the yard. The sign at the front of the wrought iron gates read: **Levond Academy 1-12**.

"Very majestic," I said. "Is this where I'll be taking the Placement Test?"

"Yes! My classroom's in the West Wing. Come on!" she stated. She clasped her hands and began trotting towards the school. I, on the other hand, stood rooted to the ground. There was only one reason I could think of when it came to Irene telling me the location of her classroom: I would be taking the test with her. That seemed like a nightmare.

Irene, who must have noticed the lack of footsteps behind her, turned around and frowned. "Everything okay back there?"

"Mhm," I said, catching up to her. "Everything's fine." We entered the school.

Irene's classroom looked like the average preschool. The desks and chairs were color-coordinated, and stickers of flowers and trees stared at me from the walls. Every desk had a name tag. The orange chair I sat in belonged to **Layla**.

Irene grabbed a packet from her desk and gave it to me. On the front page, written in thick, bold letters, were two words: **Placement Test**.

A queasy feeling began to form in my stomach. Nerves. I hated tests, especially ones that I hadn't studied for. How did they expect me to perform well if I didn't know the material at hand?

Irene cleared her throat and began reading off a sheet of paper. She sounded like one of the teachers you would take a state test with. Her cheerful demeanor was gone.

"At Levond, we believe intellect cannot be determined by age. Every individual has different strengths and struggles, both of which are detected by this test. Your performance in each topic will determine the level you will study at for the remainder of the school year. The topics are as follows: arithmetic, Soratian history, human history, modern human technology, geography, and biology. You will also be tested on the strength of your abilities or lack thereof." She stepped forward, dropping a pencil onto my desk. "You may begin."

I turned the paper and skimmed over the first section: math. The questions started off simple—basic addition and subtraction—and eventually stopped at calculus. I finished in twenty minutes (answering what I could, taking a guess of everything else) and went onto the next sections: human history, biology, and modern human technology. I worked pretty smoothly until the last two sections: Soratian history and geography.

"Excuse me, um, Irene?"

She perked up her head from the book she had been reading. "Yes?"

I pointed to the question that stated: *Explain the primary reasons behind the Soratian Human War.* "I just came here yesterday. I don't know the history of your... er... country."

Irene shrugged. "Take your best guess. I can't help you during the test, but I believe in you!" she gave me a thumbs-up and returned to her reading.

I groaned, letting my forehead slide to the table despite its putrid smell.

There was no way in hell I was going to ace this.

Chapter Eleven

Three hours after my return to the palace, I was still sulking in my bedroom. They had moved me to a different room, ensuring I wouldn't repeat the scene from last night. I didn't care much about the change of scenery; my mind was stuck on the Placement Test.

"Lucianne?" Mathias's muffled voice was located just outside of my bedroom. He was knocking.

"Ye-es?"

"Dinner's in five minutes. Can you find your way to the dining area?"

"Yeah. I'll be right there," I answered. I put on my shoes and opened the door. A part of me expected to see him standing outside. I looked both ways to make sure he wasn't standing in any of the hallways, but he was gone. The guy was extraordinarily fast. If I hadn't known he was phytokinetic, I could have sworn his ability was enhanced speed.

At this time of day, the dining room was filled with people, contrary to what it had been in the morning. All of the royal siblings were there, and one of them – Sonia- waved me over.

"Today's your last day here, right?" she asked, flipping her pale blue hair over her shoulder.

"Right. That's what Her Highness told me."

A small smile appeared on Sonia's lips. "You can call her Rina, y'know. I don't think she minds."

I wasn't completely sure about that last part, especially since I had yet to hear someone call the queen by a nickname. "I think I'll stick to 'Her Highness,'" I said. "She is the queen after all."

Sonia shrugged, shoving a piece of bread into her mouth. "Suit yourself."

I waited for her to finish chewing before speaking again. "Hey Sonia?"

"Yeah?"

"What's the Griffin?" I asked slowly, unsure of whether she would answer. Yesterday, Sorina had promised to elaborate on the subject, (or, at least, to continue our conversation), but it seemed like she had forgotten. I wasn't going to bother her during dinner; she seemed preoccupied with guests of much higher importance than myself.

Sonia took a sip from her cup, which was embroidered with red jewels. "He's the wing maker. Last one alive."

"What's that?"

"He makes wings for half-bloods. That's what your back marks are for, aside from classifying you as a half-blood. There should be two of them."

I recalled what O'Connor had said about checking my back during the night of my kidnapping. It certainly added to what Sonia was saying. But what did the rest of it mean? Weren't half-bloods not supposed to have wings?

"Could you elaborate?" I asked. "I still don't get how it works."

She looked slightly annoyed at my slow perception but decided to explain. "The wings made by the Griffin have sharp ends. You stick them into your marks, and they grow into real ones. To take them out, you just gotta press the small lever in the center and they pop right out. But they're expensive since the Griffin only makes two a year. Used to be three, but he's getting kind of old."

"Sounds painful," I said. The sheer thought of jamming something sharp into my back made me cringe.

She smiled smugly, fluttering the tips of her wings. "I wouldn't know. Only grown-ups are allowed to get them, and you have to go through rounds of testing before putting them in. But they say it's worth it since your ability strengthens by a lot. So you're almost like a real Soratian."

I nodded. "Must be nice to have them."

"Mhm."

We ate the rest of the dinner in silence, listening to the chatter of the other guests at the table. It didn't seem like a royal dinner at all, more like a fancy end-of-the-year party you would attend with a few rich friends. To me, that's what it was – a celebration of my last day at the palace.

After dinner, I found Mathias sitting on a couch in one of the rooms, sipping a cup of tea. As much as I hated to bother him, there was something I needed to do, and he was one of the only familiar faces around here.

"Hey, uh, Mathias?"

He lifted his gaze and gave me a questioning glance. "Yeah?"

"Do you have a working phone around here?"

He paused for a moment, then answered with a question of his own. "Who do you want to call?"

I told him.

"Ah. In that case, yes, we have a working phone around here. Walk straight down that hall," he pointed towards a hallway to the right, "take two turns left, and you should see it. It's pretty old, but it works."

"Thank you," I said. I deliberated asking him if he could come with me but decided against it. If he had wanted to come, he would have proposed it.

The hallway was empty except for one maid pulling her cart towards one of the rooms. Her head lifted at the sound of my footsteps, but she continued working, not bothering to say anything.

I smiled at her as I passed.

She didn't smile back.

Following Mathias's directions, I turned the two corners and walked into, yet another room filled with expensive armchairs and fancy coffee tables. My eyes landed on the phone almost immediately. It looked like something from an antique store, perhaps dating back to the late 1970s. I began turning the dial, my throat growing tighter with each number.

Done.

I held up the receiver, hearing it ring.

Once.

Twice.

Of course. Who in their right mind would answer an unknown number? The feeling of anticipation that had been building up inside my throat began to fade. I waited for the voicemail: "I'm sorry. I must be busy and can't answer the phone right now. Please leave a message."

Instead, the phone was picked up.

Chapter Twelve

The voice on the other end was hoarse, and I could tell my mother had been crying. Hearing her in such a state was enough to make me want to put down the phone. But I couldn't. Not without telling her what had happened.

"Hello? Who am I speaking with?"

"It's me, Mom," I whispered, my throat tightening to the point of suffocation. "I'm safe."

Silence.

For a moment, I thought she had hung up. But then, I heard her voice, barely above whisper. "Luce? Is that you?"

Tears began to prick at the back of my eyes. "I'm here, Mom. It's me. I promise," I whimpered. I held my breath, unsure of what her response would be. I hoped she wouldn't faint. She would have to be strong enough for the information I was about to release on her.

She began to sob. "Luce… b-baby… oh, *oh* my God… thank goodness…. I-I thought... I thought I'd-"

"Mom, I'm safe," I repeated. Her voice was making me emotional, and I was thankful for the privacy. Anyone seeing me like this would have been embarrassing. I waited for her to calm down, slowly pulling the receiver away from my ear so I wouldn't hear her crying.

"Luce?" she called. Her voice was steadier now, although I could still hear it tremble. "What happened to you?"

And so I lied. I had always been good at it, and not having to look her in the eyes made it easier. The story I came up with was something along the lines of a winged human whisking me away to a different universe, where I had spent the last few days prowling around a marble palace. I told her about the academy and Mathias, who I referred to as "my friend." I explained to her that I was what they considered a "half-blood," and that Dad was the main reason I was here. It was only half of the story but telling her about my kidnapping would have been disastrous.

"But you knew this," I said. "You knew Dad had wings."

She sighed heavily, and our connection was momentarily broken by static. It was growing weaker. "—sorry. I just didn't think they would take you so... soon. They found Mrs. Riley dead near Scott, gunshot to the chest, and that's the route you usually take when you walk home, so I-I thought you'd *surely* been kidnapped, especially after-"

"Mom, stop it. I told you I was fine."

"I know, I'm sorry," she said. Again, there was a short pause filled with static, and then I heard the end of her question. "...your father?"

"Can you say it again? I can't hear you."

"I asked how your father was, and if I could speak with him," she said. Her tone was hopeful, which made it ten times worse.

No, Mom, I thought. *Dad is dead. He was either suffocated by smoke or burned alive, and the people that killed him work for the same organization that kidnapped and beat me two days ago.*

Instead, I gritted my teeth and said, "I haven't seen him yet, but I'll call you when I do."

Which would be never.

I could hear her smiling through the phone. She was no longer crying, and that made me glad I had called. "Okay. Thank you," she said. The familiar sound of static filled my ears, this time lasting much longer than a few seconds. "...you don't, please call me anyway. I miss you."

"Sure," I said. Our connection wasn't going to last much longer. "I'll try."

Except I knew I wouldn't because after tonight I would be leaving the palace, and who knew if I would be able to find another working phone.

That made the lump in my throat bigger.

Chapter Thirteen

The next morning, Cornelia gently shook me awake much earlier than usual. She had already packed my things into several bags, all of which were lined up by the door, awaiting the courier. The fact that I spent less than two days at the palace didn't stop me from feeling hollow on the day of my departure.

As for my new residence, it was bound to be less luxurious. From what Mathias had told me, I would be sharing the dorm with another girl. That gave me mixed feelings. On one hand, I had always loved the thought of having a roommate; it was one of the many reasons I wanted to go to college. On the other, there was the possibility of said roommate not getting along with someone such as myself. The latter would make my stay at Levond a nightmare. I hoped I wouldn't run out of luck.

Mathias came up to me when I was standing near the front doors, helping the courier with my baggage.

"How are you feeling? You look pale," he said, popping a green leaf into his mouth.

I felt giddy. My leg kept bouncing up and down, and my nails had been bitten to stubs. "I'm fine," I said. "Do you know anything about my roommate?"

He shook his head. "I don't have the authority to know that," he responded. Then his eyes fell on my bouncing leg. "You're nervous."

"I'm fine."

"No, you're not. When girls say they're fine, they're usually not," he replied, gazing up at the ceiling.

"And you know that, how?"

"Experience."

The courier came back, taking the last two bags with him. "Ma'am, your carriage is ready," he informed me before walking out the door. I stared after him, my legs not wanting to move.

"Are *you* ready?" Mathias asked.

"Not really," I admitted. "But it's not like I have a choice."

He hesitated for a moment, then reached into his pocket and took out a pale blue flower. "Here. It's yours. Just don't tell Her Highness; she hates when I pick her flowers."

I took it, lifted it to my nose, and sniffed. The fragrant aroma was rich and sweet, and I placed the flower into my pocket, where it would be safe. "Thank you," I said. I meant it.

"Ma'am?" the courier's bald head poked through the door. "We're leaving."

"Right," I sighed, turning towards Mathias. "I guess this is goodbye."

He smiled, lifting his hand. "Au revoir."

* * *

The dormitory was a small square building that stood just behind the school and didn't look like it could hold more than twenty people. On the way there, I kept caressing the flower Mathias had given me. Examining the intricate patterns on its petals helped calm my nerves, so by the time I exited the carriage, my heart had stopped pounding and I was ready to meet my roommate.

My roommate.

What was she like? From the conversations I had managed to eavesdrop back at the palace, the dormitory's occupants were all parentless half-bloods, mostly from Earth. I wondered if she had also been kidnapped by the Qroes and if she had abilities close to mine. It would be nice to have a roommate with similar experiences.

Before I knew it, I was standing in front of the dorm, and the courier was hauling in my baggage. All eight bags, one by one. The door was open, but aside from the courier's footsteps, the room was silent. I looked inside.

Empty.

I walked in and sat on the edge of my new bed, studying my roommate's side of the room. The walls were covered with photos of girls, but I couldn't tell which one I would be living with – they were all group pictures. A circular mirror was attached to the wall beside the bed, and beneath it stood a small table with make-up supplies, as well as a couple bottles of perfume. That explained the sweet fragrance that wafted in the air. Her desk seemed pretty organized, much more organized than mine had been back in Minnesota. That was good. At least our room wouldn't be messy.

"Do you need help unpacking, ma'am?" the courier asked, carrying in my last bag. I wondered why there were so many in the first place. I had come to this dimension with nothing more than a single outfit, but it seemed they had already supplied my whole wardrobe. It was much more than I deserved.

"No, thank you," I said. "I'll do the unpacking. Do you know when my roommate will get here?"

The courier glanced at his watch. "An hour, perhaps more. Lessons end in approximately fifty minutes."

"Okay," I said. "Thanks. And thank you for carrying my bags. They look a bit heavy."

He chuckled. "I'm just doing my job. Have a good afternoon, Ms. Allaire."

He closed the door.

I sat still for a moment, then reached for one of the bags, curious to check out its contents. It was filled with school supplies—pencils, pens, notebooks, sheets of paper…

I closed the bag and reached into another. This one had a medium-sized crystal lamp. It reminded me of the decorations I would see displayed in the mall on the corner of my street, the ones I had never been able to afford. I put it on my desk. The other bags had clothes and shoes, long and short, thick and thin, for all seasons and occasions. Most of the garments were all modest, which made me glad—I wasn't used to wearing revealing clothing; my mother was strictly against it.

When I was in the middle of unpacking my last bag, I heard faint laughter in the hallway. It came closer, moving towards the dorm until I could hear the conversation.

"You think she's already here?" one of the girls asked, and I felt myself stiffen. They were talking about me. I pressed my ear against the door, forgetting about the clothes I had been going to place in the closet.

The other girl mumbled something indecipherable and the chatter ceased. I heard her walk back down the hall, most likely to her own dorm.

I glanced down at my nails, which had been bitten to stubs. It was a bad habit that had started at the age of eight, when I had seen one of my classmates doing it in the middle of a lesson. And now, no matter how much I tried, I couldn't bring myself to stop.

The doorknob turned.

I jumped away at once, tripping over the half-open bag on the floor. My knee hit the edge of the bed. A flare of pain shot through me as I gritted my teeth, willing myself not to make a sound. I didn't want to cry in front of my roommate. Holding onto the bed, I pulled myself into a sitting position.

The door creaked open.

Chapter Fourteen

The girl was tan and blond, seemingly frozen in shock by the scene before her. I was clearly not the roommate she had been expecting.

"Hi," I said meekly, fully aware that my face was heating up. "I'm Lucianne."

The girl stared at the open bag and its contents sprawled across the floor. When her eyes finally fell on me, they were wide. "Do you need help?"

I scrambled to my feet, reaching for the bag. "No, no, it's fine. I can do it myself. But thank you for the offer." Before I could pick anything up, however, I felt her hand grab my arm. The coolness of her skin caused goosebumps to erupt across my arm.

"It would be rude of me not to help you. I have manners."

I smiled. "Alright. Thank you."

We began picking up the clothes, and as the girl knelt down next to me, I couldn't help but feel a pang of jealousy at her outfit. It was clear that my roommate's style was far more refined than mine. A pink beret was perched on her head, and she wore a fur-lined cape coat over her crewneck sweater. The suede skirt she had on ended right above her knees, her arm holding a small leather handbag.

"Nice outfit," I said, folding up the last blouse. Putting everything away had taken us no more than twenty minutes, which was much faster than I had expected.

Her face lit up. "Thank you! It's one of my favorites. If you want, I'll take you shopping! And we'll buy the same outfit, in green or red, whichever fits you best, and then we'll be twins! We could go first thing tomorrow."

"That'd be nice," I said. "What's your name?"

"Adelaine Chevrolet," she said, sticking out a manicured hand. "Yours is Lucine, right? That's very pretty."

I shook it. "Close. Lucianne."

"So a combination of Lucy and Anne," she observed before plopping down onto her bed. "It fits you. Oh, you have no idea how excited I was when Windridge told me you were coming. Did you know I'm from Earth, too? I have so many stories to tell…"

I spent the next thirty minutes listening to Adelaine as she told me about coming to Soratia. She hadn't been in direct contact with the Qroes, nor had she spent several days at the palace, so our stories were pretty different. Hers was far more tragic. She had no recollection of her mother, who passed when she was two and lived with her aunt until the age of six. By then, her father had heard about her mother's death and took her to Soratia shortly after finding her location.

"Three days before my birthday," Adelaine said. "April third."

She lived with her father for two years. He had been killed by the Qroes in the same fire that had taken my father's life, and since she had no known relatives, she ended up in the dorms.

"It's pretty nice here, though," she said. "I've made a lot of friends. And my dad left me some cash, so I can buy a house when I'm older."

"That's good. I'm glad you're financially stable."

Adelaine kicked a frilly pillow off her bed. "Uh-uh. Now tell me about your life before you came here. You heard about mine."

I had never been too good at storytelling, but I tried my best. I told her about Huma, the only real friend I ever had, and how I had managed to qualify for the most prestigious high school in the area, despite my financial status. I told her about my encounter with Horseface, and how it had led to me being kidnapped just a day after. The second was not only recent but more interesting, which made it much easier to tell.

70

"Hold on," she said. "You're a pain manipular? How the hell did they test that?"

I was confused for a moment, unsure of what she meant. Then I remembered the Placement Test. "Oh, Irene just held up a finger and told me to make it hurt. I was pretty angry with her by that time, so she actually ended up hissing in pain. I'm not sure if it was just the finger though," I said, remembering the glare she had given me at the end of the test.

Adelaine laughed. "Serves her right. I'm sorry you had to deal with that wretch."

"Wretch? How? She seemed pretty normal. At least until the end, but I don't blame her for getting upset."

Adelaine tapped her long fingernails on the bedpost. "Nuh-uh. She's as fake as it gets. Her attitude is nice to the other teachers, but she hates her students. And I speak from experience, so you better hope you won't end up in her classroom. Speaking of which," she said, digging into her backpack and taking out a navy-blue envelope, "here's your schedule. The headmistress asked me to give it to you."

I took the envelope and ripped it open. The paper inside was a yellowish gray and printed on it was my schedule. It read:

Lucianne Allaire, 15

8:00-9:00 Arithmetic: 5W (r.15)
9:00-10:00 Geography: 3W (r.218)
10:00-11:00 Biology: 6W (r.16)
11:00-12:00 Soratian history: 1W (r. 310)
12:00-1:00 Human history 7W (r. 125)
1:00-2:00 Lunch (cafeteria)
2:00-3:00 MHT: 6W (r.4)
3:00-5:00 Ability: 7E (r. 112)

I passed the paper to Adelaine, who had been very noticeably peeking over my shoulder. She read the first few lines, and then her mouth fell open.

"No way," she said. "*No way.*"

"What-" I started to ask, but she cut me off.

"Look!" she pointed to the line at the bottom, the one that read 3:00-5:00 Ability: 7E (r.110).

I stared at the black letters for over a minute before saying, "I don't get it." None of them made sense to me. What was she so hyped up about?

"Look there." She pointed to the 7E. This time I saw what she meant. All of the other letters had a W. This one was the exception.

"It has an E. Okay. Why is the E so significant?"

"It means that you'll be practicing your ability in the East Wing."

This only made the confusion grow larger. "I still don't get it."

Adelaine pulled out a sheet of paper and began sketching. "Our academy has two wings. The West Wing, the one on the left, is for half-bloods, and the East Wing is for Soratians, aka the people with wings. I don't know why they divide us. They just do. Probably because the Soratians have stronger powers. The Shell is the only place we can meet together. The Shell is what we call the cafeteria, by the way," she added. "The numbers you see by the letters show the level you will be taught at. That's what the Placement Test is for. It finds which topics you're strong at, and which ones you need to work on. One is the lowest, seven is the highest. So, you really suck at Soratian history."

"Don't judge me," I said. "I only came here a few days ago."

"I'm not. The point is, your last class, ability practice, is in the East Wing, and you're a half-blood. *And* you got the highest level. It just doesn't make sense. Are you really that good?"

I bit my lip. "I don't think I am. I mean… I can't even control it, much less regulate its force. Maybe it's a mistake."

Adelaine shook her head. "The headmistress doesn't make mistakes, and neither does anyone in her office. Not with schedules."

"Well," I said, placing the paper back into the envelope, "I guess I'll find out tomorrow." Then I changed the topic. "Since we're talking about abilities, what's yours?"

"Telepathy," Adelaine answered. She wrinkled her nose when she said it. "I wish it was more impressive."

I snorted. "Oh, please. I'd choose telepathy over pain manipulation any day. You can literally communicate with people using your mind! How cool is that?"

She laughed, but it was an empty sound, void of any emotion. "The most I can do is tell you what number you're thinking of if you put it on the front of your mind. I don't think I'll ever be able to communicate with people. I would have to have wings to be that strong."

"It's still pretty cool," I said, flipping my hair over my shoulder. "What number am I thinking of?"

"Six. You're practically screaming it," her tone was unimpressed. "Now finish unpacking. I'll show you around campus."

Chapter Fifteen

Before my departure from the palace, the queen had provided me with fifty golden coins, which, according to Adelaine, equaled "one thousand and eighty plets." That seemed to be the currency around here. I tucked most of the cash into a bag underneath my bed and used the rest to buy a small vase for the flower Mathias had given me. I wanted to preserve it as long as possible.

"Who gave you that thing, anyway?" Adelaine asked, nodding towards the vase with the flower.

"Mathias," I replied, stroking the blue petals with my thumb.

"How romantic!"

I rolled my eyes. "I've known him for less than two days."

We were the only ones in the dormitory's lobby. Adelaine's hands were filled with bags of clothes, but mine only held the vase. I wasn't too good at shopping.

She handed me the key to our room. "Doesn't make it any less romantic. Girl, he *saved* you. He's the knight to your princess."

"He's a *friend*, and even that seems unlikely at the moment. Like I said, I've known him for less than two days, which is barely enough to have a few conversations," I replied. I placed the vase onto the drawer with a clunk.

"Then spend more time with him." Adelaine smirked. "I can find his schedule if you'd like."

I froze. "His schedule? He goes to Levond?"

"Obviously. Levond is the only school in Soratia. Everybody except the royal family has to attend."

"Oh. I guess that makes sense."

"So, want me to find his schedule for you?" she asked again. She looked completely serious.

My eyes widened. "No, no, definitely not. I don't want him to think I'm a stalker," I said hurriedly. I cringed at the mere possibility of him thinking I was one.

She sighed and shook her head, as if I had made a mistake. "Fine. But don't come crawling back to me when you won't be able to find him."

"I won't."

We washed, changed into our pajamas (hers were hot-pink and frilly, mine were blue and simple), and slept. A droning buzz woke me up in the morning, and I opened my eyes to see Adelaine sitting in front of the mirror, putting on lip gloss.

She heard the bed shift as I sat up.

"Hey girl! How do ya like the sound of the wake-up call?"

I yawned. "It sucks. When's school?"

"We've got about thirty minutes before we go to the Shell for breakfast. Here," she said, offering me her eyeliner.

"No thanks," I said, waving her off. "I don't use that stuff," I told her. I grabbed my brush and started to tame the reddish beast that had grown on my head overnight.

"Okay," Adelaine said, tapping the corner of her chin. "What brand do you use? We can go shopping after lessons," she offered. The thought of me not using make-up at all didn't seem to cross her mind.

"Errr, I don't know. I'm not familiar with any of them," I replied. That, at least, was part of the truth.

"Ohh, right!" she laughed. "I keep forgetting you came here not so long ago. Don't worry, I'll help you find one you like."

The conversation ended at that because Adelaine found a smudge on the corner of her eyelid. That, of course, needed urgent care immediately.

I got dressed into the school uniform (which Adelaine had given me alongside the schedule), which consisted of a white polo shirt and a plaid knee-length skirt. From what I had seen yesterday, the boys' uniform was the same, except the skirt was replaced with cream trousers. It was certainly better than any outfit I could pick.

The Shell was crowded with students, but Adelaine and I managed to find an empty table. It was a huge place and certainly lived up to its name—shaped like a semi-opened shell, with the glass wall in the back serving as the opening. The floor of the Shell ended at the glass, but the ceiling extended far beyond it, creating a wavy roof over a piece of the sidewalk. The architects must have really been trying to nail the ocean theme because the place was filled with shell-shaped chairs that surrounded the hundreds of circular tables. Right now, these tables were filled with an assortment of foods, so we could eat what we wanted. I chose to nibble on a waffle.

"Addie! Hey!"

I looked up to see a tall Asian girl running towards our table. Her backpack was hanging off one shoulder, and her shirt wasn't fully tucked into her skirt. She was breathing heavily when she dropped the backpack onto the floor and sat in one of the shell-shaped seats.

"Mei! You came!" Adelaine exclaimed, running around the table to give her friend a hug.

I raised my hand to wave. "Hi."

"Lucianne, this is Meiling Zhou. Mei, this is Lucianne. I hope you both get along because if you don't… well, let's just say I'll be watching the drama from the sidelines."

She sat back down and began to eat.

"You're Addie's roommate, right?" Mei asked, holding out her hand.

I shook it. "Uh-uh. You must be her friend. The one I heard in the hallway yesterday. You live in the dorms too?"

Mei shook her head. "I live with my parents. But you're right about me being in the hallway yesterday. I wanted to see you, but she wouldn't let me." She cast a quick glare in Adelaine's direction. "Anyway, nice to meet you! I heard you're from Earth, which is like, great because I'm failing human history. Mind telling me how you got here?"

I told her that no, I didn't mind, and told her everything I had told Adelaine. It took me almost thirty minutes to finish, and by that time, breakfast was nearly over, and Mei's mouth was hanging open.

"If you didn't mention Mathias, I might not have believed you," she said at last. "That's how crazy it is. I don't know a single person that's been in contact with the Qroes, aside from you and him."

"You know Mathias?"

"Yeah. I was his piano tutor a few years ago since he sucked at it and wanted to learn a piece for his girlfriend." She stood up and grabbed our plates, all of which were empty except for a few crumbs.

"What was her name?" I asked, although I already knew the answer. There was no way it was a coincidence.

"Atiana Morales. She lived in the palace since Mathias worked for the Queen. I think she was gonna work for her, too, but she was still training."

She began walking away, towards a stand near the trash cans at which the students were depositing the silverware. Without mentioning anything about Atiana going missing. I decided not to ask again.

Adelaine reached into her backpack and took out two oval leaves. She put one in her mouth and offered me the other.

"What is that?" I asked. They looked like the same leaves I had seen Mathias chew, but I had never found out what they were.

"Versicose. It's a plant that freshens up your breath. Like gum. Just swallow it before class; I don't want you to get in trouble."

I popped the leaf into my mouth and began to chew. A cool, minty taste flooded my mouth as it dissolved into a gooey substance. Adelaine had been right. It tasted similar to gum but better.

Bells began to chime, signaling the end of breakfast and the start of first period.

"What level do you have?" Mei asked.

"Five. You?"

Her eyes brightened. "Oh, me too! Wanna walk together?"

I agreed.

We took the left exit and walked into the West Wing of Levond. If it weren't for Mei gripping my hand, I would have surely gotten lost in the crowd. She pulled me past a display of shining trophies and into a shorter hallway, which was much less empty than the main hall. Apparently, not many students had Level 5 math.

Mixing in with the crowd, we walked into Room 15, where I could see several students settling in their seats. Mei dragged me towards the back and found us two empty chairs. This classroom was plain and simple, unlike Irene's colorful one. I was glad for the lack of distractions. Math required concentration.

"Is Lucianne Allaire present?" the teacher asked after everyone had taken a seat. He was a stout man, with a pale head that contained no more than a few wisps of gray hair.

"Present," I replied, waving my hand to let him know where I was sitting.

The teacher smiled. "We're happy to have you, Lucianne. I'm Mr. Berger. Adjusting to the schedule so late into the school year may be a tad bit difficult, so feel free to reach out to me with any concerns. I'll gladly assist you."

We began the lesson.

The rest of the teachers (up until the third period) were just as kind as the first. None of them asked me to stand in front of the class and introduce myself. I hoped the rest of my classes would be the same.

"What's your next class?" Mei asked. We were returning from Biology 6, which was another similarity in our schedules. I checked the sheet of paper. "Soratian History 1. Room 310. Do you know where it is? Adelaine and I didn't get a chance to see it yesterday since it's on the third level and—"

Mei snorted. She tried to cover her mouth, unsuccessfully, and burst out laughing in the middle of the hallway. I gritted my teeth but waited for her laughter to subside to giggles before speaking.

"Look," I said, "I came here two days ago. If you expect me to get anything higher than the lowest score on an unfamiliar country's *history* test, you-"

Mei wagged her finger. "No, no. Not that. What room did you say again?" She was very visibly trying to hold in her laughter.

"Three-hundred and ten. Why?"

A quick burst of air escaped her lips, but this time, she didn't laugh. "Just follow me. You'll see for yourself."

She led me up the two flights of stairs and down a wide hallway. The latter seemed strangely familiar, but I couldn't quite put a finger on it until we were standing in front of the door to room 310.

The first thing I saw were the students. They were no more than eleven, every single one of them at least a head shorter than me. Typical sixth graders. A couple older students were entering the classroom as well, but they too were much younger than me. I would be the oldest.

The second thing were the desks. Arranged by color, with chairs to match. A white slip of paper shone from the upper corner of each. Name tags.

One of them held my name.

Chapter Sixteen

"Lucianne! How wonderful to see you!" Irene exclaimed. She was grinning the same faux grin I remembered from two days ago. "Why don't you introduce yourself to the class?"

I stood in front of the board. I could feel sweat beading up on my back. My classmates stared at me, clearly surprised to see someone so old standing at the front of the room.

"Hi," I said awkwardly. "I'm Lucianne, and I came to Soratia a couple of days ago."

I looked at Irene for further instructions.

Instead of responding, she turned to the class. "Would anyone like to sit with Lucianne?"

This scenario reminded me of the day I'd met Huma. She had come to our high school in the middle of the year, and since the seating chart had been arranged, the teacher had asked if anyone wanted to sit with her. My hand had shot into the air the second these words left his mouth. Partly because I didn't want her to suffer the embarrassment of not having a seating partner, and partly because I needed a friend. Of course, once people found out about her wealth, she grew quite popular within our school. But she never abandoned me. All because I had raised my hand on her first day of school.

The class was silent. The students began looking around, trying to see if any hand had been raised.

Irene shrugged. "I'm sorry, Lucianne. It looks like none of your classmates want to sit with you right now. Maybe try being more friendly next time, eh? For now, take a seat here. I'll give you your name tag." She gestured towards the red table in front of her desk and passed me the white slip of paper. My ears reddened with humiliation, but I nodded and sat down. I could feel everyone staring at me from the back.

"Alright," Irene said. "Let's begin today with a recap of yesterday's lesson. Keisha, start us off."

A petite girl walked to the front of the room, her box braids swishing behind her. I saw her swallow as she looked at the class.

"We talked about the Griffin-Human War," she said, "and the effects it had on our species."

"What year did the Griffin-Human War begin?"

The girl hesitated. "Thirteen-seventy-two."

"Incorrect," Irene smiled as she said it, but her eyes were cold. "Detention for not paying attention in class."

Keisha sharply sucked in her breath and retreated to her seat. She looked like she was about to cry. I could see why Adelaine and Mei possessed such a strong hatred towards Irene, and why her students were so quiet. The woman was incredibly strict.

"Gregory, what year did the Griffin-Human War begin?"

Gregory, a stout boy sitting at one of the red desks in the front row, stood up at his name. "The Griffin-Human War began in the year of thirteen-seventy-four, due to—"

"Correct. Norbert, what was the cause behind the Griffin-Human War?"

A chair two rows behind me scraped against the floor as a short, freckled boy scrambled to his feet. "The cause behind the Griffin-Human War was conflict between Soratians and Griffins."

"Provide us with more information."

"Griffins bred with humans near the end of the twelfth century, producing the Griffin-human hybrids we know as Soratians. People on Earth were thinking they were cursed, I think, so they took the land of the Griffins and started the war."

Irene nodded. "Soratia was the head of the war. It only took fifty years for our population to grow large enough to defeat the Griffins. We outsmarted them with our weapons, outpowered them with our abilities. They stood no chance against us. What else happened?"

"Soratia named this nation after herself," Norbert said. "And she made herself queen after the war."

"Correct. Sit down."

The next fifty minutes were spent discussing more wars throughout the history of Soratia, but I didn't pay much attention to any of it. Irene's droning lecture was easy to ignore. I kept my eyes fixed on the stray piece of hair that was sticking out from her tight bun, watching it move from side to side as she questioned the students. When the bell finally sounded, I sprung up from my chair, eager to leave as quickly as possible.

Irene tapped her pen on my desk. "Stay a moment after class."

I slowly sat back down. Had she seen I wasn't paying attention? Was she going to punish me for it? *Could* she punish me for it? I watched with envy as the other students flooded out of the classroom.

Once the room was empty, Irene said, "We are in the middle of the school year."

"I know," I replied.

"We've had a lot of assignments over this time period." She said this slowly, as if I wouldn't be able to comprehend what she was saying if she said it normally.

"I know," I said again.

She turned towards her desk and grabbed a stack of papers. They fell onto my desk with a thud.

"I'll give you two weeks to finish the last semester's material. It should be enough to prepare you for the exam. You will take it after turning everything in."

I stared at her, then at the stack of papers, some of which had fluttered to the floor. "Two *weeks*? How am I-"

She pressed a finger to her lips, signaling for me to be silent. "You came in the middle of the year. It is only fair that you make up the work."

"What if I don't?" I crossed my arms. She wasn't being fair.

"You will be punished accordingly." She smiled tightly, pointing to the door. "Enjoy the rest of your day, Lucianne."

I ran down the hallway. My throat had grown swollen, and tears burned the backs of my eyes. I didn't notice Mei, who had been walking in the opposite direction until she grabbed my arm. She had been laughing, but the second she saw my face all traces of happiness disappeared.

She pulled me into a nearby bathroom.

"What did she *do* to you?" she asked, shutting the door behind her.

I spilled the contents of my backpack onto the tiles. "Two weeks. That's how long I have to finish this," I sighed. My jaw was trembling with anger. I regretted not replying to Irene back in the classroom, and not making a snide remark of some sort, something I was certain Adelaine would have done. Instead, I had run out like a coward, probably boosting her ego in the process.

Mei picked up one of the papers. It read: Lesson One: The Establishment of Soratia. She gasped, her mouth forming into a perfect O.

"These… aren't these from the start of the year? Don't tell me she told you to finish last semester's work in two weeks. No way."

I pressed my hands to my face and mumbled, "Precisely."

"But that's ridiculous! You have work from other classes! She can't expect you to finish all of that," she gestured wildly towards my backpack's spilled contents, "in such a short period of time! What if you just don't do it?"

"Then I will be 'punished accordingly,'" I said, trying to mimic Irene's high-pitched voice.

Mei scoffed. "No, you won't. We're going to see the headmistress. Let's go."

She began stuffing the papers back into my backpack.

"Not now," I said meekly. "Please. I don't want people to see me like this."

She sighed. "Fine. Meet me at our table in the Shell right after the final bell."

I put on my backpack. "Deal."

Human history was much better than my last class, partly because I was familiar with it, and partly because the students here were closer to my age. The teacher, Ms. Anskin, seemed strict, but she didn't force me to do last semester's work. I just started where the rest of the class had left off.

"Why are we learning this again?" a black-haired boy called from the back of the room, interrupting the teacher from her lesson on World War II.

Ms. Anskin pivoted on her heel. Her hawk-like eyes pierced into the boy's. "What did you say?"

"I asked why we were learning this. The stuff's happening in a whole other dimension, and I don't see why we need to know it," the boy responded. He cleared his throat. "I get modern human technology since some of us are interested in pursuing a career in interdimensional travel, but this? What's the point?" he asked. He was sprawled across his chair, and his voice was fuzzy and slow. I wouldn't be surprised if he had been drunk.

"Those who don't learn history will repeat it, regardless of the dimension," Ms. Anskin said, her voice cold. "Learning from someone else's mistakes is better than learning from your own. Does that answer your question, Thomas?"

I didn't need to turn around to know that it had. The silence was enough.

* * *

An hour later, I was sitting at the table in the Shell, waiting for Mei and Adelaine to arrive. Adelaine came first, grabbing her make-up pouch the second her rear hit the chair.

"Like it?" she asked, pointing to the purple and blue eyeshadow sparkling on her eyelids.

"Yeah," I said, swallowing a spoonful of soup. "It's a nice contrast."

The silence that followed didn't last long. Make-up and guys seemed to be everything she talked about, and I wasn't surprised when her next question was, "Have you seen Mathias yet?"

I shook my head. "He's in the East Wing. The guy has wings, remember?"

"So find him right now," she said, "the Shell is one of the only places in the academy where Soratians and half-bloods can be seen together."

"Gosh, Adelaine," I muttered, "I've barely known the guy for two days! Are you obsessed with him or something?"

Before she could reply, someone tapped me on the shoulder. I didn't know how long Mei had been standing there, but by the scowl on her face, I could tell she had overheard Adelaine's mention of Mathias.

"We're supposed to be planning out what we're going to say to the headmistress about the Irene situation. Not talking about boys."

Adelaine quirked up a perfectly plucked eyebrow. "What are you talking about?"

"I'm talking about what that wretched woman told Lucianne to do!" she exclaimed. After seeing no comprehension of Adelaine's face, Mei looked over at me. "You haven't told her?"

I shook my head.

And so Mei explained everything to Adelaine, down to the smallest details. That included my breakdown in the bathroom.

"She's worse than I thought," Adelaine muttered, her forehead creasing with concern. "I'm coming with you."

Mei rolled her eyes. "Of course you are."

We began planning.

Chapter Seventeen

You'd have thought a society as medically advanced as Soratia would know how to work their way around an iPhone. Seventh-period modern human technology proved otherwise. We spent thirty minutes going over text emojis.

"It's incredibly unrealistic," a girl next to me – Luna – complained. "Our faces aren't yellow. Our eyes don't turn into stars and hearts. And *this*?" she pointed to one of the laughing emojis. "Why is that face grinning and crying at the same time? How the hell are we supposed to decipher what these mean?"

I laughed. "I'm surprised we're even learning about this. Seems useless, doesn't it? Considering that we're in another dimension."

"It's not that bad on a normal day," she replied, shrugging. "Mr. Klein just wanted to prepare a bonus lesson for your arrival... and his bonus lessons always suck. No offense." Then she wrote *funny* next to the emoji she had been complaining about moments before.

"I'm not complaining," I said. "Where did you even get working phones? I didn't know this place had Wi-Fi."

Without lifting her head, Luna said, "Someone made replicas. They're much worse than the real ones."

"I can tell. The search engine doesn't work."

"Mhm."

We didn't speak again until the end of class, and by then, I was eager to leave. The East Wing was awaiting my presence.

"What room are you going to?" Luna asked once the bells chimed. "I can help you find it."

I remembered what Adelaine had told me about the two wings and that the East Wing was for Soratians only. I was an exception, of course, but Luna wasn't. And, being a half-blood, there was no way she would be allowed inside.

"I'm going with a friend," I said, "so I won't need help finding it. But thank you," I said.

The former, of course, was a lie, but I didn't feel like telling her about my schedule. Who knew what rumors it would start?

The entrance to the East Wing was on the opposite end of the Shell, and a few students shot me strange looks as I hurried towards it. A man was standing by the door. He was most likely there to ensure that half-bloods wouldn't pass through. I smirked. What would he say when a half-blood showed him her schedule?

"Good afternoon, sir," I said pleasantly, lifting my schedule up to his face. He glanced at it, muttered *good afternoon*, and moved out of the way. Like seeing a half-blood enter the East Wing was normal for him.

The hallway on the other side was empty, but I could see students milling around on the far end. I didn't want to go towards them at first, afraid of what they would think when they saw me. But my schedule clearly stated I was supposed to be here. If anyone caused trouble, I would shove it in their face.

I continued walking.

The East Wing was much cleaner than the West Wing. The intricate designs on the walls reminded me of a castle from the Renaissance, and the wooden doors, with golden knobs, looked like they cost more than my old apartment's rent. The floors were polished stone, as opposed to the beige tiles that covered the majority of the West Wing.

"What the hell are you doing here?"

I turned towards the voice, which was coming from a black girl standing on the opposite side of the hallway. Her wings—nearly twice as long as her arms—hovered over the lion tail that sprouted from her lower back.

"I'm here for class," I said calmly. "Just like you."

Ignoring my response, she turned towards a group of girls huddled near the entrance to one of the classrooms.

"Allyson," she called. "I'm pretty sure a half-blood just snuck into our wing."

The girl named Allyson turned around, her long hair whipping the person behind her in the face. Lips curling into a snarl at my sight. She, too, had a tail. She had different-colored eyes, one blue and one green, and for a second, they widened with what seemed to be fear. Then, just as quickly, they went back to normal. Except they were glaring at me with a passive hatred.

"You know," she said in a high-pitched voice, "sneaking into places you don't belong in doesn't end well."

In an instant, her hand was gripping my shoulder, and I could feel her sharp nails digging into my skin.

"I'm aware," I replied. My voice was steady, but my legs were beginning to shake. "I'm here for class. See?" I lifted the wrinkled schedule up to her nose.

Allyson grabbed it, not letting go of my shoulder, and showed it to the first girl.

"It's fake," the girl said. "Look at her other classes. All W's."

Allyson smiled, ripping my schedule into two pieces. Then she ripped it again. The bits of paper fluttered to the floor, and she once again dug her nails into my shoulder.

"You half-bloods think you're so brave." She sneered, and I felt my back pressing into the wall. "How would the headmistress feel if she knew you were in here? Oh, wait. Maybe I'll tell her!"

Go ahead, I thought. *Tell the headmistress.* I wanted the satisfaction of seeing her face when she found out the schedule was real.

But that satisfaction didn't come. Because at that moment, Mathias walked out of the door behind her.

"Zarah, what's going on out here? Hold up… Lucianne?"

Allyson's hand dropped instantly at the voice, and she swiveled around, her mouth gaping open. I stepped away from the wall and looked at the red patches of skin that had formed near my collarbone. There would be bruises, no doubt about it.

"Hi, Mathias," I said, wincing. "Could you lead me to room 112?"

Instead of answering my question, he asked, "What are you doing here?"

"I'm here for class. If my schedule hadn't been ripped to shreds, maybe I'd be able to show you."

Allyson tapped him on the shoulder. "You know her? I think she's on drugs. She says she's got class here."

"I'm not on drugs," I hissed. "Both of you saw my schedule."

Mathias squinted at me. "Aren't you a half-blood? Half-bloods are in the West Wing."

"How'd you even get past security?" the first girl, Zarah, asked.

All three of them were getting on my nerves. "Please just tell me where I can find room 112," I said.

Mathias pointed towards the room he had just come out of. "Room 112, for Level 7 Ability class. Why do you want to go there?"

"I already told you, I'm here for class. That's what was written on my schedule."

Allyson snorted. "The schedule you faked."

"I didn't fake anything. Now please move out of the way," I scowled. My anger was becoming stronger, and I feared what would happen if my ability returned. What if I accidentally hurt her? I couldn't risk doing that, not on my first day at the academy.

Reluctantly, she stepped aside, rolling her eyes as I bumped against her shoulder.

"This should be entertaining," Zarah muttered.

She was right. The class would be very entertaining. For me.

Chapter Eighteen

I sat down at one of the desks, ignoring the stares of my classmates. Like everything else in the East Wing, the desks were much higher quality. I slid my hand back-and-forth against the polished wood until the teacher spoke.

"Good afternoon everyone!" he said as his wings and arms spread out simultaneously in a welcoming gesture.

"Good afternoon Mr. E," the class echoed with much less enthusiasm.

Mr. E grabbed a stack of packets from his desk and began passing them out. "Today we begin our first project of the semester. As many of you have noticed, we also have a new student. I hope you all… yes, Zarah?"

Zarah slowly lowered her arm. "Mr. Eskerington, is the new student a half-blood?" her mouth curled back in distaste at the word.

His tone was cold when he spoke. "Is that a problem?"

"No," she said quickly, "but-"

"Then there is nothing to discuss," he said sternly. He cleared his throat. "On the first page of your packet, you will find spaces for two names. Do you know what that means?"

"We'll be working in partners," a girl from the first row answered. Her curly brown hair was draped over her wings like a curtain.

"Very good, Mallory. Thank you for paying attention." He looked at me. "The students in our class have some truly impressive abilities. If you become good enough at yours, you might land yourself a very rewarding job, even at a young age." He glanced at Mathias as he said this. "Since all of our abilities vary, it is only natural that we encounter different difficulties. The purpose of this project will be to find an area you need to improve upon, whether that be control, strength, or speed, and to do your best to improve it. The project will be due in two weeks, and I trust that you provide me with proof of your improvement. Your partner's word will not be sufficient. Understood?"

We nodded.

"Good. You may begin."

The shuffle of stools filled the room as students began to search for a partner. I stood awkwardly by my desk. What to do? Everyone seemed to know who they wanted to be with, and I clearly wasn't on their list. I deliberated going up to Mr. E and telling him that I couldn't find a partner. Just as quickly, I decided against it. Asking him for help was bound to lead to me standing in the front of the class, like a mutated dog no one wanted to adopt. I would wait.

"Hey."

It was the girl that had spoken earlier – Mallory. "Want to be partners?"

"Sure," I said, feeling a wave of relief at her question. "Thanks. I'm Lucianne, by the way."

"I'm Mallory. What's your ability?" she asked, holding her pencil inches above the paper.

"Pain manipulation," I said as I wrote both of our names on the front of my packet. There was no reason for me to tell her about my other ability. I doubted it could be measured. "What's yours?"

"Electrokinesis. I kind of struggle with maintaining the flow of it—the lights start to flicker whenever I try to hold it for more than a minute. Does that fall under 'control' or 'strength?'"

"I'm pretty sure that would be 'strength.' I, on the other hand, need to improve my control. I still don't know how to make it work without being angry."

Mallory leaned over, so close I could feel the tips of her hair against my skin. "You must be pretty darn good though. You're the first half-blood I've seen in the East Wing. How'd you do it?"

I shrugged. "To be honest, I don't know myself. The most I've managed to do is knock a girl unconscious, and I wasn't even in control at that moment. Most of the people here are much more impressive."

She slapped me on the back. "You *are* pretty darn good then! And more impressive than at least half of this class. Of course, nothing like Allyson and Mathias, but imagine if you learned to control it. Heck, I bet you could kill people!" she exclaimed. Her eyes lit up in fascination, as if being able to kill was something to look forward to.

"I-I'd focus on learning how to control it for now. That's what we're doing for the project, anyway."

Mr. E was walking around with a notepad, checking in with the students. When he stopped by Mallory and I, his smile turned into a grin.

"How's my newbie doing?" he asked, looking over to see what we had written on our packets. "Control? Nice. Are you planning to do anything for your other ability?"

"No, sir," I said. "Not yet."

He jotted something down in his notepad. "Alright. I don't expect you to work on it for this project, anyway. I look forward to seeing your results with this one."

He walked away.

Mallory tapped me on the shoulder. "You're a Multi?" she said loudly.

This caught the attention of our neighboring table. "Multi?" one of the boys asked.

"The half-blood's a Multi?" someone else said, staring at me. Several people began to murmur, casting glances in my direction. I lowered my head, knowing my face was burning red.

Mallory sucked in her breath. "Sorry! I didn't mean to say it that loud. You ok?"

I nodded, pressing my palms to my face. Their coolness helped the heat go away, and I sat back up, straightening my posture.

"I'm fine," I said. "Cat's out of the bag. It was going to happen sooner or later."

She blinked at me. "Uh, what cat? And what bag?"

Oh. Right. She didn't know the idiom.

"Never mind," I said lightly, picking up the pencil. "Let's try to finish at least two pages before the end of class. Ten minutes."

We began to work.

Chapter Nineteen

Allyson approached me at the end of class, smiling like I was one of her dearest friends.

"I think we got off on the wrong foot," she said apologetically. Zarah stood behind her, her tail swishing from side to side. "Let's start over, shall we?"

She held out her hand.

I stepped away, waiting for her hand to drop to the floor. There was no way in hell I was going to shake it.

"No," I said, lifting my hand to scratch at the back of my head. The itching didn't go away. "This is all because I'm a Multi, isn't it? Didn't you say I was on drugs earlier? Didn't you call me an idiot? I have these beautiful purple crescents on my shoulder, ones that were made by your own nails. Would you like to see them? I'll gladly oblige!"

I took another step back, this time out of shock. Where had that anger come from? It was so unlike me to say those things. Almost... almost like I hadn't been the one talking.

Allyson's tail began to twitch. "I'm trying to be kind, Lucianne. We could be friends." She was very visibly straining to maintain a polite tone.

"I'm not interested in having fake friends, *Allyson*. Even if this was legitimate, which I know it's not, I still wouldn't want to be your friend. The answer is no."

Allyson glared at me. "I'd change that attitude if I were you," she said in a low tone. "You don't want me as an enemy."

"You don't know what I want," I replied, turning away. Mei was waiting in the Shell. I didn't want to make her wait, especially since helping me out was something she didn't have to do.

Allyson laughed, a single bark, the sound echoing through the empty hallway. "Don't I?"

I didn't reply. A pounding headache was spreading through my head, clouding my thinking. Where was I supposed to go again? I turned around, stumbling through the hallway until I ran into something warm and soft.

Mathias's sweater.

"Woah, are you okay? You look sick," Mathias's voice was heavy with worry. He steadied me, letting me slide onto the polished stone.

I tried pulling away. "I'm fine. It's just a headache. It will pass. My friends are waiting for me in the Shell. Let me go."

His grip tightened. "Your friends can wait. What happened to you? You seemed alright in class."

"Nothing happened!" I said, wincing at one of the stronger throbs. "I talked with Allyson for a bit and left. Now *please*, let me go."

He obeyed, but the crease between his eyebrows did not fade. "I'll go with you."

We stood up and began walking down the now-empty hallway. I wondered why he had come here in the first place. When I bumped into him, he had been hurrying in the opposite direction, towards his own destination. Why was he taking time to escort me to the Shell? It wasn't like I wouldn't be able to find my way there. After all, the Shell was just two hallways away from room 112.

The guard stationed at the door let us pass without a second glance in our direction. Immediately, I spotted Adelaine and Mei, who were seated at our table, just like Mei had promised. My headache was nearly gone. It seemed the farther I got from room 112, the more it seemed to dwindle.

I hurried towards them, expecting Mathias to turn around and go back into the East Wing. Instead, he followed, curiously glancing at my friends.

A mischievous glint appeared in Adelaine's eyes as she smirked. "So *that's* why you're late. I see."

Mathias ignored her remark. "Pleasure to meet you. I'm Mathias."

Adelaine rolled her eyes. "I know who you are. Lucianne literally talks about you 24/7."

"I mentioned him *once*, and that was on the day we met," I replied sourly. "You're the one that constantly brings him up."

Mei grabbed both of our shoulders and pushed us apart. "Stop bickering. Lucianne is right, Addie. *You're* the one that talks about boys all the time." She looked at Mathias. "Sorry 'bout that. Adelaine is weird."

"I don't mind," he said, turning towards me. "How's your headache?"

"Gone."

He glanced at the clock. "That's good. I'll see you around?"

I nodded. The shadow of his wings disappeared behind the East Wing's entrance seconds later.

Adelaine whistled. "Damn, girl, that's a solid ten out of ten. You got so luck-"

Mei cleared her throat, cutting off whatever nonsense Adelaine was about to utter. "Have you forgotten why we're here, Addie? Here's a hint: talking about Lucianne's guy friends is not a part of it."

"Yeah," she said, "we're going to the headmistress to report one of the teachers. But we already did the planning, didn't we? We know what we're going to say."

"Exactly," Mei stated and hoisted her backpack over her shoulder. "So stop stalling. Let's go."

She led us out the large double doors and into the front yard of the academy. We went around the two wings and to the back, where the dorm building was located. But we didn't go there. Instead, we took a turn left, towards a small rectangular-shaped structure. The headmistress's office. I wondered why it was located outside and soon came to the conclusion that it was due to the separation of the wings. After all, her office couldn't be in the East Wing—the half-bloods wouldn't be able to come there. Nor could it be in the West Wing, for similar reasons. I suppose it could have been somewhere in the Shell, but I wasn't going to question the architects. It was what it was.

Mei used the brass knocker attached to the center of the wooden door and waited for a response. After about ten seconds, a voice answered.

"Come in."

It was the voice of an elderly woman, which reminded me of the one I had encountered on the day of my kidnapping. I wondered what happened to her body after she had crumpled to the ground, and how long it had taken them to find it. Perhaps the rat we had seen earlier had begun his dinner.

I pinched myself, dismissing the thought. Now was not the time to think about this.

Aside from the pale white wings that sprouted from her back, the headmistress looked like a kindly grandmother you might encounter on the street. The coffee-colored rug by her escritoire added a nice touch to the cozy room.

"Hello, Professor Windridge," Mei said. "We're sorry for interrupting you, but my friend here has a slight issue with one of the teachers."

Professor Windridge looked up, her eyes sharp and cautious. She lifted her finger and beckoned for us to come forward.

"Sit," she ordered, pointing to the three chairs lined in front of her escritoire. "All of you."

We obeyed.

The headmistress spoke again, this time to me. "Tell me about the issue. Which teacher?"

"Ms. Irene Davis," Mei answered. "She told-"

Professor Windridge held up a wrinkled finger. "I didn't ask you to speak."

Mei mumbled an apology, lightly tapping me on the arm. I picked up my backpack and took out the sheets of paper Irene had given me. Adelaine had bound them with one of her hairbands and I slid it off, just so the headmistress would see how much work I had been assigned. I placed the stack onto the smooth brown surface, watching her reaction.

She lifted her brows in amusement and waited for me to speak.

"All one-hundred and fifty-eight papers you see in front of you were given to me by my Soratian history teacher, Irene Davis. She told me to finish everything in two weeks, which I find completely unattainable," I explained. I took a sharp breath. "I'm sure you're aware that today was my first day at Levond and my third day in Soratia. I am incapable of completing such large quantities of work in such a short period of time, but Ms. Davis told me I would be punished if the work was not complete in two weeks. What do you suggest I do?"

The headmistress looked thoughtfully at the stack of papers, and an awkward silence filled the room. Mei quirked her eyebrow at Adeline, who shrugged in response. I looked at the floor. After several minutes, the headmistress declared her statement.

"Two weeks? In that case, what Ms. Davis asked of you is indeed incredibly unrealistic and inappropriate. I apologize on her behalf. However," she said, "are you absolutely certain you did nothing that could potentially anger her? There must be a reason behind this."

"Ma'am, it was my first day here. You can ask all of my classmates and they'll tell you the same thing. I honestly don't know!"

Actually, I did know. Irene's anger likely had to do with the Placement Test, where I'd accidentally caused her too much pain. That was most likely what had landed me in the East Wing. But it wasn't my fault. My ability was still new to me and learning to control it would undeniably take a while.

"I believe you," Professor Windridge said. "Leave the papers with me. I'll have a talk with Ms. Davis and promise this won't happen again. Not on my watch."

It sounded so good, I almost didn't believe her. "Thank you, ma'am. Thank you so much."

She coughed, covering her mouth with a tissue. "Anytime," she said, and for the first time, I could see a glint of kindness in her eyes.

Chapter Twenty

Adelaine and I sat on our beds, sipping a pink liquid from two identical cups. I didn't know what it was made of, only that it was considered tea around here, and I quite honestly didn't care. As long as it tasted good, I would drink it.

"So," Adelaine began, "tell me about the East Wing. I tried getting Mei to sneak in with me a few years ago but she backed out at the last moment. How was it?"

And so I said the first thing that came to mind, the thing that had been on my mind since I'd left the East Wing. "They had tails. Not all of them, but I'd estimate a good thirty percent, about ten out of a class of thirty. Real tails, just like lions, and they could move them too. Did you know that?"

Adelaine laughed. "I think you're forgetting I've been here nearly all my life. *Of course,* I know they have tails – they're a human-griffin hybrid! We're barely, like, one-fourth griffin, so we don't have wings or tails. I guess the tail gene is rarer, so only some Soratians have it."

When she said it like that, it sounded crazy. To have a lion's DNA in your ancestry was unbelievable. And yet… it was true.

"So you're telling me, one of my great-great-great something grandpas is a lion? And that my other great-great-great something grandpa is an eagle?"

She scrunched up her nose. "Ew, don't say that. It sounds weird. But yeah, I guess that if we traced down your line – both of our lines – we'd find a bird and a lion and maybe some other animal. Isn't that how we evolved into humans in the first place?"

"We're not entirely humans though. We're quarter-griffins."

"True," she said, leaning back on her bed. Then she placed the cup onto the drawer; it was empty. "But the griffin part of me is pretty much nonexistent. My 'telepathy' can barely do more than the average human's."

I snorted. "You say that like humans have magical powers."

"Everyone does. Most just don't know how to use it. Have you never seen those videos of people on Earth controlling smoke? Fire? Making small objects roll across the table? We watched them in modern human technology last year."

I recalled watching similar videos with Huma, sometime during the freshman year. We had laughed and called them fake. Adelaine, however, seemed completely serious.

"I've seen them," I said. "But can't those be easily edited? If humans did have those abilities, why would the Qroes want ours? It seems unrealistic."

Adelaine sucked in her breath, like I was some five-year-old she had been forced to lecture. "The Qroes want our abilities because they're *stronger*, Lucianne. Do humans have saliva that can heal? Can they send telepathic messages? Can they levitate items? No. They have a small percentage of what we have, and most don't even know they have it. Honestly, where did you think our abilities came from? The griffins themselves did not have any; their DNA just enhanced ours."

I felt a smile tugging at the corners of my lips. "You know," I said, "this is one of the most normal conversations we've had. You almost sound as logical as Mei."

She scoffed. "Why are we talking about this in the first place? We were supposed to be discussing your lesson at the East Wing!"

"Right, right," I said, getting back on track. "There was this one girl named Mallory, and I partnered up with her for a project. And then there was Allyson. I think she hates me. Really, there's no reason she-"

"Allyson Verlice? The one with the different eyes?"

I nodded.

"She's jealous," Adelaine said, "of your relationship with Mathias. Must be. Mei told me she got rejected by him a few years ago and now she's bitter towards any girl he likes."

"But he doesn't-"

"Lights out!" a muffled voice interrupted from the other side of the door. It was the dormitory's caretaker, Mr. Till.

Adelaine and I looked at each other.

"Tell me tomorrow," she said.

"You got it. Good night."

She turned off the lights.

* * *

The following week, Irene didn't come to class. Nor the week after that. Our substitute, a petite, brown-skinned lady, served as a wonderful alternative.

"Do you think she's dead? Would Professor Windridge even go that far?" one of the girls next to me—Isabella—asked. Since Irene's absence, the class had grown far more welcoming towards me, and I was glad. Despite everyone's young age, I enjoyed spending time with them. They seemed less problematic than the older teenagers from my other classes.

"I doubt it. My luck hasn't made an appearance for the last thirteen years; why should it now?"

Isabella laughed, flipping her brown hair over her shoulder. "Hear that, Gina? Not dead."

"You don't know that," Gina mumbled. She wasn't too fond of my company.

"Lucianne does. She's smart."

"Now, now," I said. "I never guaranteed anything. I simply stated it was unlikely for her to be dead. There's still hope."

"Ahem," a voice said. It was Ms. Teapow, the substitute. She was holding up a blue slip. "Don't you ladies think that kind of talk is inappropriate? I won't hesitate to give you this," she shook the slip of paper, making Isabella flinch, "if such behavior continues."

"Understood. We apologize," I said, giving her my best good-girl smile. That seemed to be sufficient, as she did not bother us again.

* * *

Luna, my new friend from seventh period modern human technology, grabbed my arm the second I entered the classroom. Her eyes were glazed.

"Why didn't you tell me you studied in the East Wing?" she said in a low tone. "I know you're a Multi. I wouldn't tell anyone."

My mouth dropped open. "Who told you?"

She sighed, gesturing for me to sit down next to her. "I figured it out myself. You went into the East Wing yesterday, I saw. The guard let you in without question, after you showed him a piece of paper- that was your schedule, wasn't it?" she asked. She waited for me to nod before continuing. "They wouldn't just let a regular half-blood go in there. I ruled it down to two options: you either had multiple abilities, or your ability was extremely strong. And now, you told me which one it was."

There was no denying it. The girl was smart. She would make an amazing detective. "Let me get this straight – you followed me to the Shell? Why?"

A sly grin spread across her face. "You may be a good liar, Lucianne, but I can tell when someone is lying. I knew you weren't meeting a friend. I just thought you didn't want to bother me, so I followed in case you got lost. My intentions were good."

"I never said they weren't good. I was just confused as to why someone would take the time out of their day to follow me around the school. Don't you have class?"

She gave me a pitiful look. "You'd be surprised at what people are capable of. Be more aware of your surroundings. And there's a five-minute break between seventh and eighth period, so I had time. Ugh… you don't want to be my friend anymore, do you?"

My answer was hesitant. "You can be my friend, as long as you don't tell anyone that I'm a Multi. I don't really like attention, and it's bound to come my way if people find out."

"Of course! I understand. My friend Atiana was in the same situation as you. She— wait, do you know her?"

"No," I said quickly. "Her name just sounded familiar."

"Didn't I just say I could tell when you were lying?" She slowly shook her head. "It's fine though, I won't force you to elaborate."

Good. I wasn't going to.

We didn't speak for the rest of the class period, and she didn't follow me when the bells chimed. I knew because I made sure to look around when entering the Shell.

Mathias was standing by the East Wing entrance, talking cheerfully with the guard. Their conversation stopped the second I got within six feet of the door.

"Good afternoon," I said awkwardly, feeling bad for interrupting. The guard mumbled a greeting and moved aside so I could go through. Mathias did the same but gave me a lopsided grin. I grinned back.

Upon my entry to the class, I couldn't find Mallory. Later, I found out she was absent, which was unfortunate, considering that we were nearly halfway done with our project. I had improved significantly over the last few days. Mr. E had asked me to think of something that would make me angry, since that was one of the only things that seemed to start off my ability, and picturing Irene worked wonders. Yesterday, I had made Mallory yelp, which was a huge accomplishment (although she wasn't too enthusiastic about it). She had made some improvements as well, managing to turn off the classroom's lights for more than a minute without making them flicker.

"Since your partner is absent, is there anyone, in particular, you would like to work with, Lucianne?" Mr. E asked, dragging his fingers through his ponytail.

"Uhm," I said, "I don't kno-"

"Lucianne can work with Damian and I," Mathias offered. Damian, the dark-skinned boy sitting next to him, grinned. His black hair bounced up and down as he nodded his head.

"Is that fine with you?" Mr. E asked.

"Yeah," I said.

Mr. E didn't seem to like the idea of putting a sophomore girl next to two seniors, but he didn't argue. "If there's an issue, let me know, okay?" His gaze lingered on my face for a moment, waiting for me to nod. I did, and he shifted to one of the groups nearby. I sat down and picked up my pencil.

"What are we working on today?" I asked, positioning my hand right above the sheet of paper, ready to write.

Damian chuckled, leaning back in his seat. "Straight down to business, eh?"

"Yeah, she's like that," Mathias said. "Tough crowd."

They both burst out laughing.

"You say that like you know me," I said, rolling my eyes. Maybe being in a group with them wasn't such a good idea after all.

Mathias smirked. "I know you well enough to make that observation."

Damian bit his lip and winked, which caused another guffaw. I stared. Mathias, who had seemed so mature and polite at the palace, turned out to be an entirely different person at school. I wasn't that surprised, (he was a teenager after all) but it was still strange seeing him act so childish.

"Once you're finished acting like five-year-olds, we can get started on our project. If you don't mind, I'd like to make some progress."

"Oh, she's *feisty*," Damian grinned, completely ignoring what I had just said. "I like her."

"What are your abilities?" I asked flatly. Their behavior was getting on my nerves.

Damian leaned in close, so close I could smell his minty breath on my face. "Making girls fall for me. You?"

I backed away, glaring at him. "I manipulate pain," I said, threateningly raising my hand. "My goal for today is making someone writhe on the floor. Would you like to volunteer?"

Silence. I could see fear in Damian's face. Barely there, but present, nonetheless. I smiled in satisfaction. Mathias, on the other hand, was simply looking at me with amusement.

"Mathias. Would you like to be the sacrifice?" I lifted my hand higher, pretending to gather energy.

"Yeah Mathias," Damian said, his playful mood returning. "You heard her. Be the sacrifice."

Reluctantly, Mathias stood up, his dark blue eyes focused on my face. "You won't make me writhe on the floor," he said, but it sounded like he was trying to convince himself rather than counter my statement. "You'll be punished if you do."

"I won't if it's an accident," I said cheerfully, and his reaction made me giggle. The fear in his eyes, however temporary, made up for the ten minutes of ignorance at the beginning of class. "I'm kidding. I won't hurt you. Not that severely, anyway."

Mathias nodded. "Okay. Which area are you striking? I want to prepare myself."

"Oh," I pouted, mimicking Irene's expression. "That won't be much fun though, will it?" Mathias's pupils shrank, and I snickered. "Kidding again. I'll go for the leg. Is that fine?"

Mathias swallowed. "Yeah. Let me know when."

I summoned up an image of Irene on the first day of school, when she'd told me to make up last semester's work in less than two weeks. I thought of Horseface and the kitten she had tortured with her friends, laughing as it struggled. I thought of the Qroes and how much I wanted to hurt them for making me suffer. For everyone they had killed.

All of these made the tingling return, and after half a minute, I felt my fingers beginning to twitch. The familiar pool of energy gathered at my core, and I let half of it flow to my palms. Not too much, since I didn't want to hurt him, but enough to cause some pain. My fists closed, preparing for release.

"Now."

Chapter Twenty-One

Mathias fell to the floor, gasping and clutching his leg. The flow of energy broke as quickly as it had started, and I ran towards him, feeling the blood drain from my face.

I hadn't meant for it to go this far.

I had only used half of the energy pool, the regular dose I used for practice with Mallory. Was he exaggerating? No, his expressions were too real. I knelt down next to him, grabbing his arm to help him sit up. How strong had I become?

"I'm so, so, sorry. I know what I said earlier, but I didn't mean it, I was just upset and-"

"I know you didn't mean it," Mathias grunted, forcing himself to stand. "It's fine Lucianne. It doesn't hurt anymore." Unlike me, he was a terrible liar. His body was too tense for him to be fine.

Mr. E ran over, his jacket flapping at the sides. "What happened? I heard someone fall." His gaze fell on me. "Are you okay, Lucianne?"

"With all due respect, I'm not the one you should be concerned about, Mr. E. I was the one who hurt Mathias."

"On accident," Mathias said. "She doesn't know how to control her abilities yet."

"How severely?" Mr. E asked.

"Not too severely. I'm fine now; the pain was temporary." Mathias gave him a convincing smile.

"That's good," Mr. E said. "And Lucianne, be careful next time, okay?"

"I know," I said, waiting for him to walk away before speaking. "Again, I'm really sorry-"

Mathias cut me off. "Don't apologize for something you can't control. Accidents happen." He patted me on the shoulder. "Don't worry about it."

"Aww," Damian cooed, lightly punching Mathias on the arm. "Are you flirting with her, Mathias? I thought you said she was out of your league."

I arched an eyebrow.

"I'm *joking*," Damian said. "Get that smug look off your face. He's not into gingers."

I rolled my eyes. How often had I heard that phrase? If he thought it was going to affect me in some way, he was wrong.

I decided to change the subject. "Damian, you still didn't tell me about your ability. You know mine."

"He manipulates water," Mathias said before Damian could open his mouth.

"Like Poseidon," Damian bragged, flashing his teeth. Then, in a high-pitched voice, he mimicked, "My goal for today is to make someone drown. Would any of you like to volunteer?"

This time, I wasn't excluded from the laughter.

* * *

Believe it or not, we actually managed to complete three pages from the packet, much more than I had hoped for. Mathias and I did most of the work, but Damian surprisingly made some of his own contributions. By the time the lesson was over, we were on pretty good terms compared to how we had started.

A cold hand closed around my shoulder, making me freeze.

"How's your head?" Allyson asked, turning me around to face her. Zarah stood behind her, eyeing me without much interest. Her tail smoothly swished back and forth.

I pried her vibrating fingers away from my skin. "You had something to do with it, didn't you? I thought so."

She smiled, clicked her tongue, then dragged in across the top of her teeth. "Did I?"

"Lucianne, you forgot your-" Mathias's voice faltered as he saw my company. He was holding out my packet.

"Ah," I said, reaching out for it. "Thank you."

His eyes swiveled to Allyson's trembling hand and widened. He dropped the packet and grabbed her arm, pulling her away from me. "What do you think you're doing?" he hissed, his voice furious. I could see his muscles tense beneath his skin.

Allyson seemed unfazed by his behavior. She flicked at his hand. "I'm merely having a conversation with the new student. Is that a problem?"

Mathias released her from his grip and walked towards me, placing a hand on my arm. His tone was low when he spoke. "I know damn well what you were doing, Allyson, and it wasn't having a conversation. You could get expelled. Leave before I call security."

She blinked at him innocently and took Zarah's hand. "Believe what you want. I stand by what I said," she retorted. When she walked past us, she made sure to smack his forearm with her tail. He didn't flinch.

"What was that about?" I asked. "She was telling the truth. It was just a conversation."

He shook his head. "No, she wasn't. Did you feel an itch near the back of your skull when she was speaking?"

"No," I said, "but I felt one yesterday. A few minutes before my headache started."

"I knew it." He saw my questioning glance and continued. "Allyson controls people's emotions. That's her ability, and she's good at it. *Very* good at it. She needs to get inside of your head to do it. That's what the itch is. Fortunately, if you know what she's trying to do, you can easily block it out."

"Okay," I said. "That makes sense," I affirmed. It certainly explained why I had acted the way I had yesterday. The anger hadn't been mine; it had been Allyson's. "But what about the headache? Was that from her as well?"

Mathias nodded. "The headache comes when she pulls out of your head. It isn't preventable—I learned the hard way—which is why it's important to never let her into your head in the first place."

"Good to know, but you still haven't explained how to avoid letting her in. Do I just picture something like shutting a door in her face?"

He shrugged. "Whatever works for you. Like I said, it's very simple."

I nodded, pushing open the door to the Shell. "Okay," I said. I turned around and gestured towards the doorway. "Are you coming?"

"No. Besides, I doubt your friends want to see me. Especially that blonde. See you." He walked off, the door swinging shut behind him.

Just like yesterday, Mei and Adelaine were seated at the table, waiting for me. The second was putting on what I assumed was her fifth layer of lip gloss, not bothering to lift her gaze as I came over. Mei, on the other hand, held out her fist and punched me lightly on the arm.

"Guess what," she said, reaching for her bag before placing it on her lap.

"What?"

"No, I said guess. Why do you think Addie's transforming herself into a barbie?"

I shrugged. "I dunno. I'm more surprised by the fact that you even know what a barbie is."

"Human history," she said with distaste. "Back to my question."

"Just tell me."

Finishing up her final layer of lip gloss, Adelaine said, "I'll tell you."

Then she dove for Mei's bag, snatching it up before she could react. She poured the contents—three glittery envelopes—onto the table.

"See that?" Adelaine said, pressing one of the envelopes into my hands. "It's an invitation. The party's in two hours."

Chapter Twenty-Two

The party took place at the mansion of Grace Arroyo. From what Adelaine had told me, Grace was a nineteen-year-old Soratian, one of the wealthiest in the school. I had never seen the girl in my life, so how Adelaine had managed to obtain the invitations remained a mystery... one that she chose not to elaborate on.

Like the other houses on the street, the mansion was situated high in the sky. Floating. It made sense, considering that Soratians had wings, but I wondered how half-bloods would get up there. If my only option was being carried up there by a Soratian, Mei and Adelaine would be going alone. I wouldn't risk being dropped from the height of my old apartment building.

My question was answered when we came upon a large, square-shaped box, suspended on a rope beside the building. Attached to the sides of it were two pairs of white wings.

"What is that?" I asked, nudging it with my foot.

"A plox," Mei replied, unhinging the door. It reminded me of the safety doors they had on roller coasters, but without the colorful designs. "Used for transporting half-bloods to Soratian homes. Every Soratian house has one. It's mandatory."

"Ah. How does it work?" I asked. We were all crammed into the small space, and I stared in fascination at the plox's wings.

"You pull the rope once and the wings do the rest. Going down, you just climb in; your weight should pull you to the ground," Mei explained. Mei pulled the rope, sharply, and the wings moved downwards.

We shot up.

The sudden start nearly made me topple over, and, cursing underneath my breath, I grabbed the side to steady myself. The ride only lasted about twenty seconds, but the walls were still too short for my liking.

A group of teenagers was standing by the doorway—three Soratians and one half-blood. I recognized the half-blood immediately.

"Luna!" I called, awkwardly stepping out of the plox. I tried to hurry; there were people behind me waiting to get out.

She smiled. "Hi, Lucianne. I like your dress."

I glanced down at the blue dress Adelaine had chosen for me. We had gone shopping earlier that day, and the dress had cost me one-hundred and fifty plets. It tightened around the waist and loosened at the knees, with intricate designs running down the mesh sleeves. Modest, but beautiful.

"Thank you," I said. "I like yours too."

"I picked it for her," Adelaine piped in. "I did her make-up too. Honestly, the girl would be lost without me."

I elbowed her in the side.

"Why don't you come inside?" Luna said. "We've got around fifty people so far. Go ahead and get comfortable."

"Do you know the host?" I asked. Her wording made it sound like she was the one that had hosted this party, but I knew that wasn't true. Luna wasn't Soratian.

"Yes!" Luna said. "Grace is my cousin. Would you like to meet her?"

"Later," Adelaine said, grabbing my hand. "We'd like to meet some friends first."

Luna nodded. "Have fun."

The room we entered was tall and spacious, with booming music coming from somewhere in the back. It was dark except for a colorful ball of light hovering in the center. Lined against a wall stood a table filled with pastries, and Mei made a beeline towards it. Adelaine and I followed.

"Ith good," Mei said, shoving a piece of cake into her mouth.

Adelaine wrinkled her nose. "Don't embarrass yourself. You'll get that stuff on your dress." She took a small bite out of a fruit tart and dabbed a napkin on her lips.

The room began to fill up as more people entered Grace Arroyo's home. We soon bumped into a guy holding out a tray of cups, all filled with crimson-red liquid.

"Any of y'all drink?" he asked, offering us the tray.

"Sure," Mei said, grabbing one of the cups and gulping down its contents. "Can I have another?"

He laughed. "Sure. Of course."

The band started to play an upbeat hip-hop song, and people gathered on the dance floor. A couple was flying around the levitating light, holding hands and laughing. A group of half-bloods stood below them, heads tilted up, watching with open mouths. The music grew quieter. The couple floated to the ground, still grinning and holding hands. It didn't take long for them to get lost within the crowd.

The music stopped. Now people were speaking in hushed tones, no one daring to raise their voice to more than a whisper. Lifting their head, they watched the top of the spiraling stairs with anticipation. Waiting for something.

For someone.

A beautiful woman in a fiery red dress stepped onto one of the top rails. The steady back-and-forth movement of her wings kept her from falling.

"Are you enjoying the party?!" she yelled into the crowd. The roar she received in response answered her question. "Glad to hear it! Welcome to the Arroyo home, guys and gals!" she greeted. Another round of hoots and shouts followed. She grinned, doing a graceful spin to show off her dress.

Then she jumped.

The crowd gasped in unison as she suspended herself inches above the floor, her golden curls brushing against the ground. She lifted her gaze to smile at the teenagers gathered before her. The room broke into spontaneous applause. Grace bowed, lifting the edges of her dress before making her way to a group of girls gathered in the center. That was the end of her entrance.

The next few hours passed quickly. Adelaine ran off to chat with some guys, and Mei pulled me onto the dancefloor, persuading me to dance. We had been dancing for over an hour now, twirling each other around, making up lyrics to random songs. I hadn't been to many parties, but this was by far the best one I'd attended.

She hiccupped.

"Gotta go to the bathroom real quick," she said, her words slurring. With the amount of crimson liquid she'd been drinking, I wasn't surprised. I still didn't know what the stuff was, but it seemed to have the same effect as wine, which my mother often drank after work. The liquid was much sweeter than any alcoholic beverage I had ever tried. And, just like alcohol, the more I drank, the more my mood seemed to skyrocket.

Swaying to the music, I barely noticed as someone tapped me on the shoulder.

"I didn't expect to see you here."

I grinned, doing another twirl to the music. "Neither did I! Adelaine showed us the invitations eight hours ago."

Mathias lifted his eyebrows. "Really? Grace passed them out last week. How did she get them?"

"Dunno," I said, taking another sip of the red liquid. The coolness of it traveling down my throat was refreshing, making me crave more. "Wanna dance?"

"You're drunk," he said suddenly, staring at the half-empty cup I was setting onto a nearby table. "I *knew* something was off."

"Don't be ridiculous," I giggled as I grabbed his hand, pulling him towards the center of the dancefloor. "I barely drank three cups!"

He pulled away. "You're drunk. Or you're going to be, if you keep drinking that."

I rolled my eyes, reaching for his hand again. "So what if I am? We're at a party. Relax."

It wasn't like I was going to become addicted overnight.

"Hey Mathias! Great to see ya," Mei said, running up to us. Her face was flushed, her eyes glazed over. "Want to dance with us?"

"I'll pass," Mathias said quickly, looking around the crowd. "I'm meeting with Damian."

Mei shrugged. "You do you," she told him. Then she took me by the arm, and we started where we had left off.

A few hours later, we were yawning. My feet ached. We were sitting down by the refreshments, Mei's head resting on my shoulder. I didn't know when she had fallen asleep. What I did know was that the crimson liquid had lost its charm long ago, and the thought of drinking it again made me sick. My stomach churned as I watched a boy hurl the contents of his dinner onto the floor. The party was clearly coming to a close.

I shook Mei awake, waiting for her bloodshot eyes to open in alarm.

"We're leaving," I said. "Find Adelaine."

"What time is it?" she asked groggily, hugging her arms to her chest. Goosebumps were popping all over her arms.

"Late enough to leave. We need to get Adelaine," I replied. I hadn't seen her at all over the last four hours and realized I couldn't think of a place where she could possibly be. Standing up from the wooden chair, I glanced at Mei. She was looking ahead emptily. Her eyes were still drooping.

I hauled her up. "Where is Adelaine?" I asked loudly, squeezing her arm.

"I dunno," she murmured, her head slumping to the side. "I'm tired."

I looked around the room, searching for her dress. The hot pink frills should have been easy to find in the thinning crowd, which made my panic escalate. Where could she have gone off to?

I spotted Grace standing by the door and chatting with a few girls. Damian, dressed in a bright blue suit, was sitting at a nearby table, laughing at something with a group of friends. Mathias was among them. I decided to go towards them.

The clicks of my heels as I pulled Mei along were loud enough to interrupt their voices, and they all looked up with polite interest.

"Come to flirt?" Damian asked, biting his lower lip. His friends laughed, punching him playfully on the shoulder, one of them muttering something into his ear. Mathias's face was the only one that remained serious. His eyes landed on Mei, whose knees were slowly beginning to give out. A crease formed between his eyebrows as he took in my expression.

I swallowed. "Have you seen Adelaine?" I asked. The question was meant for Mathias, but another guy answered.

"If she's a half-blood then I don't know her," he said arrogantly. "What's she look like?"

I lowered Mei onto a chair, unable to bear her weight for much longer. "Blond hair pinned into a bun, hazel eyes, red lipstick… uh-"

"You just described half of the girls at this party," Damian said. "What was she wearing?"

"A hot-pink dress. Sleeveless, frills at the hem, knee-length-"

"Hot pink dress was enough," the guy sitting next to Mathias interrupted. "I ain't inspecting every girl's sleeve frills. Save your breath."

My eyes lit up. "You've seen her then? How long ago? Where was she? Do you know where she-"

"No," the black-haired guy said flatly. "Now go bother someone else with your problems."

He waved his hand dismissively in my direction.

I looked at each of them individually, my eyes repeating the same question. They all shook their heads. Then they returned to the conversation they were having prior to my arrival, having lost interest in me. Only Mathias spoke.

118

"I'll help you look for her. You can leave Mei here; they'll make sure she doesn't run off."

"Such lovely friends you have," I grumbled. My questions had served as mere entertainment for them, and they would undoubtedly laugh about it when I walked away. I regretted coming up to them in the first place. Asking Grace seemed like a much better option.

"I apologize on their behalf," Mathias said. I opened my mouth to tell him that he shouldn't apologize but decided against it. There was no reason for me to tell him not to. Controlling the mouths of his friends may not have been his responsibility, but he had been the one hanging out with them. Plus, it felt nice to hear his apology.

"Hello, Mathias," Grace said as we approached her. "Are you leaving?"

Mathias shook his head. "Lucianne," he gestured to me, "wanted to know if you've seen her friend."

I smiled politely at Grace. "Have you seen a blond girl in a frilly pink dress anywhere? I haven't seen her for a couple of hours."

"Was she wearing dark blue eyeshadow?"

I nodded.

"She left approximately two hours ago."

My stomach dropped.

"She said she was going to the dorms," Grace said. "The girl looked tired as hell, and she told us a friend would escort her. Geez… get that tense look off your face. She's probably sleeping right now."

Relief settled over me like a blanket. "Alright," I calmed. I felt myself smiling. "Thank you."

We walked back towards Mathias's friends, where Mei was beginning to wake. Strands of hair were plastered to her face. Her lipstick was nearly gone, and a thin stream of drool was making its way down her chin. She sat up when she saw us, her dress crumpling up in several places.

"We're leaving," I told her. "Do you know your way home?"

"I'll drive both of you. I have a carriage," Mathias offered.

Mei looked emptily at both of us, fidgeting with her fingers. When she finally spoke, it was a single question: "Where's Addie?"

"She was tired and went back to the dorms," I said. I didn't want to say anything that could potentially alarm her, so I stuck to what Grace had told me. It was as close to the truth as it got.

She stood up, rubbing her eyes. "I'm tired too. Mathias, do you know my address?"

He nodded.

We left Grace's home and floated to the ground in the plox, which worked just as Mei had told me. The carriage Mathias drove us in was similar to the ones I had seen at the palace, which meant it was another one of his privileges, just like the portal stones. He had one feslin. It was much fatter than Irene's, but when Mathias held out his hand, it didn't flinch. Instead, it made a chirping sound and rubbed its head against him. I assumed that was a sound of happiness.

We went to Mei's house first. It was a small, red, rectangular building with two green bushes covering the windows at the front. She had left the window to her room open. I lifted her up to help her sneak back in.

By the time I was back in the vehicle, the house was still dark and silent. She hadn't been caught.

The dorm building was just as dark and silent as Mei's house; it was well past curfew. Mathias parked in front of the entrance, asking if I needed anything else. I told him that I didn't, thanked him for the ride, and stepped out of the carriage.

"See you tomorrow," Mathias called out to me as I closed the door. I waved back at him and entered the dorm

120

building, thankful that the front entrance was open twenty-four-seven.

Silently stepping into the room, I slid off my shoes and placed the keys in the drawer. I could see Adelaine's form on her bed as I tiptoed over to mine. I slipped underneath the covers, the remnants of my energy vanishing.

I was out in ten seconds.

Chapter Twenty-Three

I didn't see Adelaine the next morning. Considering that the wake-up buzz had gone off an hour ago, I wasn't surprised. The clock on the drawer showed me just how long I had overslept.

Wonderful, I thought to myself. *Just wonderful.*

The chime of the bells sounded when I had been waiting beside the door, ready for just over ten minutes. That signaled the end of geography. I stood up, my legs numb from sitting on them.

I had five minutes to get to biology class.

I ran outside, the wind making my hair billow behind me. It was still wet from the shower I had taken, but I didn't care. All I wanted was to see Adelaine. To make sure her form on the bed hadn't been an illusion.

I didn't spot her among the students hurrying towards their classes. Then again, Levond was huge, and Adelaine and I had no classes together except for lunch. I probably wouldn't see her for the next three hours.

I sighed. Time always slowed down when you looked forward to something.

When the lunch bell signaled the end of human history, I shot up from my seat and was the first one out the door, running to the Shell like I was in a marathon. Our table was empty. Students were just beginning to pour into the room. I grabbed lunch—curly pasta covered in white cream—and sat down at my usual spot. It wasn't long before Mei came in, waving to me as she hurried to get her lunch. I waved back, but my eyes stayed glued to the West Wing entrance.

Four minutes. That's how long it had been since the bells chimed. Where could she be?

"Hey," Mei said, plopping down next to me. "Why weren't you in math?"

"I overslept," I said, not taking my eyes away from the glass doors. "I'm surprised you didn't."

She laughed. "My mom would kill me if I did. Is that why Addie isn't here? Did she oversleep too?"

I shook my head. "No, I didn't see her at all this morning. I thought she was at school."

"I thought she was with you! None of you came to breakfast," she said. Mei's cheerful demeanor was beginning to fade. "I remember you telling me she went back to the dorms last night. Did she not?"

I swallowed a spoonful of pasta. "That's what Grace told me. I thought I saw her last night too, when I came back to the dorms. But now I'm not so sure," I replied. After all, I hadn't seen Adelaine; only a lump on her bed. That lump might as well have been her bedsheets bundled up together.

"What do you mean 'what Grace told you'?"

"She saw Adelaine leave the party two hours before us," I said. "You were passed out when I talked to her."

"Yeah, I had too much eqonilia," Mei said, rubbing her chin. "Don't blame me; everyone drank it, you included. But why would she leave without us? She could have gotten kidnapped!"

"For all we know, she *has* been kidnapped. Is there any way to report something like this?"

"Mrs. Windridge," Mei said immediately. "We have to tell Mrs-"

Two hands closed around her mouth, and a curtain of golden hair fell onto the table. The girl behind her was giggling loudly, and although her face was hidden by Mei's body, I could tell who it was.

My teeth clenched. "Adelaine."

Adelaine took her hands away from Mei's mouth and stood up. "Hello to you too, Lucianne."

I reached across the table and yanked her forward. "Sit down," I ordered. Shocked by my sudden change of mood, she obeyed.

I inhaled deeply. "Do you understand," I began, "how *worried* Mei and I were? Not only did you leave the party without us, you left without telling anyone you were leaving! If we go together, we leave together. Isn't that what we decided? Where did you even spend the night? Because I sure as hell didn't see you in the dorms this morning. You missed breakfast, you missed half of your classes, and you *dare* show up in the middle of lunch like it was some kind of joke? You better have a good explanation, Adelaine. For your sake, I'm hoping you do."

Adelaine smiled, slowly shaking her head like I was crazy. "Relax. I met a boy."

Mei's head snapped to the side, her voice trembling with anger. "You-"

"Let me finish," Adelaine said, holding up her palm. "I met a boy. His name, I think, was Jonas, and oh, you should have seen him! More handsome than everyone at Levond! I had been drinking eqonilia with him and his friends when he told me I looked like I needed a rest and offered to take me home. Naturally, I protested and told him my friends were still at the party. But he said, 'That's fine, I'll have Gabriel tell them you left.' I'm guessing he forgot, but that's not my fault. Anyway, he took me to the dorms, and I fell asleep. Didn't Lucianne see me when she came back?"

So the lump on the bed had been Adelaine's body after all. But that still didn't explain her absence this morning.

"Okay," I said. "You fell asleep. But why didn't I see you this morning?"

She sighed dreamily. "When he was leaving our dorm, he asked if I would meet him in the morning by the entrance. And I agreed, obviously. We spent the morning in front of the bakery downtown. He bought us both breakfast. He even bought me dessert, and that cost him twenty plets! He's gotta be rich. Oh, and he asked me to meet him again, tonight. After school."

"But you won't," I said.

"What?"

"You won't meet him tonight," I said firmly. "You *do* understand the dangers of meeting strangers in the dark, right?"

"But he's not-"

Mei cut her off. "Lucianne is right. He *is* a stranger, Addie. You've known him for what? A day?"

"Ugh," Adelaine said. "None of you get it! He's friends with Thomas and goes to Levond. Not a stranger. Plus, I'm a telepath! Don't you think I'd know if he had bad intentions? I already met him twice and nothing happened. If he was gonna do something, he would have already done it."

I recalled the black-haired boy from human history, the one that had interrupted Ms. Anskin during my first day at Levond. I assumed that was the Thomas she was referring to.

"No," Mei said, "because the extent of your 'telepathy' is seeing a glimpse of what's at the front of a person's head. You're not meeting with him."

She crossed her arms. "You can't stop me."

"You're right," I said, nodding. "We can advise you, but the ultimate choice is yours. So, Adelaine, we advise you not to meet him again. But what will you do? Since we clearly can't stop you, you might as well tell us."

She groaned, pressing her hands into her face. "I won't meet him," she mumbled. "There. Happy?"

But the next morning, Adelaine didn't show up for breakfast.

Chapter Twenty-Four

We went to bed as usual, with Adelaine steadily breathing next to me.

When the buzz of the wake-up call made me roll over in my bed, I expected to find Adelaine putting on her makeup in front of the mirror, as she typically did in the mornings. What I found, however, was a neatly made bed and a pink note on the drawer, that read: **See you at lunch!**

I grabbed the note and ran to the Shell, where Mei was mindlessly chewing on a bagel. Her head perked up at the sound of my footsteps, and she immediately noticed the absence of Adelaine.

"Let me guess… she went to see that Jonas guy again?" Mei said. She sounded bored, her voice slightly hinting at annoyance.

I shrugged, handing her the note. "Looks like it."

Mei looked at the note, crumpled it up, and threw it back in my direction. "I knew she wouldn't listen to us," she sighed. "What do we do now?"

I picked up the note and placed it back into my pocket. "We wait until lunch."

A couple of hours later, we were once again sitting in the shell-shaped seats, pausing every few seconds to glance up at the door. The Soratians were quite clearly keeping to the east side of the Shell, trying to stay as far away as possible from the half-bloods. It reminded me of my old high school, where the rich students would often separate themselves from the poorer ones. Huma had been an exception, and it was thanks to her that I had friends of higher class. She was probably sleeping right now, if I had correctly calculated the difference in our time zones. I wished I could call her. If only the phones in modern human technology worked!

"Where is she?" I hissed. The last students were starting to trickle into the Shell. I glanced out the glass wall, but the front yard was empty. Every student had come to lunch.

"Give her time," Mei said dismissively. "Yesterday, she showed up when lunch was halfway over."

"You're not worried?" I asked. I had been uneasy since finding the note, but now, the feeling was growing. I doubted it would subside until Adelaine walked into the Shell.

Mei shrugged. "No, not really. I was worried yesterday and look how that turned out. There's no reason for me to be worried. Not yet."

She went back to eating.

Fifteen minutes later, Adelaine still hadn't shown up. By this time, lunch was nearly over, and some students were beginning to deposit their empty dishes on the racks near the back. My own lunch had turned lukewarm, and my appetite was nowhere to be found. I kept my eyes on the door, waiting for them to open.

"Mei."

"Hm?" I could hear the rattle of silverware behind me, and I knew she was picking up my plate.

"What if she doesn't come?" I turned around to look at her, but she didn't seem worried.

"Then we wait until supper. If she's not here the next morning, we tell Windridge."

Her words didn't ease the feeling of dread that was rising inside of me. "What if it's too late? By next morning, I mean. What if she's too far away by the time we tell the headmistress?"

She stopped and put the dishes down on the table with a *clunk*. "What do you think happened to her? That she was whisked into another dimension? Seriously, Lucianne, do you know how expensive portal stones are? She probably just forgot about the time. So save your worry until tomorrow." She picked up the dishes and strutted off towards the racks, leaving me alone. I knew she was trying to reassure me, but why did it sound like she was trying to reassure herself? I sighed. Perhaps she would show up for supper.

But she didn't.

The dormitory's cafeteria (or supper-room, since that was the only meal it served) was much smaller than the Shell. The dormitory only had about thirty students, so it made sense. Adelaine and I usually sat at the largest table in the center, with her dorm friends—Gina and Teresa. Since she wasn't here, I ate in a corner. Not like her friends cared, anyway.

Falling asleep was much harder than usual. I kept turning around, my heart racing every time I glanced at the empty bed next to me. Mei's words rang in my head. *Save your worry until tomorrow.* But what if tomorrow was too late? What if she needed help now? *Save your worry until tomorrow.* I couldn't do anything about it now. Not at this hour. And so, I tried to sleep.

I'm not exactly sure when I drowsed off, but it must have been late. When the droning buzz penetrated my ears, all I wanted to do was to go back to sleep.

Until I remembered Adelaine.

And sure enough, the bed next to me was empty.

I picked up the crumpled note, running my fingers over the pink paper. **See you at lunch**! That had been the last thing Adelaine had said to me, and it hadn't even been verbal. My stomach did a flip at the thought, and I had to reassure myself that she wasn't dead. We would speak again. We had to.

Throwing on a T-shirt and jeans, I ran downstairs, only to see Mei waiting by the dorm exit. This time, she looked worried.

"She's not…?"

"No," I shook my head. "She didn't come last night, and she wasn't here this morning."

Mei grabbed my hand, and I noticed that hers was trembling. "Let's go."

* * *

Upon hearing what had happened, Professor Windridge scowled. "Why did you not tell me about this yesterday?"

I opened my mouth to speak, but Mei cut me off. "It's my fault, Professor. Lucianne wanted to tell you but I stopped her. I thought she would come back in the evening-"

"*You thought wrong*," Professor Windridge's voice was cold. "What was the boy's name? You said he attended Levond."

"Well, see," I said, "the thing is… we don't know if he was a student here. We just assumed, since—"

"I asked for his *name*." She grabbed a stack of papers from her drawer and placed them on her desk.

"Jonas. That's what she told us."

"Surname?"

"We don't know, ma'am."

Professor Windridge's mouth pressed into a thin line. She pushed up her glasses and began sifting through the papers. After a few minutes, she turned one of them towards us, her fingernail pointing to a picture of a boy. "Jonas Hudges?"

I looked closely at the boy's smiling face. His hair was blond, the same shade as Mathias's, falling way below his ears. A mole stuck out from beneath his left eyebrow, and I was pretty sure he had a nose piercing. Nothing like the Jonas Adelaine had described.

"No, ma'am," I said. "My friend described a boy with short black hair. It couldn't be him."

Professor Windridge thoughtfully rubbed her chin as she looked over the boy's image once more. Then she placed it back into the drawer. I could tell she wasn't satisfied.

"Did Ms. Chevrolet mention any other names? Perhaps someone that attends Levond?"

"Thomas," Mei said immediately. "She told us Jonas knew Thomas. They were all sitting together at the party."

"There are several Thomases that attend Levond."

"Thomas Sanchez," Mei said, "but could we see a picture of him just to make sure?"

Professor Windridge opened another drawer. She took out a paper filled with pictures of students, just like the one she had shown us a few minutes prior. It was alphabetically organized by first name, but I assumed she also had one organized by last name. Her fingernail was resting below the image of Thomas Sanchez, and I immediately recognized him as the boy from human history. "Is this him?"

"Yes, Professor," Mei and I said simultaneously.

Professor Windridge allowed herself a thin smile. "Good. I'll have him brought in for questioning. You girls hurry back to class. Your time here is up."

But he wasn't brought in for questioning because Thomas, along with several other boys his age, was absent. When Windridge called us into her office at the end of the school day, Mei was crying.

"It's my fault," she sniffled, snot running down from her nose. "I shouldn't have stopped you from telling the headmistress. I'm sorry."

I handed her a tissue. "What's done is done. The most we can do now is help them find her."

She nodded, her face contorting as a new round of tears made its way down her face. "Open the door," she whispered.

Mrs. Windridge had a theory. Her face, although appearing relaxed, was quite obviously distressed. I could tell she was trying to mask her fear. Her wings were folded behind her back, hugging close to her skin, so Mei and I could only see their edges. When she spoke, it was in a grave tone.

"This situation," she said slowly, "is not looking good for any of us."

Mei and I exchanged glances but remained silent.

She continued. "Stalling won't get us anywhere, so I'll get straight to the point. My council believes Ms. Chevrolet was taken by the Qroes."

130

She gave us a moment to take this in, watching our faces change. Mei's shaking hand reached towards mine, and I squeezed it. "We have searched through all citizen records, to no avail. There isn't a Jonas that matches the description you have given me. Unless Ms. Chevrolet lied about his appearance, it is highly unlikely he was a resident of Soratia. As for Thomas Sanchez, I doubt he'll be returning in the near future. It seems to me like he was allied with the Qroes and played a large part in Ms. Chevrolet's kidnapping."

"You're saying..." I couldn't force myself to finish the rest of the sentence.

"There are enemies among us. Impostors, if you'd like. Their exact numbers are unknown, but I would be careful. Until we find Ms. Chevrolet, don't associate yourself with anyone you don't know."

"But w-why Addie?" Mei stammered, her eyes red from crying. "Why a half-blood? If they wanted someone powerful, they could have taken a Soratian. I just don't understand-"

"Because she was an easy target," Professor Windridge said coldly. "Not only was she willing and eager to meet with one of the Qroes, she didn't suspect a single thing. I doubt she was their ultimate target, though. Perhaps they were using her as a lure for someone... like you." Her eyes pierced through mine, sending a chill down my spine.

I shook my head in disbelief. "No. I'm not powerful either. Why would they want me?"

Windridge sighed. "Perhaps they want to use you as a lure for someone even more powerful. Who knows? One thing is certain: Ms. Chevrolet is not their main target. Since she has no known family members, it is only logical to assume that their next target would be one of you."

"Okay," I said, "we'll be careful then. Do you know where Adelaine is? When is someone going to save her?"

"I don't have an answer for either question. It is beyond my power. I'll call you to my office once I get new information on the case. For now, you're dismissed."

She waved her hand in our direction, and the door flung itself open.

Mei and I didn't exchange a single word as we walked off in separate directions, me towards the dorms and her towards the street. We were both shocked by the news, and my feet practically dragged themselves to the dorm room. The headmistress's words kept ringing in my head, each one louder and worse than the former. I dropped onto the floor and began rocking back and forth, feeling the tears pool in my eyes. Gone. Adelaine was gone. I looked up at the shelf, where the purple vase stood, glistening in the afternoon light.

Mathias's flower had withered.

Chapter Twenty-Five

The next few days had no updates on the case, which made me beyond miserable. Mei was no better, and she would tear up every time Adelaine's name was mentioned, which was often. At this point, the entire school knew what had happened. Questions regarding Adelaine's kidnapping were practically unavoidable.

To make matters worse, Irene had returned from her break. Unlike the other teachers, she wasn't lenient towards me when it came to work. Two days after her return, I was already failing Soratian history.

In the East Wing, Mallory and I received a 7 on our two-week project. That was the highest grade around here (1 was the lowest). News of Adelaine's kidnapping didn't spread throughout the East Wing as quickly as it had through the West, which granted me several days of peace. Mathias told me he'd try to find out as much as he could about Adelaine at the palace, but so far he hadn't found anything helpful.

"How's that blond chick of yours?" Allyson's high-pitched voice interrupted my thinking. "Haven't seen her in a while."

"None of your business," I replied, turning away. She obviously knew what had happened. Otherwise, she wouldn't be making such remarks. Zarah, as always, stood behind her, looking at me like I was a bug she wanted to squish.

"I wonder who took her," she said softly. "How foolish of her to go around meeting strangers."

I whipped around to face her. "I wouldn't be surprised if you were in on it."

She looked surprised. "Me? No. We both share the same enemy, Lucianne. I would never assist the same people who strive to hurt me. You, on the other hand… you should be the main suspect. I'm surprised you're not. Just look at all the evidence!" she accused. Several students stopped and looked in our direction, curious to hear what Allyson was about to say. "New girl, only a few weeks in Soratia. We had no kidnappings before. Peace. And now, *bam!* A girl is kidnapped. And who is her roommate? The new girl. Say, Lucianne, that does sound a bit too coincidental, doesn't it?" she continued. A small group had formed around us now, and I could see alarm registered in some of their faces. A few more were nodding along in agreement.

I glared at her. "You don't know me. If you did, you'd know I would never help the association that tortured me into giving them answers I didn't have. You'd know I wouldn't hurt one of the only friends I had in this place. You'd *know* that I would never stoop down to that level. But you don't know me. So, please tell me, why do you hate me so much, Allyson? I can see it in your eyes. What have I done to make you hate me?" I asked. I felt the familiar itch near the back of my skull and smiled dryly. "Don't even try. I've learned how to block you off."

She laughed. "I don't hate you, Lucianne. Hatred is too strong a word to describe what I feel towards you. I hate the enemy. But you… I simply don't trust you. Give me a reason why I should. Because the last half-blood that came into our wing, a Multi, just like you, was allied with the Qroes. What guarantee do I have that you aren't the same?"

I squeezed my fist. "What was the half-blood's name? The one supposedly allied with the Qroes?"

"Atiana," Allyson said pleasantly. "Atiana Morales. Do you know her? I bet you do. Tell me how she's doing. I'd love to hear."

"She's dead," I said flatly. "The Qroes killed her. She was never allied with them in the first place."

Allyson scoffed. "I know a liar when I see one."

I opened my mouth to protest, but a moment too late. One downward movement of her wings was all it took to send her flying towards the arched ceiling.

The students gathered around me began to disperse.

As Zarah followed her out of the corridor, she turned around to glance at me. Her expression was no longer angry but filled with something else. Worry? Sympathy? I was too wound up to care.

Mathias tapped me on the shoulder just when I was about to enter the Shell, stopping me in my tracks.

"What?" I said, not bothering to turn around. I doubted it was important.

He opened the door further and motioned for me to sit at one of the nearby tables. "What did she want? Allyson, I mean. She attracted quite a crowd."

"She wanted me to know that she didn't trust me." I shrugged. "And that she thought I had something to do with Adelaine's... disappearance. I don't blame her for either, honestly. She had good reasons."

He murmured, "Of course she did." I waited for him to say more but was only greeted with silence. He seemed to have zoned off.

I snapped my fingers in front of his face. "Did you want to tell me something? News about Adelaine, maybe?"

"No news about Adelaine. Sorry."

I stood up to leave, but he leaned forward, catching my hand. "Wait. I had an idea."

I sat back down.

He looked around, as if to make sure no one else was going to eavesdrop. His voice was low when he spoke. "What's your other ability? The one that makes you a Multi."

"Seeing how people died by sleeping in their beds?" I replied. I didn't want to talk about this, not when it was making the memories of Atiana's death fresh. "Look, if you're just going to pester me with questions, I'll go."

His eyes widened. "No, no. I was just making sure it was your ability. Sorina and I discussed it a few days ago. We think you have the power to see the death of whoever last slept in that place. *If* they died, that is."

"Okay," I said. "And how does this correlate with your idea?"

He laced his fingers together. "Have you slept in Adelaine's bed since her kidnapping?"

Oh.

He waited for me to shake my head before continuing. "Sleep in her bed tonight. It will give you a quicker and faster update than Sorina's team could ever produce. At least you'll know she's not..." he let me finish the thought in my head.

"And if she is? What if I see everything they did to her? What if I see the same thing that happened to-"

The sudden look of pain in his eyes made me stop mid-sentence.

He sighed. "Then you won't have to live in uncertainty and fear. Trust me when I say this – there is nothing stronger than fear of the unknown. So for your sake and for Mei's, I urge you to do it." He squeezed my hand sympathetically. "That's my idea."

After mulling over it for hours, I decided to do what Mathias had suggested. After all, it didn't seem like an update would be coming anytime sooner, and what did I have to lose? Mathias had been right when he said fear of the unknown was stronger than any other. If we knew she was safe, perhaps Mei wouldn't be so quick to fall into a depressive state.

I lifted my hand to turn off the bedside lamp but decided to leave it on. If nightmares came, the light would comfort me.

Chapter Twenty-Six

That night, I had no dreams. Mei seemed ecstatic when I told her, as did Gina and Teresa. The news spread through Levond like wildfire. In just three hours, the academy's melancholy mood had lifted.

But not mine. Adelaine being alive meant that we knew no more about her whereabouts than we had known yesterday. Mathias assured me the people at the palace were constantly working to find her, but it did nothing to reassure me. If they didn't hurry up, she would die. No doubt about it.

"Two days," I told him during one of the afternoons. "That's how much I'll give them to get a lead on her case."

"And if they don't?"

"Then I'll take things into my own hands." I shrugged. "I can't just sit around while they do... things... to her."

I expected him to protest, to tell me that it was a terrible idea, but he just slowly nodded his head. He understood.

As expected, the next two days had no updates, and I arrived by the palace's gates on the afternoon of the third day. The guards stationed at the entrance didn't question me when I told them I was there to see Mathias Boone. Apparently, they had been expecting my presence.

I made my way down the familiar curve that led up to the heavy doors. The palace seemed larger somehow, vaster. I suppose it had something to do with me getting used to the size of the academy, which, although huge, paled in comparison.

The bald doorman, still wearing a large pair of black sunglasses, opened the door when I ascended the stairs. He gave me a small nod as I entered.

The instrument that had been standing between the black double-staircase was gone. The area seemed emptier than usual. For a moment, I stood there awkwardly, unsure of where to go.

Then I remembered what Mathias had told me: "*I'll be next door, in 116.*"

I ran up the stairs.

To my surprise, the door swung open almost immediately after I knocked. Mathias was still in his school uniform. His expression remained neutral as I walked into the room. It was twice as large as my apartment, the walls painted a light gray, the same color of my mother's bedroom back home. A picture of him and his feslin hung above his desk, which was cluttered with unfinished homework. He motioned for me to sit on his bed.

"So," he said once I plopped down onto the silky material, "when are you leaving?"

"I don't know," I said. "A few weeks, I guess. Are you good with combat?"

The question took him by surprise. "I- yeah. Everyone working for Sorina has to undergo several years of training. Why do you ask?"

If I were to fight the Qroes single-handedly, I needed proper training. The karate lessons I used to take in second grade wouldn't be sufficient. "Train me," I said. It came out sounding harsher than I intended, but to my surprise, he agreed almost instantly.

"Okay, sure. Do you have any experience?"

None, unless that second-grade karate class counted. "I'm a quick learner," I told him. "When are you available?"

"Every day after school, unless I have to assist Sorina. That's my usual training time, which should add up to approximately five hours, minus dinner and my regular duties."

I nodded. "Four hours of training. Every day. Is that too much?" I added, looking at his expression.

"No, no, it's fine. Do we start today or tomorrow?"

The sooner we started, the more training I would get. "Today."

He led me down to the foyer and into a slim hallway, which led to a long, steep flight of stairs. At the bottom was a room filled with stacks of training equipment. An array of daggers glistened from the far end. Spears lined the walls. A set of bows hung above the daggers, the arrows tucked away into cylindrical boxes.

Mathias took a small metal container from one of the shelves. He opened it to reveal a thick, greenish cream.

"The healers' saliva mixed with herbs and antiseptic solutions," he explained. "For any injuries."

"We're going to hurt each other?"

He placed the metal container down on a wooden stool. "Accidents happen," he said curtly. "Now... which weapon should we train with? I personally prefer swords, but I'll let you choose."

"How about hand-to-hand combat?" I suggested. "It's the most useful since they'll likely confiscate all of my weapons when they catch me."

His eyes widened. "You want them to catch you?"

"How else will I get into one of their bases?" I asked. I gave him a small smile and turned around, walking to the center of the room. "Focus on the training for now. There's still a chance they'll find her before my plan takes place."

But his idea of training turned out to be much different than mine. Even after our warm-up, I could tell he was still going easy on me. I had the upper hand half of the time, which wouldn't have happened if he actually tried.

"Stop," I told him.

He immediately recoiled, concern flashing across his face like a streak of lightning. "Did I hurt you? I'm sorry if I did."

"No," I said, "you didn't. You're not even trying. I want you to *try* to hurt me. Give me a real challenge. All you're doing right now is blocking my advances."

He shook his head. "I can't."

"Can't what?"

139

"Hurt you. Not on purpose. Please don't ask me to do something I'll regret."

"We have medicine for wounds," I said, pointing towards the metal container. "And *they* will try to hurt me, so I have to be good at defense." I shook my head. "We're not even training with weapons and you're already-"

His fist flew in my direction, and I ducked at the last second.

He grinned. "Better?"

"Better."

A few bruises and several hours later, I was stumbling towards the dormitory. Mathias and I had agreed to start training with daggers tomorrow since they were smaller in size and would be easier to sneak into the Qroes' base. Naturally, I still hoped they would find Adelaine before I would have to conduct my plan. But the lack of updates was making my hope dwindle.

If the plan were to take place, it would have to be a good one. I wouldn't be able to fight the Qroes by myself. Not at their own base. Unless...

Unless I wouldn't have to fight them at all. If I could stall them long enough for Sorina to bring in reinforcements... maybe fighting wouldn't be necessary.

I just needed to outsmart them.

Luna had told me I was a good liar. And if I could fool the enemy, even for a while, it would give me a better advantage than any amount of training. Perhaps lying was all I needed.

That was all it took for my plan to begin to blossom.

Chapter Twenty-Seven

Training with daggers was, as expected, much harder than hand-on-hand combat. I ended up cutting into Mathias's flesh several times (on accident), and he had cut me too, although less often. The thick green cream in the metal container worked wonders. My injuries were gone within a few minutes of dabbing it on.

"Aim like this," he said, holding my arm at an angle. "Keep your hand steady. This will be the last one for today." He stepped away and pointed to the large, red X he had painted on the wall. I had yet to hit it. All of my previous tries had resulted in the dagger either veering too far to the left or too far to the right; once, I had struck the array of spears, causing them to clatter to the ground. I strengthened my grip on the dagger, moving my arm slightly to the left to aim at the center of the target.

"Now."

I threw the dagger as hard as I could, the metal tip a mere blur as it flew across the room. It hit the corner of the X and dropped to the floor. A smile broke across my face, and I looked to the side to see Mathias mirroring my expression.

"Much better," he said. "What do we practice with tomorrow? Swords?" His shirt, wet from sweat, clung to his skin, outlining his muscular form.

I shook my head, chugging down half a bottle of water. "We practice with daggers and hand-on-hand combat. They're the only ones I'll be able to use at the base. I want to see what I'm best at."

"Fine," he said. "I'll prepare some dummies. And then, once we see what you're best at, we continue to practice it, right?"

"We continue to practice both."

There was a very slim chance the Qroes owned daggers. From what I had witnessed, most of them had guns. Perhaps I could shock them with a sudden burst of pain and steal their gun that way? I sighed. I would have to spend much more time planning out possible outcomes.

"...plan? Are you listening?" Mathias's voice snapped me back into reality. "I asked if you thought more about your plan. Because I'd like to know the details."

I raised my eyebrows. "Oh? And why is that?"

"I'm coming with you," he said matter-of-factly, as if I was an idiot to think anything else.

"No you're not," I said. "You're staying here, so you can help them track me when they take me. And then, once I'm with Adelaine, you'll bring reinforcements to rescue us."

A crease appeared between his eyebrows. "How do you know they'll take you to the same place as Adelaine? They have hundreds of bases. She could be anywhere."

I smiled. "She's in the headquarters. They'll take me there too, I think. It's what they were going to do the first time. The bases are just temporary places for us to stay in while they prepare the transport. That's my assumption."

He pondered at this for a minute. "You might be right," he said. "It sounds just like them to keep their source of power in one spot. But… how will we track your location?"

Oops. I hadn't thought about that. "Uh… insert a chip into my skin? Like a tracker?"

"That's too simple," he said firmly. "Don't you think they have detectors for that sort of thing?"

"Then make one they won't be able to detect. That doctor… Beckett, I think, didn't he make the scan I used? It's very advanced. What's his ability? If he's that good with technology, could you ask him to make a tracker for me? One that won't be detectable?"

Mathias's lips parted slightly as he stopped to think this over. At last, he said, "Beckett is a Multi, like you.

142

Enhanced intelligence is one of his abilities. I suppose I could ask him regarding your request."

"But don't tell him why you need it. He could tell Sorina."

"I'll come up with something." He smiled. "See you tomorrow?"

"See you." I returned his smile, but it was gone the second he turned away.

* * *

After six days of practicing with the daggers, I could strike the dummies in the chest nearly every time. They had been brand new when Mathias had brought them in on Thursday, but now they were ridden with holes, with bright red Xs painted on various body parts.

"Impressive," Mathias said, pulling a dagger out of one of the dummies. "You weren't lying when you said you were a fast learner."

I grinned. "Of course I wasn't." Ringlets of hair hung in front of my eyes, and I pushed them roughly behind my ear. I envied Mathias's straight hair. It looked so fluffy up close. It would be much easier to fight without having to worry about my hair getting tangled up.

I walked over to the small coffee table Mathias had dragged into our training room a few days ago. It contained four water bottles, two for each of us. I grabbed one of mine and poured the remainder onto my head. It felt refreshing.

Mathias *tsked* disapprovingly. "The showers are just a couple rooms away. Why make the mess?"

I shrugged. "Call it impulse. I'll clean up, don't worry." I looked around the room, searching for anything that might resemble a towel or rag. Anything that would absorb the water. "Where are the cleaning supplies?" I asked, pointing towards the puddle.

"Doesn't matter; we've got maids for that. Just head to the showers and get yourself cleaned up. Three days of training left."

"Do the showers have towels?"

He nodded.

Good. I would use one of them to clean up the puddle.
"Okay," I said. "Can we talk afterwards? I'd like to ask you
about something."

"Sure. I'll be by the fountain in the garden," he
responded. He headed to the left, towards the men's showers. I
went to the right.

The women's shower room was, as usual, empty, so I
went over to the bath section and poured some cold water into
one of the ten tubs lined against the wall. The cool water was
soothing for my sore muscles and I submerged myself in it
entirely, reveling in the silence.

When I closed my eyes, I could pretend I was at the
bottom of Huma's pool. We had often played in it when we
were little. My favorite way to play was curling into a ball and
sinking to the bottom, where I sat and waited for her to find
me. Most times, this ended in me having to push myself back
up to the surface; unlike me, Huma wasn't a very good
swimmer.

I blew a small stream of bubbles and watched them
float up to the surface. In water, I could almost pretend my hair
was straight. Straight and silky, like Adelaine's.

Adelaine.

A painful ache speared through my heart, cutting off
the feeling of reverie that had been there moments before. The
cool water no longer seemed welcoming. I stepped out,
noticing my fingers were wrinkled and threw on some new
clothes. How long had I been in the bath? I had agreed to meet
Mathias in the garden. Was he still waiting?

I ran into the garden. Mathias was there, all right. He
was leaning against the fountain, his damp wings slowly
moving back-and-forth, drying in the evening wind. Since his
back was towards me, I decided to sneak up on him.

"What did you want to ask me about?" he asked, still not turning around. "I can feel your presence. And what's with the heavy breathing?"

I walked around the fountain to face him, ignoring his remark about my breathing. "How did you know it was me?"

"Nobody else walks around the garden at night. It's my duty to tend to it."

"Ah, right. You're a phytokinetic," I said. The fountain was surrounded by different types of flowers on all sides, and I wondered just how much of this garden he had grown.

"What did you want to ask me about?" he asked again, tapping his fingers on the fountain's edge.

"The Griffin," I said. "Sorina didn't tell me about it." I wanted to know if what Sonia had told me was true. Even if it was, I still wanted to know more. Sonia had been too vague for my liking.

"She must have forgotten," Mathias said apologetically. "The Griffin is the most valued creature in Soratia. He was enchanted, I believe, by Soratia herself, to make half-bloods like us. To give them wings."

"How?"

"He lays them, similar to how a bird might lay an egg. I've never seen it myself since it happens two times a year, so I'm telling you what I know from Sorina. The wings have sharp ends, which you stick into your birthmark to use. All half-bloods have it. It resembles two spots in the center of your back."

"I know what it looks like," I said. "How big are the wings?"

"About this big," he said, holding up his thumb and index finger. I estimated the distance to be approximately four inches. "Once you insert them into your body, they grow to this size." He turned around and spread out his wings to demonstrate. "They also drastically improve your ability. So, if I were Mei, for instance, I would be able to lift up a whole person instead of just a pencil."

"That's nice," I said. "What does the Griffin look like?"

"He has black feathers, a yellowish beak, weighs about-"

"Can I see him?"

The question startled him. He looked at me hesitantly before slowly repeating, "The Griffin is the most valued creature in Soratia."

"Ah," I said. "So you think I'm going to steal it." I didn't blame him. It made sense for him not to trust me, especially considering Soratia's latest event. But his face was displaying a mix of shock and confusion, which surprised me.

"No, no, of course not!" he protested, holding his hands in front of him. "I know you're not a thief. I would never assume-"

"It's fine," I said. "You don't have to show me anything. Forget I asked."

"I'll show you," he said quickly. "You said you wanted to see it, so I'll show you. Follow me."

I shook my head. "Just drop it. I know you don't think I'm a thief. You don't have to show me anything to prove it."

"But I *want* you to see the Griffin. Just follow me," he said. He reached for my hand. "Are you coming?"

I crossed my arms. "You didn't want to show me a minute ago."

"I changed my mind," he said, beckoning me forward. "Come on!"

This time, I followed him. Regardless of the reason behind his sudden change of mind, this was an amazing opportunity. Most likely one I wouldn't get again.

Instead of going up the main stairs, we went to the far-left end of the palace, where Mathias opened a small metal door using his yellow card. It slid open, revealing another flight of stairs, similar to the ones we used to descend to our training room. At the bottom was a labyrinth of hallways. We were alone, except for a maid shuffling her cart in the opposite direction.

She smiled at us as she passed.

We took a few turns before arriving at a large white door. This one also required Mathias's card to unlock.

Behind this door was a plox, except much higher in quality than Grace Arroyo's had been. Instead of wood, it was made of marble, which clashed with the color of the floor.

"How deep is this thing?" I muttered as we began floating down.

Mathias shrugged. "I'd say about twenty meters."

We arrived in a small room about the size of my bedroom back home. It was bare except for the single door we were facing. Two more doors waited behind it.

This amount of security only added on to what Mathias had told me by the fountain: *The Griffin is the most valued creature in Soratia*. It also explained his reluctance when I had asked him to show it to me. Were we even allowed in this place? He must have been, since the yellow card he carried opened all of the doors. But I wasn't sure about myself.

The corridor we entered was longer than any of the others, and it took us a good few minutes to arrive at the end of it. The black door we stood in front of seemed like the sturdiest in the palace, and I got a feeling this was the end of our destination. Mathias took out the yellow card and repeated the procedure. Card in. Card out. Open door. This time, instead of another door or a corridor, I found myself facing a glass wall.

"Take a look," Mathias said quietly. "This is it."

Chapter Twenty-Eight

I didn't see the creature at first. It was hidden behind one of the larger logs in the terrarium, and I only noticed it was there when it hopped towards the glass wall. It cocked its head, opened its beak (I assume it made some sort of noise, but the glass was too thick to hear through), and then hopped back behind the log. It was about the size of a medium-sized dog, but its wings would probably add to its size if they were spread out. Like Sorina's, the Griffin's feathers were black.

"Is... is this what the original griffins looked like? The ones that humans... er... bred with?"

Mathias looked at me like I was speaking another language. "No! This one's enchanted, remember? The originals were much, much larger. Did you not learn that in Soratian history?"

"We just finished covering the Griffin-Human War," I said. "We never discussed the sizes of griffins."

"Oh," Mathias said. "Irene must be a slow teacher."

"Mhm. Not as lenient on homework, though."

We stood in silence for a bit, watching the Griffin prowl around the terrarium. There weren't any other life forms in sight, which made me pity the small creature. It must have been incredibly lonely.

The Griffin began kneading a pile of leaves with its paws. I couldn't see it very well because it was hidden behind the log, but I assumed that was its nest; it certainly resembled one. The Griffin gingerly laid down. I looked over at Mathias, who was inspecting his sweater. Watching the Griffin must have bored him.

I decided I wouldn't take much longer; I didn't want to waste Mathias's time. The Griffin was barely visible anyway. I turned towards the door, which had closed on its own, expecting Mathias to follow.

Instead, I felt a hand grab my wrist and pull me back towards the glass wall.

My eyes traveled up to Mathias's finger, which was pointing at the Griffin. The creature was frozen in place, its beak wide open. Like a scream. It stayed like that for a few seconds, motionless, still, until at last its beak closed.

It crumpled to its nest.

Mathias's mouth had fallen open. For a moment, I feared that we had just witnessed the Griffin's death.

Then he burst out laughing.

"What's so funny?" I asked. "What happened?"

Mathias's eyes were the brightest I'd ever seen, displaying a level of ecstasy I didn't know he possessed. "Funny?" he said. "Do you not know what we just witnessed?"

I blinked at him. "I dunno… a Griffin having a seizure? And let go of my wrist; you're cutting off my blood flow."

"We witnessed *birth*, Lucianne," he said, releasing my wrist. His face was filled with fascination. "We witnessed the birth of wings! Did I tell you how rare that is? Two times a year! Only two times! And we saw it. Right now, we saw the Griffin give birth!"

"How do you know it gave birth?" I said skeptically. "He was hidden behind a log."

That was when the Griffin walked out from its nest, carrying something brown and lumpy in its beak. For the first time, I noticed a golden tray lying towards the side of the terrarium, nearly concealed by a bush.

The Griffin deposited the brown lump on the tray, nudged it lightly with his beak, and retreated to his nest.

"*That* is how I know," Mathias said, his voice trembling with excitement. "Did you see that? Those were wings!" he exclaimed. He nearly ran to the door. "There's only one other person I know that witnessed it, and she's…"

From the sudden change in his expression, I knew he was talking about Atiana.

I sighed. "You still love her, don't you?" I hated that my voice sounded bitter when I said it, almost like it was tinged with jealousy. As if I had a reason to be jealous of someone dead.

"No... no, I do not," he said quietly. "It wouldn't make sense for me to dwell on her death." His eyes flickered to the Griffin, and his face once again regained the expression of excitement. "Come. We have to tell Sorina."

I walked behind him, struggling to keep up as we hurried through the dozens of doorways and hallways that led to the Griffin's lair. I didn't understand why I had felt relief at his words. I also didn't understand why he was so enthusiastic. The only thing we had seen was the Griffin's expression. Maybe I would understand its significance if we covered the topic in Soratian history... if we got to it at all.

The door to Sorina's office was locked, so Mathias had to use the golden knocker. After hearing the sing-songy, "Come in!" he burst through the door, leaving me outside. I followed suit, deciding that standing outside of the queen's office when she was speaking with someone could be interpreted negatively.

"Your Highness," Mathias bowed, "you will not believe what Lucianne and I just witnessed."

I bowed as well, fixing my gaze on the familiar patterns of the floor until I heard her voice.

"May I ask what that was?" she asked. Sorina's pale blue hair had been curled, and locks of it fell over her shoulders.

Mathias beamed. "The Griffin gave birth, Your Highness. A few minutes ago. We saw it happen."

Several expressions crossed over the queen's face before she spoke. "Both you and Ms. Allaire witnessed it?"

I noted that she referred to me by my last name, something she hadn't done before.

"Yes, Your Highness." Mathias's excited expression began to fade. He had noticed the disapproval in her tone.

"May I speak with you for a moment?" she asked. Her crimson eyes pierced through mine as she said, "Preferably alone."

I retreated out of the room, gently closing the door behind me. I pressed my ear to the wood right after, eager to catch at least a fragment of their conversation. Unfortunately for me, the door seemed to be completely soundproof. I leaned against the wall and waited.

One minute.

Two.

Three.

I lost track of time eventually, and my eyelids began to droop. My muscles were still sore from training and I longed to throw myself onto the soft mattress of my bed. I wondered why they were taking so long. It had been pretty obvious Sorina wasn't too happy about Mathias taking me to see the Griffin. Was she yelling at him? Would she punish me as well? Questions like these soared through my mind as I tapped my foot nervously against the red carpet. After what seemed like forever, the door finally opened.

"What did she want?" I asked Mathias worriedly, following him away from Sorina's office and into one of the smaller hallways. "I'm sorry if I got you in trouble."

He smiled, but it didn't reach his eyes. "She just told me to be careful with my card, or I might lose that privilege. I told her she had nothing to worry about. That's pretty much it."

I opened my mouth to tell him that such a conversation shouldn't have taken more than one minute, but he spoke first, pulling a syringe out of his jacket.

"The tracker," he said quietly. "Hide it in your pocket for now. You can put it into your arm once you get to the dormitory."

I nodded, slipping the syringe into the larger pocket of my jacket. "Thank you."

Nearly all of the lights in the dormitory were out. Tomorrow was a school day. I hurried to my room, taking out the syringe immediately after opening the door. I made sure to close my blinds before starting the procedure. I didn't want anyone from the outside watching.

The syringe's needle was much larger than the ones I was used to, but that was because it contained the tracker. I hesitated before putting it in. Jabbing needles into my skin wasn't something I enjoyed. Nonetheless, I had to muster up the courage to do it. If I were to go through with the plan, Mathias would need this in order to track me.

Thanks to the medical textbooks Huma's mother had lent me from her college years, I knew where all the major veins were located. Making sure to steer clear of any of them, I plunged the needle into my skin, pushing on the syringe. I felt the exact moment when the tracker went in. It was an uncomfortable feeling, but much better than I had imagined.

I placed the syringe in the drawer, tucking it behind Adelaine's jewelry box. Three more days until my mission. By the end of this week, we would both be back here, sitting in the dormitory and chatting about homework. By the end of this week, things would be back to normal.

That was, if the plan succeeded.

Chapter Twenty-Nine

As the day of my mission approached, the school days seemed to get shorter. I wasn't too bothered by Irene's personality either; something that surprised both me and my young classmates.

Despite my efforts not to have her find out, Mei also sensed that something was different.

"You're acting giddy lately," she said during lunch. "Did something happen? You can tell me, I won't judge."

"No," I said quickly. "A-actually yes. Mathias and I saw the Griffin give birth yesterday. To a small brown lump of wings." It sounded weird when I said it, but Mei understood.

"I *knew* something was on your mind. Lucky you. I didn't think the queen would let anyone see the Griffin. It's very valuable."

"She didn't," I said, and Mei raised her eyebrows. "Mathias showed me the Griffin, but I don't think he was allowed to. Sorina wasn't too happy when she found out."

"He must like you a lot, then," she said teasingly.

"Speak for yourself! The guy literally knows your address."

Mei glared at me. "Because I gave him piano lessons a few years ago and he had to escort me home!"

"You must be pretty good then." I smiled, hoping it would light up the atmosphere. "Play for me sometime."

"Sure," she said. "Come over to my house tomorrow after school. Does that sound good?"

I shook my head. "I'm busy tomorrow." I had training until late into the evening, and I doubted she would be awake at the time I finished.

"Oh," she said. I could hear the disappointment in her voice. "Let me know when you'll be available, okay?"

I nodded. Our conversation finished just in time because the bells chimed at that exact moment. I waved Mei goodbye as I left for modern human technology. Today, we would be learning how to use some applications on a laptop. I had never owned one, so I was just as new to it as the other students in the classroom.

At least they were my age.

In the East Wing, Mathias canceled our training. He claimed he had urgent responsibilities at the palace. I told him that it was fine and immediately ran to the Shell to tell Mei I would be able to come over after all. We made our way to her house once school was over.

Aside from the two bushes in front that had been neatly trimmed, not much had changed on the outside of Mei's house. On the inside, it was pretty clean, but I couldn't note any changes since I had never seen it before. The piano stood in the living room, right beside a dark brown couch. We had the house all to ourselves since both of Mei's parents were working and she had no siblings. I was glad for the privacy. Talking with strangers tended to make me flustered.

Mei began to play a short, upbeat piece, which I recognized as a work of Beethoven. We had studied him in music class nearly every year, so I had most of his pieces memorized.

"You know Beethoven?" I asked her, giving a short round of applause when she finished playing.

"My mom is a huge fan," she replied. "She can play every piece he wrote."

"I'm guessing she's from Earth? I don't think anyone from here would know a human musician, much less be his fan."

Mei nodded. "She came here in her early 20s. I don't know much about her life before that." She changed the subject. "Want some cookies? My dad and I baked a few yesterday, so we have to eat them before they go stale."

As it turned out, Mei was just as good at baking as she was at playing the piano.

"These are really good," I said. "You should be a baker."

Mei took a sip of tea. "I'd rather be a professional pianist."

"That suits you as well."

"What about you?"

I hesitated. Up until my kidnapping, I had wanted to be a doctor. To study medicine and gain knowledge, so that one day I would be able to save lives. The money would have pulled my mother out of debt. And so, I had spent most of my afternoons poring over Huma's mother's old medical textbooks, watching surgeries online, learning about different conditions and their treatments. I had dedicated a few notebooks to my studies. They were still lying somewhere in my room.

But now? I didn't know. Being a doctor didn't seem like a possibility anymore, not in this dimension.

"I'm not sure."

Mei shoved another cookie into her mouth. The tray was almost empty. "Think about it more often. My mom says you should have a plan of your future at least four years before you graduate, or life will be a mess. Maybe you could question people with your ability and work for Sorina."

"Maybe."

The conversation ended at that, but I stayed for a few more hours. By the time I left her house, both suns had already set.

I ran all the way back to the dormitory's iron gates. There was a slip of paper sticking out from beneath my dorm's door, almost entirely pushed inside. I furrowed my eyebrows. It was a note, and I promptly noticed that there was no signature. The wrinkled paper held one sentence, written in thin, messy handwriting.

The Griffin is gone, and you're the primary suspect.

A few moments later, there was a knock on the door.

Chapter Thirty

I slipped the note into my pocket before pressing my face against the door. "Who's there?"

There was a short pause before a girl's voice answered. "Zarah."

"Zarah?" I repeated. I opened the door a bit, just enough to peek outside. The doors in the dormitory didn't have peepholes, which was one of the few things I disliked about the place. "What are you doing here?"

Her gaze met my eyes, steady and fierce. "You get the note? Let me in. I got somethin' for you."

I opened the door a bit wider and shut it behind her.

"Is it true?" I asked. "Someone stole the Griffin? When?" I asked. I wondered if this was why Mathias had canceled our training. Did he think I was the one that took it?

Zarah scowled. "Guards are on their way here as we speak. Don't know what they'll do to you, but I don't think they're gonna let you go anytime soon."

"And you're here to… what, stall me? Make sure I don't escape? Look, if you think I had anything to do with the Griffin's disappearance, you're wrong."

"I know you didn't have anything to do with it," she said.

"Then why are you here?"

"To warn you," she replied. "And to give you this." She dropped a small orange pouch onto the carpet. I scrambled to pick it up, pouring out the contents onto my hand.

"Portal stones?"

"You're gonna save Adelaine, right? That's what you think of every day during class, so I'm guessing you will. Just don't ask how I got 'em. You won't get an answer."

I rolled one of the stones around in my fingers, feeling its smooth surface. A smile slowly made its way across my face.

"Zarah, thank you," I said. A few days ago, I had thought she and Allyson both disliked me. Clearly, I had been wrong. The stones were expensive. She wouldn't do this for me if I was on her bad side.

Zarah scoffed. "I'm not doing this for *you*."

A dull knock on the door cut off my response. My hands shot up protectively over my face—a nice reflex I had acquired during my few weeks of training. Zarah froze. I heard the faint swish of her robes behind me, but my eyes remained fixed on the door. By the time my head snapped back around, Zarah was gone, the window open and the curtains billowing in the wind. I turned back towards the door, hand on the knob. Would they force it open? Perhaps they thought no one was inside. After all, the lights were turned off. Maybe they'd leave if they thought I wasn't in the dormitory.

Another knock, this one harder, accompanied by a desperate voice.

"Open the door, Lucianne," it said. The voice belonged to a male, and I quickly recognized it. "Hurry. We don't have much time."

At once the door was agape, and Mathias slinked in, his feet padding on the soft carpet. He was breathing heavily, wearing the same cloak he had worn the night of my kidnapping.

His voice was tense when he spoke. "The Griffin is gone. They think you stole it and they're coming here, right now, left the palace not so long ago," he took in a rattling breath, "and we need to go. It was the maid. The one we saw that day. I'm sure of it. But they don't believe that it wasn't you, and we don't even know who she was. I don't have the stones, I left them in the palace, but I know someone who does." He paused to cough; his voice was growing drier by the minute. "We're going to the woods. We'll stay there for some time, and once we lose them, we can-"

I held up the orange pouch, watching as his mouth fell open.

"H-how did you…?" his voice faltered.

"Let's save the stories for later, okay?" I threw a bottle of water in his direction before picking up my backpack. "Drink up. Your voice is hoarse."

"Lucianne, we have to leave," he pressed.

I emptied the drawers, searching briefly for anything useful. It took less than a few moments for Adelaine's headband to be wrapped tightly around my thigh. The dagger I had kept from training rested inside of the bottom drawer, I tucked it into the headband. One loaf of bread lay on the coffee table, and I grabbed that too, shoving it into the backpack.

"Let's go," I told him, nodding towards the open window. Since I couldn't fly, he would have to carry me to the woods. I sat gingerly on the windowsill. My teeth gritted as some of the sharper pieces of stone bit into my thigh. The window was large enough for Mathias to kneel in, which he did, firmly placing his hands on my upper back and below my knees.

"Ready?"

"Just go."

He pushed us off the windowsill.

We plummeted towards the ground, the bricks of the dormitory a mere blur as his grip on my skin intensified. My stomach churned. I felt his wings spread out, his warm breath on my neck, and then we were soaring upwards, millions of stars blinking from the sky. The crisp night air heightened my senses as we gained speed, heading straight for the woods.

The flight was smooth. Mathias flew with incredible speed and precision, taking a wide berth around the taller buildings. I spotted a young girl in one of the windows, face pressed against the glass, mouth open as she watched us. I resisted the urge to wave.

The feeling in my stomach was no longer a feeling of fear, but a feeling of bliss. A shrill giggle escaped my lips as we flew lower, spiraling down the side of the valley.

It made me forget.

It made me forget about the guards that were entering the dormitory.

It made me forget about the danger we were bound to encounter upon my return to Earth.

It made me forget about the Qroes, and just about every unpleasant event I had ever come to encounter. I was flying for the first time in my life, the valley spread out before me like a three-dimensional map, the twinkling lights below reminding me of my first and only ride on an airplane, when Huma's family had taken me to their California house during the summer. Oh, how I longed to go back to those days.

I was so wound up in the flight that I didn't notice when it ended, and when I did, I was sitting on the damp grass, Mathias in front of me, pouring the stones out of the orange pouch.

I instantly reached out to help him.

"Where's your stick?" I asked once the oval was complete. I looked it over once more, making sure the edges of the stones were touching.

He looked surprised. "What do you mean?"

"The first time I watched you do this, you touched each of the stones with a stick to make them glow. Did you forget that as well?"

Mathias laughed. "Oh no, that was just a regular stick I found on the ground. You need to touch each of the stones with something, anything, to activate them. Want to do it?"

"Sure." I sprung up from the grass and reached for the nearest stick. It was long and smooth, and I giddily struck each stone with its tip, watching them light up. A low hum began to spread throughout the meadow as I continued activating the stones. I paused briefly once they were all glowing, then lowered my stick towards the center of the oval.

The familiar rippling surface appeared instantly, making me drop the stick into the oval. The portal cast an orange glow over my face as I grinned up at Mathias. He gave me a thumbs up in return.

"Going first again? It didn't go too well last time," he said teasingly.

"Practice makes perfect," I retorted. "How do I make it take me to the right place?"

"Just think of the address. Or picture the place. I'll go in right after you."

I looked down at the portal and tried to smile. Last time had been unpleasant, yes, but if Mathias became used to it, so would I. I didn't want to look like a coward, not when we were going on such a dangerous mission.

I jumped.

Chapter Thirty-One

The needles pierced into my skin by thousands. I gritted my teeth to block out the tears that were starting to form behind my eyelids. I was falling, my hair whipping me in the face, and I regretted not having tied it in a ponytail. That would have made things so much easier.

At last, the fall slowed, and I landed on the lush grass that was still slightly wet from the 11 AM gardener. I felt a bit sick, but nothing near as awful as what I'd felt the first time I had used the portal. Instinctively, I jumped away from the portal. I had to resist the urge to pluck out one of the stones just to see what would happen.

Mathias descended, as gracefully as ever, his cloak billowing gently behind him. He looked at me, smiled, then looked at the red-brick mansion. His cheerful expression vanished.

"You took us into someone's *backyard*?" he hissed. "We're in broad daylight! Do you understand how much danger this-"

"Relax. I know this place. Just keep your wings hidden until we get inside." I pulled a stone out of the glowing portal, the rest of the stones collapsing to the ground. The pouch was in my other hand and I quickly gathered the stones, passing it to Mathias once I finished. He would need it to go back.

I walked up the polished wooden steps to the veranda, sliding my hand along the familiar smooth barriers. The glass double-doors showed me the empty rooms of the house. It was early in the afternoon; Huma's parents were still working.

When I knocked on the door, there was no answer. That meant two things: Huma was either at school or shopping. Probably the former.

I spotted a dotted vase of flowers standing on a burlap-colored mat. It took me a while to move it aside. If it wasn't for

Mathias's training, I wouldn't have been able to move the large piece of pottery at all.

Once the vase was out of the way, I felt underneath the mat. Sharp metal met my fingers almost instantly, and I triumphantly pulled out the keys, lifting them for Mathias to see.

An expression of amusement played across his face. "We're breaking in?"

"No. We're temporarily staying at my friend's house until they come back. It would be too risky to take you to my apartment. Too many people around."

Mathias clicked his tongue. "Must be a pretty good friend if they told you where they keep their keys."

"She didn't *tell* me. I saw where she placed them when I came over one time and her parents weren't home. The vase on top changed but the keys' place is still the same."

Mathias glanced around. "Open the door, then. We shouldn't wait out here for too long."

"This key is for the *front* door. Stay here. I'll let you in from the inside."

I climbed over the fence, something I had done hundreds of times before, and boldly walked up to the front of the house. Trying to be discreet would only make me look suspicious, and the last thing I needed was to have the police called on me by the neighbors. Thankfully, Huma's family didn't have surveillance cameras in the yard. Sneaking Mathias in via the back doors wouldn't be an issue.

I climbed up the porch steps, smiled at the blinking red eye of the camera, and opened the door. If the camera notified Huma of my arrival, I hoped she would get the hint and avoid telling her parents.

The smell of expensive furniture entered my nose as I headed towards the glass doors. I made sure to shut the front door behind me.

"Where to now?" Mathias asked, looking around the modern kitchen I had just let him into. "Your friend has a nice house."

"Huma's bedroom," I said. "We'll wait until she comes home, which should be in about..." I glanced up at the neon clock hanging over the counter, "...one hour."

"Okay," he said slowly. "Where can I hide while she's here?"

"You won't hide. I'll introduce you guys to each other."

He stared at me. "Do you realize how dangerous-"

"Do you trust me?"

The question caught him by surprise. He stammered, "Y-yes. Of course."

"Good. Then you'll have to trust my plan. This is the best I could come up with," I said firmly. "Follow me."

I led him up the dark wooden stairs and into a hallway to the right. Huma's house paled in comparison to Sorina's palace, but it was still a humongous place. When I was younger and unfamiliar with the layout, I had often become lost in the labyrinth of rooms. I could never find the right one.

Now, however, I knew exactly where to go. Huma's room was third to last in the upstairs hallway, and it was one of the two rooms in the house that had a balcony. I pushed open the door and was surprised to see that aside from the walls, which had gone from baby-blue to a light purple, pretty much nothing had changed. The chandelier that hung above the lush white carpet was still there, her polished oak desk was still backed against the wall next to the closet, and her curtains were still embedded with the same flowery patterns I remembered from a few months ago.

"Sit there," I said, pointing towards the three beanbags in the corner next to a shelf. That was where Huma kept her books. We would sometimes read together, if I didn't have a sports event to attend at school. I smiled. The familiarity of this place was refreshing.

"Since we have time, why don't you tell me the details of your plan?" Mathias suggested once we were both seated. He was lazily twirling the orange pouch around his finger, his eyes resting on mine. I had told him the basic outline a week ago, but he had yet to know the rest.

"So you want me to go over the whole thing?" I asked. "Or just the details?"

"Just tell me the entire plan so I know I've memorized it correctly."

This would take a while. "I'll start with what we were supposed to do before leaving," I began. "We were supposed to train for two weeks. We were supposed to pack everything on the final night, all of the daggers, but clearly we-"

Mathias reached into his cloak. "I have your daggers. All five of them. Here."

He handed them to me.

I slid my finger along the silver blades with fascination, my lips curving upwards. Perhaps we hadn't failed after all.

I walked over to Huma's nightstand, knowing that was where she kept her headbands. Selecting three black ones from the impressive collection, I headed to the bathroom. Three daggers went on my thighs. They would be concealed by the loose material of my pants. Using another headband, I pushed one up my sleeve. The cool blade touching my skin made me shudder. This dagger would be easy to access; all I had to do was reach into my sleeve using my left hand. I placed the remaining two at my waist.

By the time I came out of the bathroom, my mood had improved significantly.

"Thank you," I said, sitting back on the beanbag.

"No problem." He reached into his cloak, producing two identical leaves. They were thick and glossy, and I recognized them as the ones Adelaine had given me to chew before class. "Want some versicose?"

"Sure." I took one from his hand and popped it into my mouth. The burst of minty flavor was refreshing. "Like I was saying… we were supposed to come to Earth, which we did, explain everything to Huma, and spend the first night in here, in her home. Hopefully, she'll manage to hide us both. The house is spacious enough. We'll leave early in the morning, you back to Soratia and me into the city. If the Qroes truly have their people everywhere, it won't take too long for them to find me." My heartbeat accelerated when I said it, but my voice remained steady. I couldn't afford to show any signs of hesitation; that could make him doubt my plan. "You'll have people watching my location every day, so you'll know when I'm taken to a base. I'll probably sit there for a day or two, and then they should take me to their headquarters. You'll know when I'm there too. If possible, find a really good telepath to send me a message that you're coming. Then I'll use the daggers to threaten some of the Qroes into telling me where they keep Adelaine-"

"They'll confiscate those," Mathias said coolly.

"Then I'll find a way to get them back. It'll work out," I said reassuringly, more to myself than to him.

"They have guns." Once again, his voice was cold.

"Then I'll take their guns. I know how to fire one. My uncle took me hunting when I was younger." He had only taken me once, and he had been the one shooting, but of course, I wasn't going to say that. "I'll find out where they keep the Griffin too. By the time you come with the others, Adelaine and the Griffin will be safe, and most of the Qroes will be wounded enough for you and the others to kill their boss." It sounded more like a dream than a plan, but I needed Mathias to trust me. I had back-ups, of course. But most of those would come when I got familiar with the Qroes' base, since there wasn't much I could do now. I had to hope it would work out. My luck was overdue, anyway.

"And if they kill you?"

"They won't. Not if they want my ability."

"You don't know that," he said sharply. "They killed thousands of us. Hell, you saw for yourself, didn't you? The bastards murdered-"

The door downstairs slammed shut.

Chapter Thirty-Two

I knew the person downstairs was most likely Huma returning from school, but that didn't stop my heart rate from accelerating. Pointing towards the white door that led to Huma's closet, I mouthed: *hide.* Mathias understood and soundlessly slipped into the closet, pulling the hood of his cloak over his head. I went in after him, slowly shutting the door to make the least amount of sound possible. It gave a small *click* before we became submerged in darkness.

I heard Mathias's shallow breathing beside me as the person began ascending the stairs. With relief, I noted that their footsteps weren't too heavy, so the person definitely wasn't Mr. Khatri. I didn't want to imagine what would happen if Mr. Khatri found Mathias and I hiding in his daughter's closet. The guy had always given me the creeps.

The footsteps drew closer, stopping right in front of the room. I heard the doorknob turn and the person walked right in, dropping onto the bed with a heavy sigh. I leaned forward to peer through the crack at the bottom, to make sure the person on the bed was Huma, and not one of her siblings.

That was a mistake. The second I leaned forward was the second the floorboard beneath me creaked, and the person on the bed stopped moving. It didn't matter who they were. We would have to show ourselves either way.

"W-who's there?" the person stammered, and I let out a quiet sigh of relief. The voice belonged to Huma.

I pushed open the door, holding up my palm towards Mathias in an attempt to make him stay. Huma was easily shocked, and I didn't want her to meet Mathias until I explained everything. "It's me," I said softly. "I'm back."

Huma's mouth dropped open. "H-how? Y-you were… what—"

I lunged at her, pulling her into a hug so tight, I felt her gasp.

"I'll explain later," I mumbled into her hair. "I missed you."

Reluctantly, she hugged me back. She wasn't the type of girl that enjoyed physical contact, but this was an exception. I could tell she had missed me.

We stayed in an embrace until the closet door behind us swung open. Mathias stood up, hands on his hips, his wings still concealed by the cloak.

"Who's that?" Huma squeaked, jumping back. Her eyes moved between the two of us frantically. She looked like she was about to faint.

"Hey," Mathias said. "I'm not going to sit in the closet forever." His eyes landed on Huma, who was turning pale. "Help her sit down before she falls over."

I lowered Huma onto the bed, waiting for her rapid breathing to slow. I wanted to punch Mathias for disturbing our moment of peace, but I knew I would never forgive myself if I did. I was the one who had dragged him here in the first place.

Finally, the color returned to her face. Huma sat up, letting out a heavy sigh.

Her hands closed into fists and she uttered one shaky word. "Explain."

* * *

I told her about everything that happened since the night of my kidnapping, with Mathias occasionally adding in a forgotten detail. It took a while, and by the time we finished, it was close to dusk.

Huma eyed me wearily; the shock had long since worn off, and nothing seemed to surprise her anymore.

"Let me get this straight," she muttered, rubbing her temples. "You were kidnapped by people that wanted to steal your magical powers, saved by a griffin-human hybrid who

169

built a portal out of stones and took you into his dimension, forced to go to school with a bunch of other griffin-human hybrids, blamed for the theft of a Griffin, and now you're going back to the same association that kidnapped you in hopes of rescuing your roommate that was also kidnapped by said association? Not to mention breaking into my home and hiding in my closet!"

I sighed. "You don't believe me, do you? That's okay, I wouldn't believe myself either. It sounds crazy."

"No, no, I *do* believe you," Huma said. "I wish I had a reason not to, but… we've literally got living proof right here." She nodded towards Mathias, who was sitting cross-legged on the carpet.

"So, you'll help us?" I asked. I lifted my eyes hopefully.

"What kind of a friend would I be if I didn't?" she rolled her eyes. "One thing though— how long are you going to stay here?"

"Just tonight," Mathias said. "We'll both leave in the morning."

"Oh," Huma sounded surprised. "Why so soon?"

But before we could answer, a woman's voice spoke from the other side of the door. "Huma, dear, who are you talking to?"

We froze.

I noticed that the door wasn't locked. How had we not heard her open the door downstairs? Mrs. Khatri could come in at any moment; there was nothing stopping her. Mathias noticed it too and scrambled to the closet, the last traces of his cloak disappearing as he shut the door.

"My friend," Huma called back. "She came over a few hours ago."

The doorknob turned, and Mrs. Khatri's head poked in. Her brow furrowed when she saw me.

"Lucianne?"

"Good afternoon, ma'am," I said meekly.

Mrs. Khatri's hand shot up to her lips. "My goodness… is everything okay? Rumors told you ran from home! Does Estelle know you're here?"

"Yeah," I lied, glancing at the wall. "I called her a few minutes ago. And everything is fine, thanks for asking."

"Oh… good," she said. Mrs. Khatri straightened her dress and smiled. "I wouldn't want her to worry." She turned towards the door. "Dinner's in five minutes. You're welcome to join us."

And just like that, we were alone.

Huma and I looked at each other, worried expressions crossing our faces. Now that she knew I was here, Mrs. Khatri could easily call my mother. I would just have to hope my lie was convincing enough.

I slowly opened the closet door to find Mathias pressed against the back wall, hidden behind an array of dresses.

"You'll have to stay here for a while," I told him. "The Khatris want me to join them for dinner."

"Must be nice," he grumbled. "My foot fell asleep."

I moved the dresses aside. "You don't have to hide right now. And I doubt anyone will come searching for you during dinner. I'll bring you some food," I added reassuringly.

The Khatri dining table was long and filled with dishes of Indian foods I recognized: masala gosht curry and flatbread (lacha paratha), among others. Their cook was extremely talented, and I always enjoyed the food he served. Thanks to him, I had come to know a wide variety of dishes from Huma's mother's home country.

After prayer, we sat down and began eating. Huma had two twin brothers: Rishi and Rohan, who sat on either side of me.

"You were kidnapped, Lucianne?" Mrs. Khatri said softly. "When did you come back? How? Who took you? I have so many questions."

I swallowed. "I'm sorry, ma'am. I don't really feel comfortable talking about it."

"Of course! My apologies. This must be a touchy subject for you." She continued chewing in silence, averting her gaze from mine.

Mr. Khatri cleared his throat. He was a tall, broad man, with a nice beard and thick-rimmed glasses perched on the bridge of his nose. Unlike Dr. Beckett's, they didn't slide off.

"If you don't mind me asking," he said gruffly, "do you have any idea who those people were?"

I did. But telling him that my kidnappers specialized in stealing the powers of an interdimensional species would make me look like a lunatic. "No, sir. I don't know."

"That's a shame," he said, brushing several crumbs off his shirt.

And that was when I noticed the design embedded on his right breast pocket.

The same design that had glared at me from Alfred Stellinger's shirt when I'd been strapped down to the metal table.

The crow's eye looked at me teasingly, as if to say, *Oh, Lucianne! What an idiot you are. Straight into the enemy's home!*

My appetite vanished.

"Something the matter?" Mr. Khatri inquired politely. "You look quite pale."

"I should go," I mumbled. "My mother is expecting me." Leaving the food on the table, I hurried up the stairs. I heard a chair scrape behind me. *Most likely Huma*, I thought to myself as I moved forward, my head pounding. Did Mr. Khatri know what I was? If he did, great. I wouldn't have to search for the Qroes in the city. But Mathias wasn't supposed to be captured. I had to get him back to Soratia.

A hand touched my shoulder and I swiveled around, holding my hands in front of my face.

It was Mr. Khatri.

"What happened?" Mr. Khatri spoke softly, slowly moving towards me as I backed away from Huma's bedroom. I couldn't lead him to Mathias. "You told us you were heading home."

"I am, sir," I told him, willing my voice not to shake. "I'm getting my things."

"Should I come with you?"

"No, sir," I said quickly. "I don't really feel comfortable around men. I'm sorry."

"And yet you brought one into my house."

My breath hitched in my throat. He knew.

"Sir," I said slowly, "I have no idea what you're talking about."

He smirked, his cold eyes penetrating through my skin, making me shiver. "Your face deceives you."

My legs trembled beneath me as I lunged at Huma's door. Locking it behind me, I turned towards the closet. Mr. Khatri was pulling on the knob harshly, and I could tell it wouldn't hold for long. Mathias would have to build the portal quickly.

But when I opened the closet door, it was empty.

A sinking feeling infiltrated my stomach as I staggered backwards, eyes on the door. Just like Adelaine, Mathias was gone. The portal stones were gone, too. It was my fault. He had trusted me, and I had foolishly led him to the enemy's lair.

The doorknob stopped moving, and I heard Mr. Khatri's footsteps retreating back down the stairs. He would come back for me. That was certain.

Gone. The word kept replaying in my head, and I pulled at my hair, watching several orange locks come off. Gone. I ripped the hair in half, feeling a burning sensation forming behind my eyes. Gone. My fault. I let out a high guttural sound, but no tears came. Instead, my throat felt as if it had been stuffed with cotton balls.

I heard keys in the lock, and I knew why Mr. Khatri had gone downstairs. Of course. It only made sense for them to have keys to each room.

Two men came in, Mr. Khatri a few feet behind them. One of them held a rag. I instantly recognized the foul smell of the knock-out drug. *Good*, I thought. *Let them take me.*

I knew I would have to put up some kind of a fight. It would look strange if I didn't.

I threw myself at the man closest to me—the one with the rag—and clawed at his face, turning my pointer finger into a hook. This was a move Mathias and I had practiced often enough for me to be good at it. My finger sunk into something wet—his eye—and the man let out a raspy groan.

The satisfaction didn't last long.

Something hard and heavy collided with my head, pushing me off the man. I tried to stand up. Mr. Khatri was pinning me down, the man next to him pressing the rag to my face.

The last thing I remembered was thrashing beneath their grasp.

Then I blacked out.

Chapter Thirty-Three

The mossy cell they threw me into was a hundred times better than my last one, whose walls had been caked with the blood of the previous prisoners. I flexed all of my limbs, but aside from my pounding head and aching body, I didn't seem to be hurt anywhere.

Unfortunately, I couldn't say the same for my companion.

A large cut ran along Mathias's cheek. His knuckles were bruised and bleeding. He was slumped on the floor across from me, his eyes blankly gazing at the wall. When I sat up, they flickered to me, but his expression remained blank.

"They didn't hurt you, did they?" he asked. "You don't look hurt."

"No," I mumbled.

"Good."

"Mathias, I-"

"Don't," he said, holding up his palm. "I know what you're trying to say. Don't bother apologizing." His voice was seeping with anger, anger that was most likely directed towards me. But how could I blame him? I had led him straight into the filthy claws of the Qroes.

"I'm an idiot," I blurted. "I'm sorry. I should have never taken you to Huma's house. It was a mistake, but a grave one. I won't blame you if you hate me. I deserve your hatred." I slammed my fist onto the stone floor. "Damn it, Mathias! Your expression is angry. Say something."

"I'm not angry at you," he said. "I'm sorry if I gave off that impression. The only people here that deserve hatred are the enemy. You were just as clueless as I was." He sighed. "The fault is equally ours."

I gritted my teeth. "How, exactly, is the fault yours?"

"Simple," he said indifferently, shrugging his shoulders. "I insisted upon coming with you. Had I not done that, none of this would have happened."

"But I told you that you could come. I should have done more to stop you."

He laughed bitterly. "You think you could have stopped me? Look, Lucianne, if I wanted to-"

A familiar man walked up behind the bars, sliding a long loaf of bread through the metal. It fell to the floor, and he grunted, "Dinner." The eyepatch on his left eye made me recognize him as the man from yesterday.

I picked up the loaf and walked over to Mathias, shooting a glare at the man. "So now you're going to starve us?"

The man's lower lip curled up, revealing an array of yellow teeth. "Be thankful you aren't dead."

Mimicking his tone, I said, "Be thankful I didn't poke out your other eye."

The expression that appeared on his face was priceless.

He snarled. Droplets of spit sprayed from his lips. "Watch that mouth. You're lucky he wants you alive."

With that, he pivoted on his heel and walked off, head raised high.

I turned towards Mathias, who had broken the bread in half and was beginning to chew on the smaller piece. "What does he mean?"

"He's probably referring to his boss," Mathias said, his voice hinting at amusement. "What you said to him… was it true? Did you actually poke out his eye?"

I picked up the larger half of the bread and sat down next to him. "Yeah. It was the move you taught me during hand-on-hand combat—the one where you turn your finger into a hook and pull out the eye. It wasn't as precise as I wanted, since my finger went straight *into* the flesh, but it was satisfying nonetheless." I placed the pad of my finger just above the cut on his cheek. "Looks like you put up a fight as well. How did it go?"

"Not as well as I would have liked, since… you know… I was crammed into a closet. They climbed in through the window. Two went to hide across the hall. I tried to take on all of them, but there were too many, and they advanced too quickly. One had a knife. I threw a few punches, but they pretty much knocked me out after that." He smiled. "Yours sounds much cooler. I never poked out someone's eye."

"It wasn't an experience I'd like to repeat," I said. "Now… how do we get you out? Can't you use your ability like last time? Grow some branches out of the floor and break open the wall?"

He shook his head. "They took care of that. Didn't you notice the armband they put on you?"

I glanced down at my arm. Sure enough, there was a metal armband right above my elbow. I tried pulling it off, to no avail.

"Great," I muttered. "I'm guessing this prevents us from using our abilities?" I noticed that the armband had a lock, which meant that someone had the keys. If I could find them, both of us could escape.

"Precisely. They most likely got rid of your daggers too."

I pulled up my sleeve. As expected, the skin underneath was bare. All that remained of the dagger was the red indentation, and even that was almost faded. The same went for my hips. Both daggers were gone, two red indentations where the handles had been.

I sighed. "Right."

"Did you check your thighs?" he asked. His voice was low.

"No, but-"

"Check them."

My hand traveled down the thick material of the pants, to the area where the daggers had rested. Two on my right thigh, one on my left. I had placed them there because these areas were covered by pockets, which made the daggers practically invisible.

And my hand met a hard surface.

My hands flew up to my mouth to muffle the cry of joy I was about to utter. Mathias dropped his loaf of bread. The corners of his lips tilted upwards as he took in my expression.

"How many?" he whispered, his voice quivering with excitement.

"All three," I whispered back, and I couldn't suppress the smile that appeared on my face. "Want one?"

He shook his head. "Too risky. Don't take them out yet. We don't know if there are cameras at this place."

"True." I finished chewing my bread. It was stale and hard, the opposite of the crispy, fresh loaves we were served at the Shell for breakfast. The mere thought of fresh food made my mouth water. It couldn't have been more than a day since I'd eaten that chicken curry, but it felt like ages.

I instantly regretted those thoughts, remembering that Mathias didn't have dinner at all. He was certainly hungrier than me, and yet he had given me the larger half of the bread. I decided I would let him have the next meal. That would be fair.

"Entertain me."

My head swiveled towards Mathias, who was lying on the floor, his wings spread out beneath him. "What?"

"Entertain me," he repeated, gazing up at the ceiling. Dozens of cobwebs stretched across it, and I wondered when it had last been cleaned. "Tell me a story or something. I'm bored."

"You sound like a child," I said. "Like a child begging for stories during nap time."

Mathias picked up a small rock and rolled it towards me. "I'm past the point of caring. You tell me a story and I'll tell you a story. Fair?"

"I'm not good at telling stories," I protested. "My imagination is about as complex as… a rock."

"Rocks *are* complex," Mathias said. "Take granite for example. It consists of many different parts. Quartz, mica, potassium feldspar-,"

"Show-off," I murmured. "My point still stands. I suck at coming up with stories."

He smirked. "Then tell me one from your childhood. That's easy and takes no effort. You don't have to come up with anything."

"I wouldn't want to bore you."

"You won't," he assured me. "I want to know about your life before... all of this. I'm not from here, remember? Tell me about your friends. Or your school. Anything is fine."

"And what will you tell me about?"

"An event from *my* childhood. Story for a story."

"Fine," I said at last. "But don't say I didn't warn you."

He waited patiently as I searched my mind for a semi-interesting event. Unlike Huma, I hadn't traveled to many places as a child. I had occasionally gone on road trips with my aunts, who were in a much stabler financial situation than my mother and I, but none of it was worth mentioning. At last, I settled on a number of surprisingly vivid memories from fourth grade.

"When I was nine," I began, "there was a pretty girl in my class. Her name was Victoria Hill. She was one of the richer girls in school, and she used to make me cry for fun."

Mathias raised his eyebrows. "A bully?"

"No." I smiled softly. "My best friend."

And then I told him of the night that had ended our friendship.

* * *

A huff of exasperation escaped Victoria's lips as she watched me burst into tears. This was a scene she had witnessed hundreds of times before, and it wasn't one she was particularly fond of.

"Are you finished?" she snapped impatiently. Her face blurred as a new round of tears welled up in my eyes. "Stop acting like such a crybaby!" she hissed. "My mom's gonna hear."

I swallowed, desperately trying to get rid of the lump in my throat. "Y-you said you didn't want to be my friend anymore. What did I do?" I asked. My face contorted as I said it, and another tear made its way down my cheek. Crumpled tissues were scattered on the floor around me, my sleeves wet from snot and tears.

Victoria leaned back and pursed her lips. "You're weak," she said simply. "You keep crying at little things. My dad says being a crybaby won't get you far in life. And that's what you are. A crybaby."

I wiped my eyes with my sleeve and stood up. "I'm leaving."

But before I could touch the doorknob, Victoria's arm yanked me back. I yelped as I dropped to the floor, my knee slamming into the wood. The dull pain of the impact made me wince. I pressed my palm onto the spot where a bruise would later emerge.

"You're not going anywhere," she said, throwing a tissue onto my lap. "It was a joke, okay? My dad says that the more you cry, the stronger you become. I'm just making you strong, Luce. You're still my best friend."

"You keep making those stupid jokes. I hate them," I mumbled, pulling away from her. Once again, she yanked me back to the floor, this time by my hair. "*What do you want?*"

"You look like you've been crying."

"I *have* been crying."

She rolled her eyes. "You don't want your mom to think you're a crybaby, do you?"

I shook my head. My mother already had enough problems to deal with, and I didn't want to be one of them. If faking my friendships was going to make her life easier, I would do it. Regardless of how difficult it was.

180

"Lemme see your eyes."

I leaned forward, waiting for her to examine my face.

"Can I go home now?"

"Wait for your eyes to dry. They're still wet and red."

And so I sat in the corner for the next five minutes, staring at the princess stickers on her walls. Victoria had a nice room, not as beautiful as Huma's, of course, but still a hundred times better than mine. A pink carpet was spread across the floor in front of her bed, which had a white frame and fancy designs at the head. Victoria had no books (she hated reading), so her shelves contained dolls and stuffed animals, neither of which she was willing to share.

"Can I please go? I was supposed to be home two minutes ago," I said nervously, looking at the neon clock placed on her bed stand. I didn't want to worry my mother, especially when she was working several jobs.

Victoria clicked her tongue. She flipped her slick brown hair over her shoulder. "Mmm... you look sad."

I forced a smile. "Better?"

"Mhm."

I was out the door before she could say another word, sprinting down the street towards the complex of apartment buildings. This late at night the streets were empty, but I wasn't scared of being alone. My apartment was only one block away from Victoria's home, a short distance compared to the one we took to school.

My mother wasn't home when I arrived, and by the time she did, I was asleep. She was friends with Mrs. Hill, which was one of the main reasons Victoria and I had become friends in the first place. I had deliberated talking with her about the things Victoria said to me. But that would probably get Victoria in trouble, which would cause entirely new problems. I didn't want to ruin my mother's and Mrs. Hill's friendship... nor did I want them to worry. In the end, I decided to put up with Victoria's behavior until I found another friend.

Said friend came the following day, by the name of Huma Khatri.

* * *

When I finished, Mathias was silent, most likely mulling this over in his head. At last, he said, "You should have dumped her earlier."

I nodded. "I should have. But, like she said, I was weak, young, and stupid."

"Why didn't you?" he asked. Mathias's eyebrows pinched together. "I mean... aside from not wanting your mother to worry about your well-being."

"Two reasons," I said. "She was popular, and our moms were good friends. Everyone at school liked her, so I thought that I should too. She told me I was lucky to be her best friend. In a way, I was, since she was the reason I was invited to most of the parties her friends threw."

"So she manipulated you," Mathias said.

"Pretty much," I replied. My body had stopped aching, and now I only had a mild headache. "But in a way, she did make me stronger. After befriending Huma, I didn't cry for the next three years. She was my 'real' best friend. Until..." I sighed, looking around the mossy cell, "today. Or yesterday; I don't know what time it is. Looks like I've never had much luck with people."

Mathias gave me a wry smile. "Since we're on the topic of best friends, want to hear the story of mine and Damian's friendship?"

"It's not as bad as mine and Victoria's, is it?"

He chuckled lightly. "No, no. It's time we moved on to something more positive," he said. Lifting his hand, he ripped off a chunk of moss from the wall and began kneading into a ball. "We met four years ago, and started off as... er... enemies, I guess. I thought he was a pretentious prick. Always trying to impress the girls, never focusing on his studies. The opposite of me. One time, when I was demonstrating my ability to the class—growing a small tree out of a patch of earth—he

182

got jealous. I had already started working with Sorina at that time, so he challenged me to a duel, coming up to me when I was packing up to leave and claiming I was scared if I declined. Since I didn't have any duties that day, I accepted." He paused, pointing to the thin scar running across his left eyebrow. "Can you guess which weapon he chose to fight with?"

"Daggers," I said instantly. A scar that thin couldn't have been done by a sword, whose edge was much thicker.

"Correct. Guess who won."

"You," I replied, just as quickly. "You had experience in combat whereas he had none."

"Precisely," he said, snapping his fingers. "I did win, but he still managed to hurt me slightly. It was an accidental cut, one that didn't really bother me, but the guy was so wound up, he almost broke down on the floor. He must have been expecting some sort of consequence for hurting Sorina's assistant. Fortunately for him, nothing would have happened even if he had caused a major injury since I had willingly agreed to the duel," he said. He threw the ball of moss across the room. "And then we became friends. I can't tell you exactly how it happened because I don't know. It just… happened, if you know what I mean."

"I do." I couldn't remember how mine and Huma's friendship came to be either. I had offered to sit next to her on her first day of school, and things just went on from there. Neither of us had offered friendship. That was something characters did in movies. Huma hadn't told me she considered me her best friend until one year of knowing each other, but by then, we both knew it was mutual.

Now, I had mixed feelings about her. A part of me wanted to forgive her, wanting, *needing* to hear her side of the story. Maybe she hadn't known of her father's involvement with the Qroes. Maybe she was crying right now, not knowing what had happened to me. The rest of me, the more brutal side, wanted to do what I had done to Horseface for such betrayal.

"Mathias," I said softly, "how will we get out of here?" Despite the daggers resting against my thigh, I felt more vulnerable than ever. Mathias should have returned to Soratia yesterday, leading the operation that would both rescue me, Adelaine, and the Griffin, and destroy the Qroes' headquarters. But now, with the metal armbands that prevented us from using our abilities, how would we get past the hundreds of men milling around the building?

"They'll come for us," he reassured me, placing a gentle hand on my shoulder. His voice lowered as he said, "You told me not to, but I informed Mei of our plan. Just in case something like this would happen. I told her that if I didn't return by midnight of the following day, she was to go into the palace and request Sorina's presence immediately. I left her a note with my signature, so she should have no problem getting past the guards. Beckett knows too since he's in possession of the tracking device, but he doesn't know what it's for. I told him it was to test out an important mission but didn't go into too much detail. If my estimations are correct, they should arrive three days after we're taken to the headquarters."

A smile cracked across my face and I reached out to Mathias, engulfing him in a hug. "Thank you," I mumbled into his shirt. "You're a lifesaver."

Quite literally, he was.

184

Chapter Thirty-Four

The guards came for us during the night, eight of them, but were met with no resistance as they pressed the filthy rags to our faces. I knew what this was for—our transport to the headquarters.

My new cell had no window and was much cleaner than both of my old ones. It had a large wooden slab that substituted for a bed, with a thin grey blanket crumpled up against the wall. The blanket was a godsend, since the room's temperature was so low, I woke up shivering.

Contrary to my previous cell, this one had a guard stationed just outside the thick metal bars. I hit my fist against them, causing him to turn around with mild interest. He seemed to be in his mid-twenties, with an olive complexion and jet-black hair neatly slicked back. Like the others, he wore a black shirt with the outline of the crow's head embedded on it. The long hallway he was standing in was empty. A semi-opened door was right behind him.

"Problem?" he asked, glancing at the watch on his wrist. It read 5:00. Whether that was morning or afternoon, I didn't know.

"Where's Mathias?" I growled, grinding my teeth. "What did you do to him?"

The man gave me a smug smile. "The blond boy? He's in the south sector with the other Soratians."

"Let me see him."

The guard threw his head back and laughed, baring his pearly teeth. "Now, now, sweetheart. You're in no place to give me orders."

I fought back the urge to slap him. "Where am I?"

Perhaps the guard would slip up and drop some useful information.

"In a cell," he replied, flicking one of the bars with his finger to demonstrate.

"And where are you?"

"Outside of your cell," he said simply.

Since beating around the bush didn't get me anywhere, I asked him exactly what I wanted to know. "Are we in the headquarters?"

At this, he stiffened, turning around to face me. "You don't need to know that. Why are you asking?"

"Just curious," I shrugged. "This place is cleaner than any of the other ones I've been in."

The man didn't reply to this statement, and once again glanced down at his watch. I searched my mind for another tactic to approach him, settling on friendliness. Maybe he'd be more talkative if he grew fond of me.

"What's your name?"

"You're annoying," he muttered, taking a step away from my cell.

"I'm Lucianne," I said, ignoring his insult. "Who are you?"

The man fisted his hands. "I'm your enemy," he said, pronouncing each word with slow precision. He looked strangely familiar when angry, but I couldn't quite put my finger on it. I wondered if I had seen him somewhere.

"You can tell me your name," I said, crossing my arms. "It's not like I'll be going anywhere anytime soon. Plus, it's not even valuable information! There are probably millions of men on Earth with the same name as you. I told you what my name was. It's only fair that-"

"Octavius," he snarled. "Now shut up."

"Octavius is a nice name," I said. "Sounds professional and manly." If none of my other tactics worked, inflating his ego would have to.

"I told you to shut up," he said, but his tone was softer. I bit back a satisfactory grin. Inflating his ego it was.

186

"How old are you?" I asked. "You don't look a day over seventeen!"

The vein on his neck began to bulge as he swiveled around to face me. "You think I'm a boy?" he snapped. His voice was seeping with anger.

"N-no," I stammered. "Not at all! You look very..." I faltered as I searched for a word to describe him, "er... manly." I cursed myself inside my head. Did men not view youth as a compliment? I remembered my mother, who had always beamed whenever someone said something along the lines of, *You don't look a day over twenty, Estelle!* Maybe I should have said he looked several years over thirty. It would have been much more accurate, anyway.

The man gave a loud *tch* and walked away, shaking his head aggressively. *There goes my chance at getting information,* I thought as I flopped down onto the wooden slab and gave the ivory wall an imposing stare. The translucent panel that stretched from the back wall to the bars was making my eyes hurt. I sighed, throwing the blanket over my body. It had grown cold.

And that was when I remembered the daggers.

My hand flew to my thigh, and I could feel my heart rate starting to accelerate. I was still wearing the clothes from yesterday, which meant that unless they had undressed me, the daggers would still be underneath Adelaine's headband. I felt around the thick material, searching for a hard point.

There was none.

Adelaine's headband was gone along with the daggers, both of which provided me with an ugly feeling of emptiness. Mathias had been right when he said they would confiscate my weapons. It made sense, considering that this was probably the most secure building the Qroes owned, but that didn't stop the disappointment from crawling up my throat.

The following hours stretched on for what seemed like eternity, dragging on and on as I stared at the blank white wall. To pass some time, I began counting the holes the wall in front of me had. One big hole. Three small holes, almost forming a triangle. Two medium-sized holes right next to that.

I was at nine-hundred and seventy-eight when a voice ripped me from my thoughts.

"Hey wench." I recognized the unpleasant voice of the guard from earlier. "I've got your dinner."

He was holding a small plastic tray, filled with a Styrofoam cup of water and a brown pulp. He passed it through the slit in the middle of the bars, waiting for me to take it. When he realized I wasn't going to, he mindlessly dropped the tray to the floor, the water sloshing out from the sides.

I reached towards it and drank up the remnants.

"I'm thirsty," I complained, holding out the empty cup. "You gave me too little water."

"Deal with it," Octavius replied.

"But then I'll die of dehydration," I said, "and you'll get fired."

He hesitated. Then he reached his hand through the slit. "Give me the cup."

I did. He moved to the wall on the left side of the cell, holding the cup like it was infested with germs. Which, I suppose, it was since I hadn't showered for more than twenty-four hours. The wall must have had a faucet attached to it because I heard the sound of pouring water as it hit the bottom of the cup.

Octavius turned off the faucet and passed the cup back through the slit, his face wrinkled in disgust.

I chugged down the water. It tasted surprisingly fresh for something that had come from such a filthy place. When I was done, I passed the tray towards him, the brown pulp left untouched. The unpleasant smell emitting from it was enough to make me want to vomit. There was no way in hell I was going to eat it.

Octavius raised his eyebrows. "You're not going to eat your food?"

"I'll pass," I said. "I'm not that hungry."

"Suit yourself," he replied, shrugging his shoulders. "Your next meal won't be here until morning." He grabbed the tray and walked off, his footsteps echoing on the stone floor. I sat down. Hunger was gnawing at my insides but knowing I would have to eat the brown pulp sooner or later made my stomach churn. I tried to tell myself that it couldn't be that bad; after all, the rest of the prisoners in this place most likely ate it. I wondered if Mathias had.

Yes, a tiny voice in my head piped, *and he would want you to eat it too*. If the rest of my plan was to take place, I would need all the energy I could get.

Using my arm as a pillow, I lay down on the wooden slab and pulled the blanket over my body. It was coarse and itchy, but I was thankful for its presence. The thin material would keep me warm, however minimally.

I thought about Mei back in Soratia. Had she already gone to Sorina's palace? Were they preparing a rescue mission right now, as I lay freezing in a cell? That was what Mathias had told me would happen, and I trusted his word; it was the only thing that gave me hope. Adelaine, who, for all I knew, could have been resting a few feet away from me, was probably just as freezing as I was. As long as the tracker worked, and Mei had told them what it was for, they would find us.

I wondered about my mother back home. I had promised to call her again, and I regretted not having done so when I was at Huma's house. She was probably worried about me. I would see her after all of this was over, just to explain things to her. If I made it out alive, I would tell her about my father's death. I would tell her about the Qroes, and about my kidnapping, and about the Griffin. If my plan worked, Sorina would owe me a favor. Maybe she would make an exception and let me take my mother to Soratia. That way, I would be able to take care of her. The other option was me moving to Earth permanently. Deserting my mother after all she had done for me would be cruel.

That was what I decided as I drifted off to sleep, the steady hum of machinery slowly taking me into the endless abyss.

Chapter Thirty-Five

When I awoke it wasn't because I was rested, but because I heard two voices speaking just a couple feet away from my cell. Unsurprisingly, both of them were male, and I recognized one of them as Octavius's. I strained to hear what they were saying.

"...wants her alive?" one of the men was saying. His voice was gruff, which made him sound to be at least fifty. "She had no significant ability. Not like the boy. We have Soratian pain manipulators dozens of times stronger than her. She's disposable! I told him five times today, 'Question her. If she don't cooperate, gun to the head.' But no! Tells me to keep her alive and hangs up."

Octavius spoke, his voice much lower and harder to hear. "The girl's pretty. I don't blame him for being hesitant. I would want her to myself too."

"Pretty? Pah! Average at best. And that attitude she's got is repulsive. I don't want nothing to do with her."

I rolled my eyes at the insult, biting my tongue to prevent myself from opening my mouth. Opening my mouth would likely lead to me giving away my position.

"Careful, Casper," Octavius warned. "Her cell's right there. Don't wake her."

"She got the sedative, didn't she? It should keep her out 'til morning," the man named Casper grunted. "And I took her daggers. She won't be able to reach across the hall."

I smiled with satisfaction. Their conversation was giving me more information by the second.

"She refused," Octavius said, almost inaudibly.

Casper scoffed, and I imagined him flinging his hands into the air in exasperation. The image was comical. "Then *make* her eat it. Force it down her throat. Threaten her. Hell, I'd make sure she choked on it!"

Damn, I thought, *this guy's more sadistic than Stellinger.*

"He wants her *alive*, Casper," Octavius snarled, emphasizing on the word. "I'm not about to risk my life. If she wants to starve herself, so be it."

"He ain't coming back 'til Wednesday. You said you wanted her to yourself, right? She's yours for three days," Casper drawled. His voice in itself made me want to cut off his airflow. If time allowed, he would meet his death the moment I got out of this cell.

"She won't be as easy as the others." Octavius lowered his voice, and I had to strain to hear the rest. "You said so yourself. Her attitude is a difficult one to manage."

And that was when my brain must have started working because the idea that popped into my head was pure genius. Manipulative, but genius, nonetheless.

I felt a grin slowly spreading across my face and had to press my mouth shut to stop laughter from escaping my lips. He wanted me? Very well.

I would give him exactly what he wanted.

* * *

Three hours later, another pale blue tray slid through the slit. Octavius wasn't the only one delivering my meals; this one was delivered by a short, broad-shouldered man whose bulbous nose was peppered with blackheads. He muttered something indecipherable under his breath before strutting off.

I looked at the contents of the tray. It held a bottle of water, which was an upgrade compared to the Styrofoam cup I had drunk from yesterday and a stale loaf of bread. I had to stop myself from calling out to the man to ask if the food was drugged. That would reveal my eavesdropping, and who knew what they would do with that information? One thing was certain—they would stop having important discussions near my cell. Or, like Casper had suggested, force the drugs down my throat. Neither seemed appealing.

I lifted the bread up to my nose but couldn't find any abnormal smells. Either the drug was undetectable, or there was none. I bet on the latter. My hunger made it nearly impossible to resist.

The water relieved my parched throat as I chugged down half of the bottle, chewing up the remaining half of the bread. Octavius stood outside of the door, as stoic as always, and I dropped the tray back to his side, leaving the half-finished bottle in the cell. The Qroes made sure I wouldn't die of thirst and hunger, but I wouldn't have the luxury of having those necessities whenever I desired. I would have to preserve my rations.

"Hey, Octavius," I said, plastering on a smile. "I like your hair today. It looks good on you." In truth, I couldn't notice a difference between yesterday's hair and today's, but it was a decent start. I needed to see how he reacted to compliments. *If* he considered them compliments, that is.

"What's gotten into you? Are you gonna beg for handouts?" His tone was heavy with irritation.

"Not at all," I said. "I'm just pointing out the obvious."

Octavius didn't reply to this, and so I asked for the next thing that would make my scheme more believable.

"How old are you?"

"None of your business," he replied, crossing his arms. "Why do you want to know?"

I shrugged. "Curious. I'm turning sixteen in three months." I wouldn't make the mistake of saying he looked terribly young. Not after his outburst yesterday.

"Twenty-one," he said after a minute. "What is it you want from me?"

A few months ago, I had read an interesting novel. It revolved around a brave woman who, after being illegally imprisoned, managed to escape using nothing but her intellect. She flattered the men who would deliver her meals, creating a unique bond with one of them. The man grew so fond of her he helped her escape. Once she was out, the woman found the nearest police station and led them to her kidnappers' base, which resulted in most of them getting arrested.

That was the novel that had inspired my plan, except I'd have to tweak a few things. Our situations weren't the same. I didn't have months to form a bond with Octavius; my time was limited to less than two days. It was obvious he wouldn't help me escape. What I would do would be manipulative, and a tactic that I had seen done dozens of times before. I would just have to hope he would be gullible enough to fall for it.

"I don't want anything, Octavius," I said, pronouncing his name like he was my significant other. "I'm just trying to get to know you since we'll be spending some time together for the next few days." I cursed myself for saying the last three words, certain that he would catch on. Certain that he would know I knew. But instead, he smiled slyly, leaning against the wall.

"In that case," he said slowly, "what is it you want to know?"

There were hundreds of things I wanted to know, primarily concerning the location of Adelaine and the Griffin, but decided to ask him about something that had bothered me from the start—his strange familiarity. It was the safest option. "How did you get the job here? Do you have relatives that also work for this er... association?"

The vein on his forehead instantly made its appearance. "You think I wasn't qualified?" he snapped. One of his hands had been closed around one of the bars to my cell, and now the knuckles were turning white.

"No!" I protested. "You just looked familiar, a-and I wondered if you were related to... any of the men here."

Octavius was like a ticking bomb, one that could explode at any given moment. I would have to choose my words carefully.

194

He raked his hand through his hair. "Alfred Stellinger. He's my uncle. You know him?"

Lovely, I thought to myself, forcing my face to remain straight. Showing any signs of disgust to Stellinger's nephew, especially when he was interested in me, would be disastrous.

"Y-yeah," I said. "But you're much more impressive than him. Everyone can see it."

Bingo. The expression on his face was one of pure satisfaction.

"Oh I know," he gloated. "I know."

* * *

I spent the rest of my afternoon mulling over my plan. I had deliberated asking him about more important things, such as the locations of my friends, but deemed it too risky. If he suspected that I planned to use him in order to escape, he would never open my cell.

For the first time since my arrival, I ate dinner. Octavius eyed me with mild interest as I forced globs of the brown pulp down my throat, trying not to gag. The food might have had a sedative, but it was still food. It would give me enough energy to ensure I wouldn't faint in the middle of action.

"Did the hunger finally get to you?" Octavius asked, his sour mood returning. His mood swings seemed to be worse than Irene's.

"You expect me to starve myself?"

"You women are so weak," Octavius snorted. "I could survive a week without food, and you can't last nine hours? Pathetic."

I opened my mouth to say, *I'd like to see you try*, but what came out was, "Of course you could. You're a strong man." Until tomorrow, it was best to stay on his good side.

Octavius gave me a triumphant smirk and snatched the empty tray from my hands. Already, I could feel the effects of the sedative on my body. My eyelids drooped and began to tingle, as if hundreds of tiny pebbles were weighing them down. I sunk to the wooden slab, nearly forgetting to cover myself with the blanket.

The only thing I heard were Octavius's retreating footsteps as he walked away from my cell.

Chapter Thirty-Six

Three years ago, Huma and I had gone sledding at the largest hill in our neighborhood. Her mother had driven us there at eleven o'clock on Sunday morning, which gave us five hours to sled before dusk. The hill had two sides the children used for their winter entertainment—the north side and the south side. All other areas were covered with patches of rocks. The north side was much steeper, mostly occupied by teenagers and adults. The south side, on the other hand, was pretty gentle, and almost always crowded with toddlers and kids learning how to ski. Huma and I were both twelve at the time, so we didn't exactly fit into either category. For the first hour or so, we stuck to the south side of the hill.

But then I got bored with it. I wanted to experience the shrieks of joy coming from the teens on the north side. I wanted to feel the thrill of an insanely fast ride, certain that we were experienced enough to do it unharmed.

And so I pulled Huma along with me. I can still vaguely remember the anticipation building up inside of me as we trudged up that hill, our faces red from the cold. We had looked down just to see how steep it was, but it was so steep, we couldn't see the slope. Huma had been logical. She had begged me to back out, but I couldn't allow myself to act weak in front of all the teenagers waiting for their turn. I suppose that was a result of what Victoria had said to me all those years ago, but it was still a thought I regret to this day.

Because that thought made me go down the hill aiming straight for the patch of trees.

Aiming for the trees wasn't something I had done on purpose. I just didn't know how to turn the sled away from them, nor how to stop. Everyone else did.

That night, I had woken up in a hospital bed, with my mother asleep beside me. Huma came in later, too, with a get-well-soon package that contained a gift card and four stuffed animals—all dogs. As it later turned out, I had a broken arm and a concussion and would have to spend the next two weeks resting in bed until the latter subsided. In those weeks, I often suffered from headaches and dizziness, accompanied by nausea and fatigue on the worser days. Most of it, though, was just dizziness.

That was how I felt when I woke up on the wooden slab, my movements slow and sloppy. I instantly noticed the tray with the bread that had been dropped to the floor, and the brand-new bottle of water. I still hadn't finished the one from yesterday, so I gulped down the remnants, my throat parched from the lack of fluids.

"Had a nice sleep?" Octavius smirked, dangling a cluster of keys from his finger. "It's two in the afternoon."

"What did you put in my dinner?" I snapped, too tired to put up a polite act. Today was the day my plan was to take action, but I surely wasn't feeling like it. Food or no food, skipping dinner would have benefitted me.

Octavius put on an expression of innocence, but he wasn't a very good actor. I could see the evil triumph he felt in his eyes. "Nothing. You were tired."

I ignored him and picked up the bread. It was just as stale as yesterday's, but I didn't care. It was still a hundred times better than the brown pulp I had been served for dinner. And hey, maybe the bread would help the dizziness that was still clouding my senses. The sooner it disappeared, the sooner I would make my move, and the sooner we would get out of this wretched place.

"Hey Octavius." I smiled. "You look good today."

It was time for my plan to begin.

After breakfast, my dizziness slowly began to fade. I decided to take a short nap to speed up the process. If I were to have a chance against Octavius and the men around here, I would need to preserve as much energy as possible. Hopefully,

the training I had gone through with Mathias would be
sufficient.

Chapter Thirty-Seven

I woke in a cool room of whirring machinery. It was the same room I remembered from my dream about Atiana. This time, however, I was the one strapped to the table. Hovering above me were two faces—Huma's and Stellinger's. The latter held the polished black cane that had ripped open the flesh on my ankle.

"Where is the Griffin?" Stellinger growled, holding the cane threateningly above my head. I opened my mouth to say: "You took it," but no sound came out. In this nightmare, I was a mute.

"Gun to the head," Huma said quietly. "Gun to the head. If she don't cooperate, gun to the head."

I heard Stellinger unholster his gun. "*Where is the Griffin?*"

"Gun to the head," Huma kept muttering. "Gun to the head. Gun to the..."

The cane crashed down on my ribcage. I was still mute, but tears were now flooding my eyes, blurring my vision. I pulled at the restraints, feeling them bite into my wrists.

"Gun to the head," Huma was saying, louder each time. "Gun to the head. Gun to the head..."

A third person came into view. Her silky brown hair brushed against my foot as she moved next to Stellinger. Despite my blurry vision, I managed to recognize the monster from my childhood.

"You're weak, Lucianne," Victoria purred, sitting down on the metal table. "Don't be a crybaby." My ribcage was burning, and I could see blood beginning to stain my shirt where Stellinger's cane had struck my skin. Each of my breaths was getting shallower. He had done something to one of my lungs.

"Gun to the head. Gun to the head!"

200

I felt the barrel of a gun press against my temple and looked straight into Stellinger's face. The vein on his forehead was bulging, his skin red with anger. And that was when I heard Mathias's scream, dull and far away, as if it was coming through a thick coat of plastic.

"*Gun to the head!*" Huma shrieked. "*GUN TO THE HEAD!*"

Stellinger pulled the trigger.

***

I shot up from the wooden slab, my shirt soaked with sweat and clinging to the skin on my back. My ribs were sore. It all had felt so real, I had to look down to make sure I wasn't bleeding. There was one part about the nightmare, however, that didn't fit in.

Mathias's scream.

I stood up from the slab, fully aware that my hands were trembling. My legs wobbled beneath me, and I had to grab onto the wall to stabilize myself.

"Did the boy's scream wake you?" Octavius asked, crossing his arms. "Don't worry, they're just questioning him. I could have them move to another room if you find it distracting."

I felt the color draining from my face. I had assumed the voice was too different—too clear—to be a part of that nightmare, and now Octavius was confirming my assumptions. He seemed completely unbothered, which made me want to wrap my fingers around his throat and squeeze.

"No, I don't find it distracting at all." I forced my voice not to tremble as I walked towards the bars. My legs were no longer wobbling, the long-awaited feeling of adrenaline coursing through my body. "Could you do me a favor?"

"What do you want?"

I had no time to waste. Somewhere nearby, they were hurting Mathias, and their boss would be arriving in a matter of hours. It was now or never.

"I want you, Octavius," I said pleasantly, plastering on a fake smile. I silently prayed he was in a good enough mood to overlook the panic in my eyes.

Octavius took a step back, his brows furrowing.

"You're handsome," I said, reaching towards the bars. "One of the most handsome men I've seen." Then, realizing that boosting his ego too much could make him think he was too good for me, I quickly added, "Men compliment me too, you know. But I reject them. You're one of the only exceptions."

For a moment, I feared that he wouldn't buy it. That he would put two and two together and rid me of my last hope at escape.

But to my surprise, he took a step forward.

And the door to my cell flung open.

Four years ago, I would have been afraid of a man his size advancing on someone as small as me. I would have feared the way his lips spread into a coy smirk, the way his eyes twinkled with desire. In the best-case scenario, I would have sunken to the floor, begging for mercy.

But I was not the girl that had cowered before the person she considered her best friend. I was not the girl that would spend her evenings crying on the divan, thinking having friends was next to impossible with her status. I was not the girl that would flinch when someone barely raised their voice.

I was the girl who created a trap, and Octavius had been the one to fall straight into it.

His hands brushed my arms and I pulled him into an embrace, my palms traveling down his back. The shirt was so thin, I could feel the outline of his spine. My fingertips danced around his belt, searching for the cool steel surface of his gun. He was too wound up to notice.

My fingers latched around the handle of the gun and I pulled it out of the holster, pressing it to the back of his head. This, he felt, and his eyes widened as he realized what was happening.

"Hush, hush," I said quietly, a small smile cracking across my face. "Make a sound and I press the trigger."

He was too stunned to speak, and I grabbed the collar of his shirt, turning his back towards me. This way, it would be easier to walk towards the door on the other side of the hall. I couldn't be sure if the gun had a muffler, so shooting him right now would be risky. It would be better to have a second option—my daggers.

"Are my daggers still behind that door?" I murmured, loudly enough for him to hear.

He began to tremble. "H-how do you-"

That was all the answer I needed. "Take two steps forward," I said. "Very carefully. If you make any sudden movements, I won't hesitate to shoot."

He obeyed, and we began to make our way towards the door. The process was slow and awkward, but there was no way I was losing hold of his collar while we were moving. Holding it was the only thing preventing him from jumping aside.

At the door, though, I needed to use one of my hands to retrieve the daggers.

"Stand still," I ordered him, hesitantly taking my hand off his collar. "The gun is still pressed against your head."

Thankfully, the room wasn't large—the size of an average closet. It also had a light switch, which I flipped with my finger the second I spotted it on the wall. The single lightbulb hanging from the ceiling flickered, and light flooded the room. At once, I spotted my daggers. They were shoved into a cylindrical container, the blades hidden behind the plastic.

"Take a step back," I told Octavius. The daggers were near the back, and I couldn't reach for them without taking the gun off Octavius's head. That was something I couldn't risk doing.

Octavius took a step back, flinching as the gun's barrel collided with his head. I grabbed the daggers, whose number had dwindled to three, and slid two of them into my waistband. The other, I kept in my hand.

"Now," I said, "Walk back to the cell. Once again, be careful with how you move. Anything sudden will result in you getting killed on the spot."

Now it was his legs that were wobbling as he took the next six steps forward. Mine were steady, the adrenaline still pumping in my veins.

"Sit down," I said, raising my foot to push his knee towards the wooden slab. Once he did, I had to readjust the gun's position on his head, but I didn't have to worry about him escaping. The words *no sudden movements* seemed to be drilled into his brain, and Octavius was far too scared to risk losing his life.

I stood next to him, my body turned towards the door of the cell. If anyone passed us, it would be better to face them than to have them attack me from behind.

"I have four questions," I declared. "If you don't answer them, you die. If you tell the truth, I'll let you go. You know that I'm a Multi, right?"

He shook his head, momentarily knocking off the gun. I gritted my teeth.

"I told you not to move. Next time, just say yes or no. As for me being a Multi, my second ability will let me know when you're lying. So unless you're interested in dying, I would tell the truth."

He gulped. "O-okay."

"Good." My palm was growing sweaty, and I yearned to put down the gun and wipe my hand. If I didn't hurry up, the smooth handle could slip out of my grasp. "First question. Where is the key to the armband I'm wearing?"

"In my pocket," he said shakily. "I'll reach for it."

"No, you won't. Which pocket is it in?"

"Front left."

"Stand up, hands behind your back."

I had to readjust the gun again, this time moving it to his forehead. The knife had to be tucked into my waistband too, in order for me to be able to reach into the material of his pants. The key was there along with two others, meaning Octavius hadn't lied. This also meant that he believed what I had said about my other ability. Good.

"Which of these keys unlocks my armband?" I asked, pushing him back to the slab with my knee. The gun was once again rotated to the side of his head.

"The smallest one. It unlocks a-all armbands," he stammered.

"And I assume all guards have it?"

"Yes."

I slipped the keys into my pocket and grabbed the dagger from my waistband. "Second question. Where are they questioning Mathias?"

"In the questioning room."

"Specify," my voice was harsh when I said it.

His face grew paler. "D-down the hallway and to the right. It had a r-red door."

"Is it guarded?"

"It shouldn't be," he answered. His hands were squeezing each other nervously, and I saw beads of sweat glistening on his forehead.

"Third question," I said, my own hand incredibly sweaty. "Where is Adelaine Chevrolet?"

"I-I don't know who that is," he replied. The gun pressed further into his head, and his eyes widened. "Tell me what she looks like! I can try to identify her."

"Blond hair just below the shoulders," I said flatly. "Blue eyes. Average figure. High-pitched voice. She came here approximately three weeks ago."

A stream of sweat made its way down Octavius's cheek. "It's close to five, so she'll be at testing with most of the others. In the heart."

"And where is that?"

"In the center of the building. Follow the red lines."

My other hand was growing sweaty too, and I had to place the dagger back into my waistband to wipe it on my shirt. Octavius just eyed me wearily, all signs of excited anticipation gone from his face.

"The center of the building is definitely protected. Is there another way to get to the heart?"

Octavius swallowed. "Use the vent in the questioning room. They're joined together. It should be large enough for you to fit. Head north from the door and you should be in the testing area after five minutes."

That sounded too specific to be false. And it wasn't like I could check if he was telling the truth, anyway. I had to take his word for it.

"Last question," I said, my arm starting to hurt from holding the gun horizontally for so long. This was the question the Qroes had sought the answer to for years. "Where is the Griffin?"

Octavius stiffened at this, and blubbered, "I don't know."

"If you don't tell the truth, you'll die," I warned, pushing the gun further into his hair.

"I'm s-serious," he stammered. "It's probably in the heart. Ask my uncle or anyone of higher rank. I really don't know!"

"Does Casper know?"

He didn't even bother asking how I knew. "I-I think so."

Lovely. So I would have to find one of the two men in this place that made my blood boil the most. But what to do with the man I held at gunpoint?

"Let me go," Octavius said, as if reading my thoughts. "I answered your questions. Now let me go."

"But then you'll notify the others," I said bluntly, my heartbeat accelerating as I realized what I would have to do. There were too many things at stake. I couldn't just let him go—he could promise not to tell anyone, but I knew that promise wouldn't last. Even if I wounded him, he could scream for help. Gagging him wouldn't work either—not only did I lack materials for that sort of thing, but he knew where I was heading. And if someone found him, he would tell. The hatred burning in his eyes spoke for itself.

"The gun doesn't have a muffler," he gasped suddenly as my finger moved to the trigger. "You can't shoot me. Guards nearby will hear. You'll give yourself away." The desperation in his voice made it clear that he was lying, but there was still a slim chance he was telling the truth. And that was a chance I couldn't risk taking.

"That's why I got my daggers."

Chapter Thirty-Eight

I tried not to think about what I had done as I pulled the dagger out of Octavius's chest. It had been lodged there pretty deeply, and I cringed as I wiped the crimson liquid onto his black shirt. *He was a terrible man*, I told myself. *He deserved to die.* But a part of me knew that killing him made me just as bad.

Octavius crumpled to the ground, his eyes emptily looking at the fluorescent light above. I pulled the blanket over his body. Looking at his emotionless face made me shudder. Even if he still had a heartbeat, which I doubted, it was clear the stab had been lethal.

Shakily, I slid the dagger back into my waistband and exited the cell, gun raised. The hallway was empty, just like it had been minutes ago. I hoped Octavius had told the truth when I questioned him. Even if he hadn't, I didn't have another choice. Trusting his word was all I could do.

Remembering my armband, I reached into my pocket and took out the keys. The smallest one was a paler shade of silver, which made it even easier to recognize. I momentarily placed the gun on the floor as I turned the key in the lock. The armband split into two and clattered to the ground. I kicked it back into the cell.

One side of the hallway had a dead end, so I walked in the opposite direction—left. I paused in the intersection to peek around the wall. Surprisingly, no guards were milling around the area. I turned right. The hallways here reminded me of a hospital, minus the chairs that were often lined outside every doctor's door. Fluorescent ceiling panels seemed to be the only source of light; I could see no windows anywhere. Either this place was deeply underground, or the Qroes didn't want anyone looking in through their windows.

Octavius hadn't lied about the red door—it glared at me from fifteen feet away, the neon shade hurting my eyes. I slowed my pace, pausing to look around again. The headquarters seemed to be deserted.

Placing my hand on the doorknob, I felt a brand-new surge of adrenaline. Wonderful. That would come in handy since there were bound to be people inside. I pressed my back to the wall and slipped out two of my daggers, remembering the training I had undergone with Mathias. He had told me I had good aim. This would be similar to striking those dummies, except those people would be moving. And they would probably be armed.

Better sooner than later, I thought, pressing down on the doorknob. The door creaked open, and a voice called out a rough, "Who's there?"

I peered over the side of the door, trying to locate the man that had spoken. There were two of them in the room, both of them sitting in cushioned chairs and sipping something from two brown mugs. One of them, a middle-aged man dressed in a white suit, resembled a doctor. Unlike his companion, he wasn't looking at the door, but instead, reading a magazine that rested on his legs.

The man that I assumed had spoken stood up from his chair and placed the mug on a clear table. He was staring at me, and an expression of surprise crossed his face.

My dagger struck him in the chest before he could utter a word. He crumpled to the ground, gasping for air, his fingers wrapping around the handle. A dark spot appeared on his shirt.

This, the doctor noticed, but he too was struck with a dagger. He didn't even have enough time to stand up. I didn't feel as much remorse for these men as I had for Octavius, partly because I didn't know them and partly because they had more than likely hurt Mathias. I stepped into the room and shut the door behind me, moving towards the men to retrieve my daggers. It was easy to picture them as dummies, ones that could be thrown out after I was finished training. Thinking of them as people, ones who had lives and families and children, would make me see myself for what I was becoming—a monster thirsty for blood. That was something I couldn't allow myself to see, at least not until all of this was over. Not until Mathias and Adelaine were safe.

The second dagger was wedged deeply into the doctor's flesh. I had to use both of my hands to pull it out. Once the blood was wiped onto the doctor's white uniform, I turned towards the center of the room. Right away, my eyes landed on the metal table backed up against the wall, and the boy strapped onto it.

"Mathias," his name escaped my lips as I rushed forward, the dagger I had been holding dropping to the floor. He was bleeding in several places, the most visible cut on his forehead. I rushed to untie the straps, praying he was still conscious. When my finger touched his wrist, his eyes fluttered open.

"Lucianne?" he croaked, pushing himself up onto his elbows. "What are you doing here?" he asked. His hair was plastered to his face by blood and sweat, his normally clear blue eyes outlined with red.

"Saving you," I replied, my own voice hitched in my throat. My hands shook as I took out the keys and unlocked his armband. He looked like he could pass out at any given moment.

Mathias sat up, groaning as his leg hit the side of the table. "Hide," he said. "The blond one will come back soon."

I ignored him. "Do you know where they keep their medicine?" I asked. He was in no condition to fight, so fixing his wounds was my greatest priority.

"The doctor has some in his jacket," Mathias said, lowering himself onto the floor. "They used it to keep me from bleeding out."

I hurried toward the man's corpse, hauling him off the chair. I dropped him to the floor as I took off his jacket. He fell face-first, probably breaking his nose in the process.

There was a hard lump in the jacket's front pocket, and I found a small aluminum container inside. I unscrewed it,

Mathias watching the door behind me. Inside was a clear liquid. Mathias and I both knew what it was.

Saliva. Not just any saliva, but saliva belonging to a healer. I had no idea how the Qroes had managed to lay their hands on it, but it didn't matter. I needed to shove the stuff into Mathias's wounds as soon as possible.

"Lay down," I ordered him, in the same tone I had used when speaking to Octavius several minutes before. He did, and I knelt down next to him, dipping my fingers into the spit. The texture was slimy and watery, the opposite of the thick cream Mathias and I had used during our training. I poured a fourth of the container into the wound on his leg, which, although hidden by his jeans, was by far the most severe one he had. His knuckles went white as he gripped the side of the table, gritting his teeth to prevent himself from crying out. I did the same for all other wounds, emptying nearly the entire container. Only a thin layer remained at the bottom.

Mathias stared at me in astonishment. "I can't believe you just... killed those guys."

"Would you rather I let them live?" I snapped, crossing my arms. "They wouldn't have *hesitated* to shoot me if I hadn't reacted as quickly as I did. They-"

"I know," he said quietly. "You did well. Much better than I could have." He rubbed his bloodshot eyes with the back of his wrist. "Thank you for saving me. I owe you one."

"We're even," I muttered. "It's my fault you're here in the first place."

He squeezed my hand reassuringly, turning the aluminum container over in his fingers. "We can blame each other later." He cleared his throat. "What do we do now? You *do* have a plan, correct?"

"Oh. Right." I stood up from the floor and brushed off my shirt. The vent Octavius had mentioned was on the ceiling, right next to one of the fluorescent panels. It looked wide enough for both of us to fit, Mathias's wings included. "We're going to wait for the blond man you brought up earlier, and then we'll go through that vent and to the heart of the headquarters, where they're keeping Adelaine."

Mathias began to massage his temples. "I'm not even going to ask how you know all of that. Just tell me—why do we have to wait for the... blond man?"

"He might know where the Griffin is," I replied. "That's the only piece of information Octavius... er, my guard, wasn't able to give me."

His eyebrows knotted at the name, but he didn't say anything.

I continued, "I took off your armband, so you should be able to use your abilities. Hide behind the table while I wait in front of the door. When he comes in, I'll distract him, and you'll immobilize him with a plant of some sort. Then we'll question him, hopefully find out where the Griffin is, and go through the vent. Can you do that?" I asked. Of course, we would have to kill the guy before we left, but I assumed Mathias already knew that.

"Can we switch roles?" he asked. "You've already done too much. I can handle him alone." His worried gaze met my eyes, and I had to lower them to the floor. I wouldn't let him risk his life.

"No," I said firmly. "Your ability is stronger. If I work as the distraction, you can focus better on immobilizing him. That's something I wouldn't be able to do—if anything, I'd only make him scream, and that would attract guards toward us."

I could see the hesitation on his face. His hands balled up into fists four times as he thought this over, and I thought surely he would argue. But then, I heard him utter a barely audible, "Fine."

"Okay," I said. "Now try to grow something from the floor, so I know you can do it."

He rolled his eyes. "I can grow things from *earth*."

"There's earth underneath this floor. Grow a plant or something. *Quickly*," I hissed, shooting a glance at the door. The man could return at any moment.

Mathias laid his hands on the floor, and I saw the familiar glint of concentration in his eyes. The tips of his fingers began to tremble, and he began slowly raising his hands, as if pulling something from the earth. That was when I noticed the first crack break across the stone floor. Two seconds later, a sprout poked through.

He had grown a blue flower, just like the one he had given me the day I left the palace. I brushed the tip of my finger against the soft petal, a warm feeling spreading through my chest. That day had felt like an event of another lifetime, like it had occurred to another person. So much had happened since then.

"I'm surprised you still remember," Mathias said, noticing my expression. "Keep it. It's yours."

I plucked the flower from the floor and placed it in my pocket. "Thank you."

As I moved towards the door, I could see Mathias crawling below the table out of the corner of my eye. I sat down in the chair that had been previously occupied by the black-haired men. The doctor's corpse lay beside me, and I averted my gaze to the door. Looking at it made me shudder.

"Can you see me?" Mathias called. His hands were readily placed on the floor.

"Yes, but only because I'm sitting down. You're good." My throat was practically begging for water. The man wasn't returning fast enough. I remembered the bottle I had left in my cell and wondered if we could risk going back to retrieve it.

No, my mind replied. *Too dangerous.*

The sound of the turning doorknob made me jump. Gun in hand, I stood up, nudging the doctor's head aside with my foot. It was getting in my way.

"Stef got us some cof-" the man's voice faltered the moment his beady eyes met mine. "What the…"

I recognized the voice almost instantly. "Hello, Casper."

He was an average man of a stocky build, with a round pink face that reminded me of a pig's. His pale blond hair was short and scraggly, the opposite of Mathias's, whose hair was fairly long and luscious. I remembered him as one of the men from Huma's house.

"You," he huffed, jabbing a chubby finger in my direction. "The hell are you doing here?"

I raised my gun the second he took out his, and said, "I'm armed." Then I noticed the green vines creeping up behind him, and added, "I also have to tell you something. Octavius asked me to relay some information to you."

"Then say it. Say it, woman. Say it or I'll kill you. What'd you do to Octavius?" he asked. He shook his gun threateningly but didn't step forward. That was good. As long as he stayed in one place, the vines creeping around his torso would be able to tighten.

"Relax," I said lazily, but my heart was thumping. "Do you know how the Griffin's powers work? Octavius did. And he told me to tell you," I lied. I hoped that he didn't already know. That would just be a waste of time.

Casper scrunched up his nose, and I was once again shocked at how much he resembled a pig. "Nah," he said, not taking his eyes off my gun. "You gonna tell me just like that?"

I shrugged. "I mean… you caught me. And you probably called reinforcements already. I'm pretty much dead. So why not reveal the information Octavius wanted me to tell you?"

The vines were nearly circling his entire body, but Mathias was being careful not to touch Casper's skin. Just a few more seconds of stalling.

"Why'd he tell *you*, out of all people?" Casper sneered. "You're nothin' but a distraction."

I smiled. "He trusted me. I may not have a good attitude, but manipulation is something I'm pretty decent at." That was true. While Octavius hadn't willingly given me any secret

214

information, he still trusted me enough to open the door of my cell.

"You… manipulated…" he froze. One of the vines had touched his hand. Mathias noticed Casper's realization, and the vines tightened.

Casper stared at his body, which was wrapped in a cocoon of stems and leaves, both of them a lively green. They kept growing up to his neck, where a rose sprouted from one of the vines next to his head. The sight made me want to laugh.

"I manipulated Octavius, yes," I admitted. "Just like I manipulated you into standing still." I noted that the vines had crumpled up his gun, which was probably the only reason he wasn't shooting.

"What'd Octavius want you to tell me about the damn Griffin?" Casper growled, his face growing red. There was no fear in his eyes. "I'll make you starve to death, you ugly witch."

Calmly, I walked over to the vines and picked off the rose. Then I placed it behind Casper's ear, just to make him look a bit less threatening.

"I'll tell you if you tell me the location of the Griffin," I said. "Where is it?"

Casper spat at me, the foamy drops of saliva absorbed by my shirt. I didn't react. If he saw that his actions didn't bother me, maybe he would be more afraid than he was.

"Where's the boy?" Casper asked as he glared at the empty metal table. "He's the one growing this crap, ain't he?"

"That's not your concern. Where is the Griffin?" I asked. This reminded me of how the Qroes had questioned me and numerous others—by immobilizing us and threatening us with death. The roles were now reversed, which brought a strange feeling of satisfaction into my body.

Casper spat at me again, then began to choke. The vines around his neck had tightened.

"Mathias," I said, still looking into Casper's beady eyes, "loosen the vines around his neck. Slightly. He won't be able to talk like this." I flicked the side of Casper's head. "Answer the question, please. If you don't, I'll kill you."

The hatred pouring from Casper's eyes could have been felt within a fifty-mile radius. His voice shook when he spoke. "You'll kill me anyway. Get lost."

"Tighten the vines, Mathias," I said calmly. "Only a little bit."

Casper began to choke, and his face turned a deep shade of red. Like a beet that had been freshly harvested from a garden. He gasped, his eyes bulging from their sockets.

"I'll tell!" His voice was raspy, barely a whisper, and I had to strain to hear what he was saying. "I'll tell. Just... j-just make... it... stop."

"Loosen the vines," I told Mathias. "Quickly. We don't want him to pass out."

The vines slithered away, and I could see the red markings they had left on Casper's neck. He gulped up the air like a fish out of water. Color returned to his face as his rapid breathing slowed.

"It's in the...in the center... of the building," he breathed out. "The heart. In a l-large safe... closet... behind machines."

While some of his words were difficult to interpret, he had told us the general area of the Griffin—the heart. Where Adelaine was.

"So it's in a safe," I said, "and I presume that safe is locked?"

Casper nodded.

"Does it need a key or a passcode?"

"Passcode." He was straining against the vines, as if trying to break through.

"Okay. What's the passcode?"

Casper snapped his head to the side, making the rose fall off. Mathias had loosened the vines a bit too much. "Figure it out yourself. Six digits. I already told you where the Griffin was."

"Tighten the vines, please."

216

I could see Casper writhing, trying to get away from the vines circling his neck like hungry serpents. When he realized he wouldn't be able to escape, he choked out, "Two five eight six sev-"

His head lolled back.

Mathias rushed out from beneath the table, his eyes wide with worry. "I'm sorry Lucianne. I'm so, so sorry. I didn't--"

"Doesn't matter," I said, reaching towards the vent. "We know the first five digits. Let's go."

"You first," he said, kneeling down and cupping his hands. I stepped onto them, grabbing onto his shoulder for support. Mathias stood up and lifted me so far my entire torso was inside the vent. I looked around. The area was tall enough for Mathias's wings to fit, and wide enough for both of our bodies, if we crawled in a line. I managed to pull myself halfway in, leaving my bottom half hanging. Mathias gave my feet a push. That got me all the way in.

I peeked outside through the vent, trying to locate the door. It was facing me, meaning that if I turned around, I would be heading in the right direction. Perfect.

"Do you need help?" I called down to Mathias, who was trying to pull himself up.

He shook his head. "I'll be fine," he replied. But his hand slipped just when he grasped the edge of the vent, and he tumbled down to the floor.

"You don't *look* fine," I said skeptically. "Can't you use your wings?"

"Oh." His face turned red as he facepalmed himself. "Right. Sorry. I can't think straight."

"Just get up here. Fast."

His head came poking through a second later, but there was an issue—his open wings didn't fit through the opening. He would have to fold them for them to fit, and there was nothing he could use to pull himself up in the meantime. The inside of the vent was bare.

"Grab my hands," I said, holding them out. "Grab my hands and fold your wings. Come on."

"What if I pull you down with me?"

"Then we'll have to repeat this process until you get up here. I'm not leaving without you."

He took my hands, intertwining his fingers with mine. I pressed my feet to both sides of the vent as he pulled himself up, to prevent myself from sliding off. The moment his stomach touched the floor of the vent, I let go, knowing he would pull up his legs by himself.

"Thanks," he said. "Now I owe you two favors."

"Oh, shut up. You don't owe me anything." I began crawling forward, hoping the vent was strong enough not to collapse underneath our weight.

He was silent for a bit. Then he said, "Lucianne?"

"What?"

"If, like you said, we save Adelaine and the Griffin, what will we do next?"

"We'll get out of here," I replied. Wasn't it obvious?

"How? This place is filled with hundreds of guards. That's what the area around my cell looked like. We can't fight them all."

I felt a sinking feeling at the bottom of my stomach. I had been so preoccupied with saving Adelaine and the Griffin that I hadn't thought about what we would do *after* their rescue. Mathias was right—we wouldn't be able to get past all of the guards. And I hadn't asked Octavius where an exit was. The only thing we could do was go on with the plan—once they found the bodies and Casper passed out in that cocoon of vines, there was no doubt they would search everything.

"I don't know," I said. "You said Sorina would come here after three days. Today is the third day."

"I said she would come here after three days if my estimate was correct. There's a chance it wasn't."

I sighed. "We'll have to hope it was. There's nothing else we can do."

The vent stretched out for what seemed like miles in either direction, and I wondered just how vast this place actually was. Octavius had said the journey wouldn't take us longer than five minutes. Had he meant five minutes of walking or five minutes of crawling through the vent? If he had meant the former, then getting to the heart would take us forever.

Mathias broke the silence. "Who's Octavius?"

"I already told you," I said. "He was my guard."

"Was…?"

"He's dead now," I said. The word sounded hollow when I said it. I didn't want to think about what I had done until later. Why did Mathias have to bring it up?

"Oh," that was all Mathias said. My tone made it obvious I wasn't interested in revealing the details, and he seemed to understand. For now, we would focus on the task lying ahead of us. Storytime would come later, after all of this was over.

If all of this came to be over.

Soon, my knees grew sore from crawling. My arms were aching as well, which showed just how much I had been weakened by the lack of nutrients.

"I think this is it," I said, pointing ahead of me. Slashes of light illuminated my face as I moved toward the opening, Mathias shuffling forward after me. I peered through the plastic vent. I couldn't see much of the room below, since my vision was limited to the white-tiled floor, but I was certain I heard voices nearby. Several of them.

"You hear them too?" Mathias murmured, moving closer to the vent's opening.

"Uh-uh. How will we get past them?"

Mathias clicked his tongue. "Same thing we did before. You distract them, and I immobilize them. Unless you'd like to switch roles…?"

"No," I said. "My ability requires anger, and I'm pretty sure my supply ran out. Plus, I still haven't mastered it. We'll go down there, immobilize the guards, save Adelaine, and get the Griffin. We have to act fast. Casper could wake at any given moment," I told him. It sounded so simple when I said it. Reality would be different.

"Here," I said, reaching into my waistband and taking out a dagger. "You should be armed too."

"You're the one doing the fighting," he said but took the dagger anyway. His fingers brushed mine when he did so, sending an electrifying feeling through my body.

I placed both of my feet on the vent, knowing the thin plastic would break underneath my weight. The people below wouldn't see this coming. I turned around to face Mathias and gave him a small wave.

Then the plastic gave away, taking me with it.

Chapter Thirty-Nine

Jumping down from the vent took the guards by surprise and bought me enough time to pierce two of their chests with my daggers. The third guard lunged at me from the side, and because Mathias had my last dagger, there was nothing I could use to stab the man on top of me. And as luck would have it, his hands clamped around my throat.

I lifted my leg and slammed my heel into his lower back. I hit the tailbone. His hold on my neck loosened, granting me enough time to push him off with my foot. Now, I was the one on top.

I heard a heavy thud behind me, followed by a soft *oomph.*

"Are we in the heart?" I asked the stone-faced guard.

He grunted in response.

Mathias knelt down next to me, placing his hands on the cool tile. The guard furrowed his brows. He was still trying to push me off, but my grip was too firm. Mathias used one of his legs to help me hold him down.

A thin stick poked out from the floor near the guard's feet, and soon a vine snaked around his back. He felt this and continued straining against me, foams of spit dribbling from his pasty lips.

The vines circled his body, and the man's eyes grew wider. They had reached into his mouth, serving as a muffler in case the man dared to scream.

Getting off the man, I cleared my throat and repeated the question. "Are we in the heart of your headquarters? The center?"

The man frantically tugged at the vines around his mouth.

"Just nod or shake your head. Yes, or no?"

The man nodded. He was still desperately pulling at the vines, but Mathias and I weren't stupid enough to fall for it. As long as he could breathe, he would be fine.

Mathias tapped me on the shoulder. "This room isn't the heart. It's too small. Adelaine isn't here, nor is the Griffin," he observed. He jutted out his chin towards the two doors on the back wall. "The heart must be behind one of those." He pointed to one of them and turned to the man. "Is the door on the left the one that leads to the heart?"

The man shook his head.

"So it must be the door on the right."

The man nodded.

"Alright," Mathias said. "Let's go."

The second I looked at the room, my mouth fell open. Not because of its vastness, which in itself was jaw-dropping, but because of the dozens of machines that lined the walls, people attached to every single one. The whole place had a vibrating hum about it. It droned out our footsteps as we made our way forward. I looked at the boy nearest to me, my heart doing an uneasy flip at the sight.

The boy's hair had been shaved off, as was everyone else's. Tubes and electrodes were attached to his head in numerous places, and his wings were strapped to the wall with black bands. His eyes were shut.

Testing? I thought. *How could Octavius have spoken of this so lightly?*

"Let's split up," Mathias suggested. "I'll take the left side and you take the right. We'll find her quicker that way."

I hesitated. "The lack of security feels weird. Don't you think they'd have guards inside places like this?"

"Yes," Mathias admitted, "that's strange. So let's be quick. The sooner we find Adelaine the quicker we can go."

"And the Griffin," I added.

"Right."

I moved to the right side of the room, scanning each individual face. The absence of hair on each of their heads made the task more difficult, and I found the hope within me dwindling as none of them were recognizable. Ruling out the ones with different skin tones made the task easier, but barely. The task seemed unachievable.

Just when I felt the tears burning at the back of my eyes, I heard Mathias call out from the opposite side of the chamber.

"I've got her."

I rushed over to his side. Adelaine's face had paled significantly, her tan completely gone. She looked sick, as if all of her energy had been seeped away, leaving nothing but an empty shell. Her beautiful blond hair had been shaved off, and only a light fuzz remained on the top of her scalp. Like all of the others, she was unconscious and covered with tubes and wires. The sight made my stomach churn.

"Pull them off," I said, my voice tight. "All of the wires. We have to wake her."

Mathias took a deep breath, and I could tell he was just as nervous as I was. Nonetheless, he began pulling the cords and tubes from the left side of her body. I worked on the right.

When the last tube was out, Adelaine's finger twitched. It took another five minutes for her eyes to flutter open. She gazed emptily at the ceiling before focusing her eyes on me.

"L...Lucy...Anne?" her voice was faint as she squinted at my face. "Lucianne?"

"Oh, God," I whispered, taking in the hollows beneath her eyes. "What did they *do* to you?" I sighed. Her cheeks had lost their red tint, and her eyes were glazed over, like a doll's. I turned towards Mathias. "We're leaving."

"What about the Griffin?"

"Ah," I let out. I pressed my palms into my eyes, desperately trying to clear my mind. "She's in no condition to go with us."

"Clearly," Mathias said. "Whatever drugs they put into her system are still wearing off. Let her stay here; we'll get the Griffin ourselves."

As much as I didn't like the idea of leaving her by herself, I knew Mathias was right. She would only slow us down.

"Okay," I said wearily. "Look for a door near the back and see if it has a safe. I'll search right, you search left."

"On it."

We ran to the back of the room, our footsteps echoing on the stone floor. The faces of Soratians and half-bloods strapped to the strange machines blurred as I moved past. *So many kids.* Sorina hadn't been lying when she had said these people were a threat. And if they were gathering the abilities of such large amounts of people, who knew how strong they had really become?

The first door I tried to open was locked. Mathias would be able to break it down, no doubt, but if more than one door was locked, we'd be in trouble. Getting through all of them would be too time-consuming.

The second door opened to reveal an air conditioner and metal equipment that reminded me of an operating room. A section of it was covered with vials, most of them filled with red liquid. Blood. Unlike most of my friends, I didn't find the sight of blood gruesome. Unappealing, yes, but looking at it didn't make me sick. I had watched enough medical documentaries to make me insensitive to its sight.

The third room was small and dark, and my hand slid across the rough walls for a minute, trying to locate the light switch. After a while, I gave up, but by that time my eyes had already adjusted to the dark. In the corner of the room was a square-shaped box.

The safe.

"Mathias!" I called. "I found it!"

He ran in a moment later, breathing heavily. "Where's the light switch?"

"There's none. We'll have to do without it."

Attached to the safe was a combination lock, and just like Casper had said, it had six digits. We knew the first five.

"Two… five… eight…" I muttered as I put in the digits, "six… what came next?"

"Seven," Mathias said. "His voice cut off at the end, but I'm pretty sure he was going to say seven."

I rotated the plastic circle to seven. "And now?"

"Now we try all ten digits. Zero to nine."

I put zero into the last slot and pulled. The lock didn't budge.

"Now try one," Mathias said.

I did, to no avail. We continued with the next five numbers, getting the same result—a locked lock. My fist hit the ground in frustration.

"Keep going," Mathias said encouragingly. "Try seven, eight, and nine. Want me to do it for you?"

"No. It's fine," I said, rotating the lock to seven.

And the safe clicked open.

The creature inside was cowered against the back wall, looking so much sicker than it had when I'd last seen it. In Soratia, it had been thriving in its habitat, well-fed and taken care of, but now it had lost its magical aura. The Griffin's head was bent, its wings protectively folded over something I couldn't see.

But when the Griffin gave a weak croak, I knew.

"Wings," I gasped. "Mathias, the Griffin birthed wings!" I exclaimed. Before I could say another word, Mathias was pulling out the Griffin. He handed the frail creature to me, and it nuzzled its beak into the crook of my arm.

"It knows you're a half-blood," Mathias said, reaching inside the safe for the wings. They were a mix of black and dark grey, a color that reminded me of shadows. "That's why it trusts you."

I gently ran my finger along its back and felt the Griffin shudder from my touch. "Let's get out of here," I said. We turned towards the door.

If I had paid attention, I would have noticed that the door to the room with the Griffin was slightly more ajar than it had been when Mathias had pulled it open last. I would have noticed the faint muddy footprint just outside of the threshold, a footprint that hadn't been there before we had gone inside. I would have noticed the six men standing off to the side, only partially concealed by the machines.

But I didn't.

And my carelessness allowed us to be captured.

Chapter Forty

The men led us to a small room that resembled an office, where we stood in silence for the next five minutes. Mathias had slipped the wings into his pocket.

"What are we waiting for?" Mathias asked, receiving a slap on the cheek moments after the words left his mouth. The Qroes had taken the Griffin from me, but it was still in the room with us; one of the guards was holding it in his arms. Judging by the way he held it, they must have been instructed to be careful with it.

The room had two doors—one of them located behind the large wooden desk we were standing in front of, and the other behind us. The former opened, and a tall man came through.

The first thing I noticed was his hair—it was thick and curly, the color of a ravenous fire.

My hair.

His eyes, although partially hidden beneath his red locks, were a deep, dark shade of green, just like the foliage of an evergreen tree.

My eyes.

A short gasp escaped my lips as I noted these similarities, knowing the chances of this being a coincidence were too slim. The man that had been a mystery to me for nearly sixteen years, the man I had longed to meet for as long as I could remember, the man I had thought was dead, was standing in front of me.

And that man was a monster.

Mathias must have noticed the similarities too because he gave me a confused look, furrowing his brows. I mentally begged him to see that I was just as confused as he was.

The faintest smile appeared on the man's face as he looked at me. "Lucianne," his voice was soft and kind, like he was glad I was here. But I wouldn't fall for it. This man was responsible for everything those innocent kids had endured.

"It's a pleasure to finally meet you." He extended his hand, but I just glared at it. His guards still had my arms pinned back.

"Release her," the man said. "My niece is in no state to hurt any of us."

"Niece?" The word came out before I could stop it.

He chuckled. "Surely you must have made the comparison between our features by now. Is 'Vladimir Allaire' not a name you were acquainted with?" Noticing my surprised expression, he said, "Oh, did you mistake me for Francis? Aside from the lack of wings on my back, we do have similar features, I admit. But he was a fool, and death took him pretty early. Did they not tell you he passed?"

I stayed silent.

"So stubborn! How pleasing it is to see my genes flourishing within you." He smiled. He sat down, leisurely placing his feet on the desk.

"That's not a compliment," I said, noticing the guards' hands instinctively moving towards my arms.

Vladimir waved them off, but his expression hardened. "I'd be careful with my words if I were you. Wouldn't want anything unnecessary to scar that pretty skin of yours."

"Liar," Mathias hissed, his eyes threateningly cold. "If you truly cared about her well-being, your men wouldn't have beaten her." His words immediately resulted in another slap, and I could see him clenching his jaw, undoubtedly, to prevent yelling out.

Vladimir leaned forward, his cold eyes making me shudder. "Surely, you can see the reason behind that. Pain is temporary. It strengthens you, provides you with resistance. I don't cause it without purpose."

"In that case," I said through my teeth, "what was the *purpose* of having Stellinger slash open my ankle during my first night in one of your bases?"

He smirked. "Preventing you from escaping. Pain always works—it cuts off one's rational thinking, minimizing their chances of finding a way out."

"It didn't work that night."

"No," Vladimir admitted. "But it would have, had your boyfriend not intervened."

I opened my mouth to correct him, to tell him that Mathias and I were mere friends but said something of much higher importance. "What do you want from me?"

"Your alliance."

Two simple words, and yet they still managed to send chills down my spine.

"My *alliance*?"

He raised his eyebrows. "Are you surprised? Correct me if I'm wrong, but I'm quite certain you're a pain manipulator, just like your father and I. That sort of skill is rare to find these days, so you could be a useful asset." He sighed. "Finding a trusting heir to lead this on is a difficult task. Nobody is nearly as skilled as I am. You're close. After all, my genes are in your possession. With the proper training, you could be working alongside my finest men within months."

"I don't understand," I said. "Why? Why do you do this? You're a Soratian. You shouldn't be working against your own people. And why… why don't you have wings?"

I didn't really mean to say the last part, but curiosity took hold of me.

Vladimir propped up his chin, as if he was finding our conversation amusing. "For the latter, it's simple. Francis and I shared one father, but our mothers were two different women. I wasn't aware of my brother's existence for most of my life. That should explain the lack of empathy I have for him. As for the former, I was raised on Earth. My friends were human, as were the people I considered family. *Those* are my people. The society your father is from is alien to me. I don't care about it. I found out about my power when I was your age, and shortly after, I began my work here, advancing ranks, proving to be so resourceful that I inherited the company after the former owner passed. You must understand, Lucianne, that what we do here is not what it seems. The abilities of those that have a Griffin's blood flowing within their veins are crucial to the development of today's society. Can you imagine how many diseases we could cure with the saliva of the ones you consider healers? Can you imagine the technological advancement that would come once we've harnessed enough power? *We* would be the ones credited for it, Lucianne. *We* would be credited for those innovations. Worldwide fame, riches, anything you could imagine. If only you agreed to work alongside me, it could all be yours."

For a second, greed made me want to consider. Then I cursed myself for thinking about considering working for such a treacherous man. Family or not, Vladimir wouldn't become someone I worked with.

"No," I said. "You expect me to work for you when I have experienced your treatment first hand?"

Vladimir's mouth thinned in frustration. "Perhaps you're just as foolish as my brother after all. Look at it this way— hundreds of lives gone, but how many saved? Success never comes without sacrifice, Lucianne, and that is something both you and your father failed to understand. How many of your friends have relatives dying of sicknesses that would be curable if we captured enough of those healers? How much would conditions improve for people struck by hunger and poverty if we harnessed the powers of someone like the boy standing next to you? Everything we do is done to improve humanity. And if that means sacrificing the lives of a few, so be it."

I could see his point. I could see the reason behind everything he did, but that didn't change the fact that it was *wrong*. He wasn't doing this to improve humanity. That was just an argument he had come up with to bribe me, to *manipulate* me to be on his side. He was in it for the benefits. For the fame and money that would come from all those murders. He didn't care about the people. He cared about himself.

"I have questions."

"Go ahead and ask. We've got plenty of—"

His walkie-talkie emitted a low buzz.

Vladimir picked it up, pressed the large red button near the side, and snapped, "What?"

A voice spoke from the other end, but I couldn't hear any of it. Vladimir's face went from confusion to shock, then momentarily flashed fear, and at last, settled on a determined seriousness. He kept nodding and muttering underneath his breath, none of which I could decipher.

"How threatening?"

The voice on the other side gave a short reply, and Vladimir's face relaxed.

"Okay," he said. "Bring her to 301. I've got my niece and the phytokinetic in here."

There was a burst of static, and Vladimir put the walkie-talkie back in his pocket. His expression was strange, nearly pleased.

"What was that?" I asked.

"An intruder," he replied. "Nothing to worry about. She's been taken care of."

Mathias and I exchanged glances, both of us thinking the same thing: Sorina's rescue team had arrived. But why had Vladimir said there was only one intruder? Was it to cause a distraction? Neither of us knew, but I hoped Sorina's team had things under control.

This was our sign to act.

"My questions," I began, forcing myself to look into his eyes, "have to do with a couple of things. First, the money. How much would I get? My allyship is valuable. I won't work for free."

A smirk appeared on Vladimir's face. "You'll get your share. It will be enough to buy you anything you'd like. If we capture enough of them, you could have billions at your disposal."

"What about my mother?"

"I could bring her here, as long as you provide me with her current address."

"In that case, if everything you said is true, I'll work for you," I said. "Under one condition."

Vladimir raised his eyebrows. "Go on."

"Let me say goodbye to Mathias. Preferably now."

He smiled, but it didn't reach his eyes. "Alright. You can say goodbye."

"No," I said. "I want to hug him. Here's what I propose: put an armband on his arm, the one that prevents us from using our abilities, and then your guards will let him go. If they do, I'll know I can trust you. It's a simple exchange."

Vladimir considered this, furrowing his brows. "Why, exactly, should my guards let him go?"

"I need to hug him," I repeated. "And I can't do that with your men holding him still." I decided to use Vladimir's perception of our relationship to my advantage. "If you truly want my allyship, let me hug my boyfriend. What do you fear? It's not like I can run away."

Vladimir tapped his chin thoughtfully. Then, to his guards, he ordered, "Put the armband on the boy. Fifteen seconds, you said? I'll give you twenty. No privacy."

I watched as one of the guards grabbed an armband from his belt and clasped it around Mathias's arm. Mathias stared at me in confusion, still not catching on to what I was planning.

The second the men let go of Mathias's arm, I lifted the back of my shirt, showing him the two circular birthmarks on my lower back. If this didn't make him understand, I didn't know what would.

I heard the shuffling of his coat behind me and knew that he had. My eyes were focused on Vladimir, whose brows were furrowed. But he didn't move from his position. And by the time he did, it was already too late.

232

I felt Mathias step forward, the velvety black feathers of the wings brushing against my back as he gripped my shoulder. It didn't take more than two seconds for the sharp tips to touch my birthmarks.

He pushed them in.

Back in the dormitory, when I had imagined the pain of plunging those honed edges into my back, I had greatly underestimated the agony of the actual deed. What penetrated my skin was a hundred times larger than a regular needle, and I felt it lodging deep within my flesh.

A fire began to burn at my lower back, and I crumpled to the floor, my mouth opening in a silent scream. I didn't see Mathias, or Vladimir, or anything around me. My whole world went black. There was only the fire, burning at my core, spreading to my shoulder blades as it devoured everything in its path.

Pain. Oh, so much pain.

The thin skin on my back started to rip as the wings expanded, and I bit down on my lower lip. Hard. The metallic taste of blood flooded my mouth as another scream ravaged my lungs, and I shrunk into the floor, wishing it could absorb me. Anything to make the fire stop.

I could feel the wings growing, like something was being pulled out of my core at an excruciatingly slow pace. Somewhere in the distance, I heard the muffled *thud* of a door opening, accompanied by several shouting voices.

One of them was Mei's.

Chapter Forty-One

Despite the fire still burning inside of me, I forced myself onto my knees. They had all been staring at me, stiff with shock, but now their attention had shifted to Mei, who had been hauled in by two tall guards. She looked like a nightmare. Her clothes were torn in several places, most likely from defending herself against the men, and her hair was a wiry, tangled mess, dangling over her shoulders like a drape. Cuts and bruises were scattered across her face, far too many to count. And yet as she saw me stand up, she grinned, dragging her tongue along the top of her blood-caked mouth.

But her happiness didn't last long. For at that moment, Vladimir's hand drew back, and I could see his fingers beginning to twitch. Building up his power.

I surged forward, but my knees buckled beneath me, sending me to the ground. My head spun around to Mathias, who had been pinned to the wall by a guard, and I grasped at the desk, desperate to pull myself up.

The scream that followed shattered all feelings of empathy I had for my uncle.

My eyes landed on Mei. Young Mei, beautiful Mei, Mei that now lay motionless of the hard, cement floor, her black hair fanning around her head like a halo. Mei whose eyes were empty, like little glassy orbs, looking at the fluorescent ceiling without a single emotion. Mei who had smiled despite being beaten, laughed despite being afraid for her life, whose lips still held the faintest smile as the color drained from her skin.

Mei was dead. Not just gone, like Adelaine had been, when there had been hope for her rescue. There was no hope here. She was dead, like Octavius and the doctor and those guards, except she didn't deserve it in the slightest, didn't deserve to die at the hands of such a monster.

The fear that had rested inside of me vanished. For a moment, I was numb, the world around me seeming to slow. Then the familiar sensation of anger burned through my core. It wanted to take control of my body, to wake the electric sensation from its slumber, to destroy the monster that had mindlessly taken Mei's life.

And, in the state I was in, I let it.

The wings had made me powerful. I had been told they were capable of increasing one's ability drastically, and now I could feel the change as I flexed my newest muscles. My anger was stronger, by far the strongest it had ever been. And so was my power.

The expression on Vladimir's face became replaced with terror, and I knew he wouldn't be able to use his ability any longer. That required anger, a feeling that wasn't registering anywhere on his body.

My hands glided forward, like they had done dozens of times in Mr. Eskerington's classroom. Except this time, the motion was smoother, more elegant, as if I had already perfected this act. My wings were pulsing with tension. I could see the tips of their black feathers at the edge of my peripheral vision.

The guards stood still, as if held back by some invisible force. Vladimir had flattened himself against the wall, hands raised up, and I could see him shouting something at me. But all I could hear was Mei's scream, echoing in my head without an end. Her scream was feeding my anger, growing it into a monster far more powerful than the one that had scarred Horseface.

This monster would kill.

The warm sensation flowed to my arms, taking the warmth out of the rest of my body. It gathered in my palms, pooling up into two identical orbs, making my skin tingle. I brought my hands together. The energy inside was burning with desire, pleading me to release it all onto the monster cowering in front of me. Begging me to murder the man that had murdered thousands. Begging me to murder the man that had mindlessly tortured kids, stripping them of freedom without batting an eyelash. He had taken my friends, killed their loved ones, not once regretting what he was doing. He was a selfish, greedy man, whose hands had always been stained with the blood of his victims.

Now, the blood staining his hands would finally be his.

The twitching spread to my arms, and I struggled to keep them still as I aimed for Vladimir's chest. For a moment, I wondered if I really wanted to do this. If this incident would destroy me. But then, Mei's scream echoed in my head once more.

That was all it took.

The force of the energy leaving my palms threw me backwards and I slammed into the back wall. Vladimir crumpled to the floor. His eyes blankly at the ceiling, devoid of life. A drizzle of blood made its way down his chin, splattering onto his half-closed hand. It had been a merciful death. A death exempt of even a second of suffering. A death much better than what he deserved.

I remembered Mr. Eskerington's lesson, when he had warned us of using too much power.

"Your abilities take up energy," he had said. "Be wary of how often you use it, and how much you spend. The consequences of recklessness could impact you severely."

I had disregarded his warnings, thinking I would never use my ability on such a large scale. Today, of course, this had been proven false, and now I could see the room spinning around me. I was spinning too, but much slower, not quite catching up with the speed of the room. I heard the doors bursting open again. I was too dizzy to care. Then came brand new voices and shouts, so many I couldn't decipher them from one another. Darkness began to creep at me from the corners, welcoming me into its arms.

My world was fading, and I was fading along with it.

Chapter Forty-Two

The first thing I noticed was that I was lying in the infirmary. The second was that Mathias's head was resting right next to my hand, fast asleep. The third, most disturbing thing, was Dr. Girble's face, staring at me from above. It startled me and I flinched, quite upset to find two aching spots at my lower back. My wings were gone, and so was the feeling of power. Both realizations made me feel glum.

Upon seeing that I was awake, the doctor jotted down something in her notebook and strutted off. Her shiny heels clicked on the white tiles.

I turned and closed my eyes again, wanting to go back to sleep. But Mathias must have sensed the movement because his eyes fluttered open and he sat up.

"You're awake," he observed, moving the chair forward.

"Clearly."

"How are you feeling?" he asked. Although his voice was slightly groggy, his eyes were alert.

"I've been better," I replied. "Why are you here?"

"Waiting for you to wake up."

"Oh," I said. How does one respond to that? "I'm awake now. So… you can leave."

"Do you want me to?"

Did I? That depended on how long I'd be stuck in here for. If I would be spending the next couple of days in this room, I wouldn't mind having company. And I yearned to know what had happened after I blacked out. However, I didn't want to keep him with me against his will. So I said, "Do what you want. I don't care."

"In that case, I'll stay."

"And Sorina will be fine with that? What about your parents?" I asked skeptically.

The corners of his mouth lifted slightly. "I told them everything. They're very understanding. Sorina is, too."

"You have to tell *me* everything," I said. "How long have I been out for?"

"Approximately three days."

"Three days? Sheesh. That's long. Is Adelaine okay?"

"She's safe," he assured me. "Adelaine's in the infirmary, same hallway as you."

"I want to go see her," I said, sitting up. As soon as I did, the pain in my back made me wince.

Mathias's hand gently pushed me back down. "You'll see her later. For now, try to rest. What you did back in the headquarters must have been extremely draining."

"Mhm. Now tell me everything that happened."

Mathias leaned back, crossing his arms above his head. "You passed out the moment Sorina's team came barging in. They had sent Mei in as a distraction, to lessen the number of guards at the entrance. Mei wasn't supposed to be a part of the team but wanted to help us anyway. And since she was in possession of important information, thanks to me, they had no other choice but to let her take part."

"I wish they hadn't," I said, my throat growing swollen. "She's not with us, is she?"

Mathias's gaze saddened. He looked older, as if last week's events had made him age five years. I probably didn't look any better. "No," he said quietly. "She's not. And she wasn't the only one that volunteered to go."

"What do you mean?"

"Do you remember Mallory? From ability practice?" he asked softly.

I nodded.

"They needed someone to cut off the building's power, partially, and she was the only electrokinetic willing to do it. The others were either busy or too scared to go."

"Is she… with us?" I tilted my head towards the door. "In the infirmary?"

Mathias shook his head. "Her part of the team held off the Qroes while the others advanced. From what Sorina told me, they put up quite a fight," he replied. I didn't like the direction this was going in.

"Are they…?" I couldn't force myself to finish the sentence.

"Dead," he confirmed. "Mallory included."

Since I couldn't bring myself to speak louder, the question that followed was whispered. "How many others?"

"Fifteen. If it makes you feel better, the fatalities on the Qroes' side are much higher."

"Oh," I muttered. The air seemed much colder than it had been when I'd woken up, and I pulled the blanket further over my head. Fifteen people. That was nearly as large as my MHT class, which had twenty-four students. Fifteen people who had woken up that morning with hopes of tomorrow. Fifteen people that wouldn't live to see another sunset.

Tears burned at the back of my eyes, and before I realized it, I was crying. My body heaved with sobs as they grew heavier, and I pressed my face into my bedsheets as it contorted. Crying in front of Mathias was the last thing I wanted to do.

Without saying a word, Mathias's arm slid around me, and I felt his wings folding over the both of us. They were soft, just like the Griffin's. The feathers were silkier than any material I had ever touched.

We stayed like that until my sobs subsided, and even then his wings didn't leave my side. It wasn't until my last tear had dried that I dared speak. My voice was hoarse from crying.

"What happened then?" I asked. "After I blacked out."

Mathias's forehead creased in concern. "Are you sure you want to hear about it today? You just woke up. You're in a weak state. We'll have plenty of time to discuss this tomorrow."

"I want to hear about it today. I'm sure. So will you tell me?" I asked, pushing a loose strand of hair away from my face.

He sat down on his chair and scooted forward so that he was right next to my bed. "Yes. I'll tell you."

My breathing grew quieter, the drowsiness fading as anticipation replaced it. For the first time since I'd woken up, I could see eye bags beneath Mathias's eyes and wondered just how much time he had spent by my bedside.

"After you fainted," he began, "Sorina's team barged into the room. They killed the guards, and Mr. Fuji—one of our healers, stayed with you while the rest of them moved to the heart. Since I was in a stable enough condition, I went with them. The effects of Adelaine's drugs had worn off by the time we arrived, but she hadn't moved from her spot. The things she experienced at the headquarters have taken a toll on her, both mentally and physically, and Beckett told me it will take her a while to recover. Once we-"

"Wait," I said. "Back to the time I was fainting—why didn't the guards try to kill me? They had guns, didn't they? They could have easily killed me since I wouldn't have been able to defend myself, but they didn't. Why?"

Mathias reached over to a wooden stand, where a cup of water was resting. He took a swig and said, "That was Sorina. She paralyzed everyone within fifteen feet of her that didn't have Soratian blood. It only lasted for a minute, but that was enough for the men to drop dead. Believe me, if they could have killed you, they would have." He cleared his throat. "Anyway, we took the wires off of all of the kids and searched the headquarters for any leftover men. Most of them managed to evacuate after their boss was killed, thanks to you, but we still caught a couple hundred. Once Sorina called for reinforcements, they didn't stand a chance. Speaking of which," he paused, searching for the right words, "I didn't know their leader was your uncle. Did you?"

I shook my head. "Not until he told me."

"I thought so. Sorry that you had to go through that. Killing a family member, regardless of how wicked they might be, is not an easy task."

"Don't be," I said. "Had I been attached to him, it might have been different. But what I viewed him as was nothing more than a monster. That made him easier to kill."

Mathias nodded, his expression solemn. "That makes sense," he said.

"What happened then?"

"We teleported everyone here. First the children and then the Qroes. The children were ushered into the infirmaries upon their arrival, the Qroes imprisoned in the palace's dungeons. Out of the hundreds of Qroes that escaped, I managed to track only one. Once again, this is thanks to you. Can you guess which one?"

The moment the words "*this is thanks to you*" left his mouth, I knew who he was talking about. "Mr. Khatri."

"Mr. Khatri and Mr. Khatri's daughter. His wife and remaining children fled before we could get to them. Huma wishes to see you, but only if you allow her to. Since we can't prove that she was a member of the Qroes, she's residing in the palace, in a windowless room with guards stationed outside of her door at all times. Her father awaits his execution in the dungeons, along with the others."

"I'll see her," I said. "I want to hear her explanation."

"How do you know she has an explanation?"

"Because she wouldn't want to see me otherwise," I said. "Can she come over now?"

"Tomorrow," Mathias replied, standing up. "I'll bring her over tomorrow. And then, if you're feeling well enough, Dr. Girble might allow you to visit Adelaine."

"Dr. Girble hates me," I muttered.

"Then I'll help you sneak out, and you'll see Adelaine anyway," Mathias said. "Deal?"

"Deal."

Then he walked out of my room, closing the door behind him.

***

That night was another dreamless sleep, (they had undoubtedly ensured that my bed hadn't been slept on), and I woke with the cool surface of a lady's fingertips pressed to my forehead. I recognized the pretty auburn-haired lady as Mrs. Hearn, the first woman that had greeted me when I had come to the infirmary with a wounded foot. Her hair was a bit longer now, almost down to her shoulders, but the rest of her face was just as I remembered it.

"Rise and shine!" she chirped when my eyes opened. "No fever today. The doc will be here shortly. She'll be happy to see how much your health has improved! How are you feeling?"

"I'm okay," I replied. Although my back was still aching slightly, it was much better than yesterday.

Mrs. Hearn grinned. "Great!" she said. Then, holding her head high, she walked out of the room, her wings folded behind her. Their shape resembled a heart, which was something I didn't recall from the last time I'd seen her.

There was a sharp knock on the door before it swung open. Dr. Girble. I wondered why she had knocked in the first place if she was going to open the door anyway.

"Good morning, Lucianne," she said, her face as stoic as always. "Have you been experiencing any abnormal pain in your lumbar region?"

"No, ma'am. It's gotten much better."

She jotted something down on her notepad. "Aren't you going to ask why it hasn't healed yet?"

"Huh?" I frowned. "I'm sorry, ma'am, but it would be quite rude of me to do so, wouldn't it?"

"No." She shook her head. "I find it surprising that you haven't asked, considering that you're aware of our saliva's ability. It heals most wounds almost instantly."

Oh. Now that she mentioned it, I realized that I hadn't thought about that at all. I could see why it surprised her—I had asked lots of questions during our first visit, not to mention being incredibly untrusting towards her. Now, it was clear that my behavior had changed, but she still seemed to dwell on the way we had started off. As the saying goes, first impressions matter most.

"The last few days have been tiring," I said, wincing as the memory of Mei popped up. I tried to avoid thinking about her as much as possible, though it was getting difficult. "But since you want me to ask, I will. Why hasn't my wound healed yet?"

She made a soft *tch* sound. "Two reasons. Deeper wounds take longer to heal, and if the wounds come from wings it slows down the process significantly. Had your organism been stronger, you'd be healed by now. However, you used an excessive amount of your power, resulting in your defensive system weakening. I urge you to be more careful. Excessive use of power seldom leads to death, but I've seen it happen."

"I doubt anything like this will happen again."

She didn't respond to that and instead said, "Turn around. I need to apply another coat to your wounds."

I did, and she lifted my shirt, pausing to jot down another note. Then I heard her spit, and her wet finger landed on my back. I gritted my teeth as it touched my sensitive flesh, but the cool liquid's effects soon began to take place, stopping the burning sensation completely.

I lay back down as Dr. Girble rushed outside to clean her hands, feeling much better. The healer's saliva had soothed my skin. It allowed me to lie on my back comfortably, at least until it wore off.

A few minutes later, I heard another rapid knock on the door. This time, however, my visitor wasn't Dr. Girble.

It was Zarah.

Chapter Forty-Three

The girl opened the door and walked in, her box braids swishing behind her. She looked awkward just standing there, wearing a black pair of jeans and a white tank top, which made me wonder why she had come in the first place. It wasn't like we were friends. She had barely acknowledged me at all during my few weeks at Levond, and the most we ever exchanged was when she'd come to my apartment with the portal stones. I still didn't know why she had done that.

"Hey, Zarah," I said, raising my hand in a wave. "What are you doing here?"

She reluctantly stepped closer, her brows furrowing as she examined my face. Her dark skin glowed in the sunlight that shone through my window, and I found myself marveling at her beauty.

"Sorry about your friend," she said. "I'm here to thank you. For saving Adelaine. I didn't think you were gonna do it, but you did."

I raised my eyebrow at this but allowed her to continue.

"Look," she said, "don't get me wrong, but you just don't seem like the type of girl that knows how to fight. So I had my doubts about you. But you were also the only girl that was gonna try to save her in the first place, and my brain told me it was gonna turn out good, so I thought, 'Why not?' And my brain was right, cause you actually saved her. Don't know how but thank you. Means a lot."

I smiled. "All thanks to you, Zarah. I'm not sure what we would have done if you hadn't given me those portal stones."

"Least I could do."

"If you don't mind me asking," I said, "why did you do this for Adelaine? It doesn't sound like you know each other too well."

She frowned. "My past... is none of your business. She ain't gonna tell you either; we agreed to keep things between us."

I nodded understandingly. There were just some things people didn't deserve to know, and I would respect that.

Zarah turned back towards the door and yelled, "You gonna come in? I'm not sitting here forever."

I was surprised to see Allyson step into the room. Her head was bowed, her arms wrapped around a basket. When she looked up at me, her expression was sad.

"I've come to apologize," she announced, placing the basket onto the floor. "I'm sorry for treating you the way I did. You reminded me of someone from my childhood, someone I hated, and that brought up some unwanted memories, and then Mathias grew fond of you, and I know I shouldn't have been jealous, but I was, and-"

"I understand," I said. "I had someone like that, too. From my childhood, I mean."

"Oh. I'm sorry. I-I brought you a gift... to make up for the things I said, I guess." She picked up the basket and placed it on my bed. I lifted the light blue cloth that had been covering its contents and gasped. On the bottom of the basket lay three porcelain figurines, each dressed in pretty dresses. Me, Adelaine and Mei.

"Allyson, this... this is *beautiful*. Wow."

Allyson's face turned red. "Thank you. I'm glad you like it."

Another knock came from the door, and I called, "Come in!" as it opened.

At first, the only thing I could see was Mathias's head poking into the room. But then I saw the line of people behind him, and my mouth fell open.

Huma was in the middle, two men holding her by the arms. Two others trailed behind, their eyes fixed on her back. I came to the conclusion that they either had too many men on hand or they were stupid enough to think Huma was a dangerous criminal. Why else would they have four grown men escort her to the infirmary? Mathias was more than enough; the girl was about as strong as a stick. And even if she did manage to run off, where would she go? She didn't have portal stones in her pocket, and they weren't particularly easy to steal. Sorina had nothing to worry about.

From the large purple bruise on her cheekbone, I knew Huma hadn't been living luxuriously at the palace. The men were looking at her like she was a parasite they wanted to swat. That made me want to smack them… until I remembered that Huma and her family were the reason Mathias's life was put on the line. This made the empathy go away in seconds.

"Hi," Huma said quietly to the floor as she was yanked forward. "I know you probably hate me, and you have every reason to, so I won't take too much of your time." Her eyes lifted up to my face, and I could see they were wet. "I need to explain."

Instead of replying, I pointed to the guards at her sides, my face wrinkling in distaste. "Is this really necessary?" I asked Mathias. "Huma won't do anything. She's not dangerous. She's a teenage girl, probably scared out of her wits. So for my sake and for hers, please tell at least half of those men to leave the room." It was getting extremely cramped, and I didn't want everyone listening to our conversation.

"Sorina's orders." He shrugged before turning to face the men. "Rodriguez, Krol, and Smith, head outside into the hallway. Takahashi, stay with us."

"I'll leave too," Zarah said, inclining her head towards the doorway.

I sat up. "Wait. Can you tell if a person is lying?"

Zarah stopped in her tracks, slowly turning around to face me. "Yeah. Why?"

"Stay with us," I said. "Please. Your ability could be useful."

Hesitantly, she walked back towards my bed and took a seat at one of the two chairs meant for visitors. Huma took the other, and Mathias and the guard remained standing behind her.

"Alright, Huma," I said. "Let's hear your side of the story. I'll decide whether to hate you or not afterwards."

She gulped and sat up straighter, flinching as she felt the guard's hand touch her arm. "I'm sorry. I'm so, so sorry for everything those people put you through. It's difficult seeing you like this, like-"

I lifted my palm, and she immediately stopped talking. "You can apologize later. The only thing I want to hear at the moment is your explanation."

"O-okay." She gulped again. "When you came to me... to my house, I mean... I-I didn't know my dad would hurt you and that boy. I didn't know about my dad's work, either, I swear! He was always vague when I asked, telling me I was too young to know. All I knew was that he worked for the government. My mom knew, but every time I tried bringing it up she would end the conversation, so after a while, I stopped asking. I wouldn't have told you to stay if I knew my dad would hurt you."

"Doesn't look like you tried to stop him," Mathias muttered.

Huma looked down at the floor. "I didn't know what was going on. Our house has soundproof walls, so I didn't even hear anything from upstairs. After you were gone, I asked my dad, 'Why is Lucianne not with us?' and he told me you had to go home. Then I checked my closet, and your friend wasn't there either. And since you mentioned you had to go during dinner, I believed him. I thought you changed your mind about spending the night with us.

"But that night, after I showered, I found droplets of blood by the threshold to one of the guestrooms. They were dried by then, and I was convinced they were paint or something. But lying next to them was a white feather. I knew

248

the feather was from your friend since it was identical to the ones he had. That was when I figured out my dad hadn't told me the truth, but I was too scared to confront him. I thought I would be punished."

"What a coward," Zarah sneered. "Afraid to confront your daddy when the life of your best friend is at risk? What sort of punishment were you afraid of? Because I know for sure that your own daddy wasn't gonna kill you. And what he did to your friend was much worse than a good ole' beating, if that's what you feared."

"I did confront him," Huma whispered, almost inaudibly. "He told me it was all for the better good. He told me they were working on vaccines for serious diseases. That they were trying to stop people from going hungry, and that they only needed you for a little bit. He said that you guys were all well-fed and living in nice rooms and that you wouldn't be hurt at all."

"And you believed him," I concluded flatly.

Zarah shrugged and leaned forward, saying, "She's telling the truth."

Huma shrunk into her chair. "I know I was wrong. But he made it so convincing! I wanted to believe that you were fine because that made things so much easier for me at home. I didn't want to see my dad as someone evil." She paused, and tears crept up into her eyes. "You guys are going to kill him, aren't you?"

I sighed. "Huma, your father-"

"Yes," Mathia answered. Mathias's eyes met mine for an instant before averting to Huma. "Your father will be executed by the end of next week, along with his comrades. Prior to the execution, he will be questioned for the locations of the other members. He's currently residing in the dungeons."

Huma took a sharp breath, her hand trembling as she raised it up to wipe her eye. "Is there... is there anything I can do? I want – no, I-I *need* to see him."

"You'll be able to visit him before the execution takes place, but I'm afraid there is nothing you can do to prevent it,"

Mathias said. "I'm not a liar, and I certainly won't sugarcoat things for you. Your father most likely won't be in a good condition when you see him. I'd suggest you prepare yourself. That is, if you still want to go."

"I do," she whispered, her cheeks glistening with tears.

"I'm sorry, Lucianne. For putting you through this."

"I forgive you," I said, despite Zarah's glance of disapproval. "If you're telling the truth, and Zarah claims you are, then I have no reason to hold a grudge against you. Your father's actions aren't your own. He may have not been a good man, but it's rational for you to love him."

Huma sighed heavily. Considering the drastic changes she had undergone in the past few days, I was surprised she was still managing to stay sane. Just last week, she had been attending classes at Kindred High School, chatting with her friends, reading books at the mini library in her mansion. She had been living the life I had always dreamed of, careless and free of worry.

Now, she was awaiting her father's execution.

"S-so… what happens now?" she asked uncertainly, her bottom lip trembling just like it had on the day we had seen Horseface torturing the cat. How much time had passed since then? A mere couple of months, and yet I felt like an entirely new person.

"We can start over," I said. "As for your stay here in Soratia…" I glanced over at Mathias. He was the only person here that had information on that topic.

"She'll stay here for the time being," Mathias said. "Sorina has already prepared her quarters at Levond's dormitory. If she wishes to return to Earth, she'll have to earn Sorina's trust first, and that won't be easy. Staying here permanently would be safer; some of the Qroes are still out there. Once they catch her, they'll have access to valuable information."

Huma swallowed. "I won't go back. It's too dangerous. They know where I live."

"Then it's settled," Mathias said, stretching his arms. "I'll have the guards escort you to your new quarters. Once you're comfortable enough, you can come to the palace and see your father."

She gave him a small nod. "Okay. I will. And Lucianne... thank you. For giving me another chance."

"Don't mention it."

After she was escorted out, I thanked Zarah for her time and waited for her footsteps to disappear down the hallway as she left. Mathias was the only person remaining in the room, and for a moment, neither of us spoke. I thought of the expression on Huma's face when she'd found out about her father's execution. It must have taken everything she could muster to remain so collected. I tried to picture myself in her position. What would I have done if I found out my mother worked for a sadistic association that tortured and killed kids? It was a difficult question, but I knew one thing—I wouldn't have reacted as calmly as Huma had.

Mathias must have sensed my discomfort because he asked, "What's the matter?"

"I'm just thinking about Huma's dad," I said.

"He was a monster, Lucianne. Don't tell me you're feeling empathy toward him."

"I'm feeling empathy towards Huma," I mumbled. "And, in a way, I'm a monster too."

"Don't be ridiculous," Mathias snapped. "The only monsters around here are those murderers rotting in the dungeons. You're not one of them."

I sat up. "But I am! I'm a murderer. A torturer. The way we questioned that man— Casper—it makes us just as bad as them. *I hate it! I hate everything!*"

His lips parted slightly at my words, a shadow of pain etched upon his face. "Lucianne-"

"I'm sorry," I said. "I don't know what's going on with my emotions. One minute I'm happy, and the next I'm bawling my eyes out. What's wrong with me?"

He knelt down next to my bed, squeezing my hand reassuringly. "Nothing is wrong with you. You're a human experiencing the aftermath of a traumatic event." He smiled softly. "Tell you what. Tomorrow, if you're feeling well enough, we can do anything you'd like. Is there anything you want to do?"

There were many things I wanted to do. I wanted Mei to be alive. I wanted my life to go back to the way it had been a month ago, when my greatest worry was earning a decent grade on a school project. But none of those things were possible. So I settled on something that was.

"I want to see my mother."

Chapter Forty-Four

After paying a quick visit to Adelaine in the Infirmary (she was asleep but looked a lot healthier than she had when I'd last seen her), Mathias and I departed for the palace. It took hours of begging Sorina to let my mother permanently reside in Soratia until she finally agreed. She was pretty reluctant to allow yet another human to venture into her dimension, but Mathias and I convinced her that my mother was trustworthy and wouldn't do anything she wasn't supposed to. I suppose me being the reason the leader of the Qroes was dead helped too. Mathias did his part by reminding her that she did in fact owe me a favor… and an apology. After all, she had sent people to arrest me, hadn't she?

"Here," Mathias handed me the orange pouch. Although I protested, Sorina had insisted on sending two people with me—Lady Hunt and Mr. Bernard. They were both half-bloods, which would make them blend in with the rest of Earth's population, but the powers they possessed were strong enough to defend me against any possible danger.

Lady Hunt was a muscular woman with a dark complexion and even darker hair. She was watchful and silent, a combination that made her look intimidating. It was clear why Sorina had chosen her.

Mr. Bernard, on the other hand, reminded me of my old English teacher—he was in his mid-thirties, and the top of his head was already beginning to bald. I was pretty skeptical about this choice—the man didn't look like he could hurt a fly—until I learned that he had been on the team that had stormed the Qroes' headquarters. Not because he had to, but because he volunteered. That made him ten times more likable.

"Thanks," I said. I began laying out the stones, thinking back to the last time I had done this. Back then, my movements had been hasty, my mind focused only on the possibility of escape. Today, my hands were still moving at a fast pace as I placed down the stones, but this was due to excitement. Excitement and anticipation.

Today was the day I would finally see my mother.

After the stones were all spread out into an oval, Mathias ripped a stick from one of the nearby trees and handed it to me. One tap later, the rippling orange surface made its appearance.

"I'll go first," I said, sliding onto the portal's edge. The soothing warmth felt refreshing on my bare skin. I kicked my feet a little—like a child in a swimming pool—to rid myself of the adrenaline building up inside of me.

Mathias gave me a small wave. One side of his mouth lifted into a crooked smile. Then he moved so swiftly that I didn't notice until I felt his firm hand on my back, and by then it was too late.

"Don't you-" I began to say, but my warning was cut short as I was pushed over the edge and into the thick substance.

It wasn't as bad as last time. The pain of the needles felt like it had reduced by fifty percent. Like Mathias had said, you got used to it pretty quickly.

Halfway through, I realized that I hadn't thought of a place to teleport to, but my subconsciousness had taken care of that. I emerged into the playground from my childhood, right next to the swing set. It was fortunate that the place was pretty much in the middle of the woods; otherwise, people would have seen us, and that would have brought trouble.

The playground was four blocks away from my mother's apartment. That was slightly less than the distance I usually had to travel in order to get to school. Good enough.

I rolled away from the glowing oval suspended in the sky as Lady Hunt descended, followed by Mr. Bernard. They were dressed in normal attire, but the way they looked around with interest was likely to earn us some stares from the locals. Typically, humans weren't too fascinated by the average playground.

"This way," I said, pointing to a thin road cutting through the tree line. "We'll be on my street in ten minutes."

The array of apartment buildings on Clark Street seemed greyer than usual, but I suppose *everything* looked greyer when compared to the bustling streets of Soratia. Aside from the occasional passerby, the streets here were pretty much empty, the air infected with the smoke billowing from someone's cigarette. That someone turned out to be a group of smokers gathered right outside of our apartment complex, the same ones I was used to seeing every day on my way to school. Lady Hunt glared at them as we passed.

We entered the building, and I saw Lady Hunt wrinkle her nose at the stale smell of the foyer. I had become so used to it over the years that it didn't bother me at all. I stopped right in front of my mother's door, waiting with my fist raised until Mr. Bernard joined us.

I knocked.

There was some commotion on the inside, which took me by surprise. It was uncommon for my mother to have guests. It was also uncommon for her not to be at work, so I came to the conclusion that today was Sunday. It had to be. She had work every other day.

The doorknob jiggled and my mother's face poked through, traces of laughter disappearing as soon as she saw my face. For a moment, she was still in shock. Her eyes swiveled to the people standing behind me. Then back to me.

Then the glass she had been holding dropped to the floor, spilling wine all over her carpet.

"Estelle?" a woman's voice called from our living room. "Is everything alright? I heard something break."

My mother either didn't hear her or pretended not to. Instead, she pulled me into an embrace so tight all remaining air was ripped from my lungs. I hugged her back, my chest flooding with warmth as I inhaled the lavender aroma of her perfume. Five months. That's how long it had been since I'd last seen her in person. But it felt like much longer, like years had passed since we'd last been together.

The woman from the living room must have deciphered the silence as a negative sign because she ventured into the hallway where my mother and I were standing. I lifted my gaze to see just who this visitor was.

And my heart dropped when I saw her.

The woman was one of my mother's best friends from high school. She had cut her hair, and it now hung just below her ears, the brown locks curled into a style similar to the ones I often saw on magazine covers. The baby-pink sweater she wore was expensive-- I could see the designer brand's logo on the collar. But her wealth hadn't changed her personality—she was a kind woman, one that I had always been very fond of.

She was also the mother of Victoria, the girl that had bullied me throughout my childhood.

"Lucianne?" she said. Her face was shocked for a second, and then her mouth spread into a wide grin. "Back so soon! Did you enjoy your stay with your auntie?"

I glanced at my mother, raising an eyebrow. She avoided my gaze and rushed to the kitchen to get supplies for the scattered glass. *Great,* I thought. *So this must be the story she made up to excuse my absence.* The only problem was that I wasn't particularly skilled at making up stories.

"Yes," I said quickly. "Of course. But I'm on a tight schedule right now, and I need to talk to my mom in private, if you don't mind. Maybe you could come over later?" I offered, looking behind me to see if Lady Hunt and Mr. Bernard were still behind me. They were.

Mrs. Hill nodded. "Of course I don't mind, dear. I'll let you gals catch up." She gave me a reassuring smile and leaned back to look into the living room. "Honey, we're leaving. Get off that phone and come here."

The girl that emerged through the doorway looked so different, I almost didn't recognize her. Her sleek, brown hair had been bleached blond, and two purple highlights glared at

256

me from the front. She was wearing layers of lip gloss and foundation, her arms covered with bracelets of various designs. Her eyes seemed to be glued to her phone, and she wore an expression of annoyance as she lazily walked into the hallway. When she saw me, they widened in surprise.

"Lucianne." She inclined her head in my direction, acknowledging my existence.

"Victoria," I replied coolly. My hands fisted and pressed into my hips. It was all I could do to prevent them from trembling. Mrs. Hill didn't notice; she was chatting with Mr. Bernard, who must have been making up some pretty funny story, because she kept laughing at every other sentence that left his mouth.

Victoria pursed her lips. "You've changed," she noted.

"So have you." My fingers were very visibly pulsing, and I gritted my teeth. As much as I wanted to smack that smug look off her face, I couldn't risk hurting her. It would cause a commotion, and that would waste our time.

"Come on, Vicky! What's the hold-up?" Mrs. Hill called from the front entrance, sparing me from Victoria's company.

"Coming," Victoria grumbled. She was gone without another look in my direction. The door shut behind them, Mr. Bernard and Lady Hunt moving to stand just inside of the threshold.

My mother ushered me into the kitchen and pointed to the chair I always sat in.

"What is it?" she asked, her worried eyes scanning over my face. "I wasn't expecting your visit, Luce. Your father told me his people rarely allowed others to exit the dimension. What happened?"

I smiled, hoping it would minimize the effect of what I was about to say. "Nothing serious, Mom. I just realized that you must have been pretty lonely down here on your own, so I want you to come live with us in Soratia."

Her eyebrows raised at this, slightly. "For how long?"

"Forever."

Chapter Forty-Five

Sorina demanded to see my mother immediately after our return, so I led her up the marble steps, politely bowing my head at the bald doorman. She had agreed to live with me with no hesitation, and I promised I would tell her everything that had happened to me after I was taken.

Mathias was waiting just below the steps. He greeted my mother with a handshake. She was nearly as amazed as I had been during my first day in Soratia and managed to survive the portal ride without throwing up. That was an accomplishment worthy of praise.

Room 106, marked with the letters "SOR", had the same golden knocker I remembered from the few times I had seen it. Because Sorina had asked us to meet in the dining hall this morning, this would be the first time I entered her office since running off to rescue Adelaine. I picked up the knocker and dropped it, the dull thud of its impact with the eagle's head making my mother flinch.

"Door's open," Sorina's voice called out. Mathias reached the door before me, holding it open for us as we walked through. I gave him a small smile as I passed.

"Good evening, Your Majesty."

I bowed, squeezing my mother's arm to tell her to do the same. She took the hint.

I heard Sorina stand up and walk toward us, her footsteps slow and steady. "It is a pleasure to meet you, Ms. Allaire. Your daughter is a hero." She extended her hand, waiting for my mother to shake it.

"A hero?" My mother stared at me. "In what way?"

Sorina placed her hand on my mother's shoulder, her crimson eyes shining with pride. "Your daughter defeated the danger that ravaged my people for decades. She risked her life, allowing herself to face the unthinkable, leading us to the place we had always searched for-- the enemy's lair."

My mother's lips thinned. "You forced my- my... you forced Lucianne... to-"

"No," I said firmly. "*I* was the one that wanted to do it. These people took one of my friends, Mom. I knew the risks. But," I jabbed my thumb into my chest, "I'm alive. So whatever you are about to say won't change things because what's done is done."

I saw her swallow. I hadn't gotten a proper look at her ever since we left Earth, but now I could see that the gray strings of hair had nearly tripled on her head, and her skin seemed almost as papery and frail as the skin of that old woman that had been shot by the Qroes all those months ago.

She grasped my arm. "You have to tell me *everything*, Luce. Please. I don't understand a thing these people are saying. What enemy? W-what did they do to you? Where-"

"Mom. Relax." I held her gaze, taking her hands into mine. "I promise I'll tell you everything you want to know after you rest. Speaking of which," I turned towards Sorina, "where will my mother reside? My quarters are at the dormitory, but I'm pretty sure that's for students only."

"Both of you will stay at the palace," Sorina said. "It's the least I can do to represent my gratitude for your bravery. I will have Cornelia escort you to your rooms."

She pressed the bell on her desk. No sound came out of it, but someone must have heard something because Cornelia arrived moments later, flushed and out of breath.

"Yes, Your Highness?"

"Please escort Ms. Allaire and her daughter to their chambers. You have prepared them, I assume?"

"Yes, Your Highness." She did a little bow and beckoned me towards her. "Follow me."

*   *   *

Our rooms were conjoined, something that both my mother and I were grateful for. I missed living with her and was glad that we would be able to do so again. The rooms had balconies that looked out onto the city, where I could see hundreds of homes lighting up as the two suns set below the valley. Peaceful. My mother gazed in awe at the view, unable to take her eyes off the window.

"It's getting late, Mom," I murmured, wrapping my arms around her. "You should rest. I know how exhausting it is to travel inter-dimensionally."

She nodded slowly but didn't move from her spot. "That blond boy we just saw… who is he to you?" she asked. Her words were beginning to slur, and I could tell she was struggling to stay on her feet.

"Just a friend," I replied. "You're tired. So… get yourself to bed. I don't think I'll be able to carry you, and I certainly don't want to leave you here on the floor."

She nodded again, and this time, her feet began to shuffle toward the door that led to her room. "Doesn't seem like a friend to me," she muttered.

This was not the type of conversation I enjoyed having with my mom late into the evening. Things tended to get deep when you talked about them at night, and I would surely say something I would later regret.

"Go to sleep, Mom. Your mind will be clearer in the morning."

"Are you trying to avoid me?" she said accusingly, but her words were becoming more slurred by the second. I doubted she would remember our conversation tomorrow.

"Yes. Goodnight," I said. I closed the door in her face, knowing she would have no energy left to re-open it. That gave her only one choice—going to sleep.

I changed into my nightgown, drowsiness settling over me like a blanket. A fluffy blanket, one that I wanted to wrap around my body, allowing it to absorb all my thoughts as I gave in to the blissful slumber.

But instead of slipping beneath the covers, I headed onto the balcony, wanting to feel the fresh breeze tousling my hair once more before I retreated to my room. The city was spread out before me like a map, the twinkling lights reminding me that I was looking at thousands of different lives. Most of them, I would never get to know. Most of them would never know me either. It was safe to say that I was insignificant.

"Beautiful, isn't it?" a voice drifted to me from the balcony to my left, pulling me from my thoughts.

Mathias was sitting on the edge of his balcony, leaning over so far, I was worried he would fall off. Then I remembered that he had working wings, which made me feel like an idiot. Exhaustion had clouded my thinking.

"I thought your room was 116," I said. "What are you doing out here?"

Mathias shrugged. "I like the view. My room looks out over the garden, so I typically come here to look at the city. It's almost always empty." Then, as if sensing my thoughts, he jumped off. He shot down so quickly, I couldn't see where he went until his head popped up from below my balcony. "Mind if I join you?"

"Not at all," I said, moving away from the edge to let him pull himself up. He was wearing nothing but shorts, and I averted my gaze from his bare chest. Staring would have been ill-mannered.

Mathias moved up next to me, and I could feel the tips of his wings brushing against my back. "I like your nightgown."

"Thanks," I said. "I like your… shorts."

He laughed, so clearly and loudly, I was certain it would wake my mother. That would be the last thing I needed—what would she think of me sitting alone on the balcony with a shirtless boy? Whatever it was, it wouldn't be good.

"I should thank you," he said, changing the subject. "Properly. For everything you did back in the headquarters. If it wasn't for you, I would be dead."

"If it wasn't for me, you would have never gone to the headquarters in the first place," I said, imitating his tone.

He cracked a smile. "True. But back there, you didn't have to save me. Keeping yourself alive should have been your priority."

"If I was the reason you were out there, the least I could do was to prevent you from dying," I said, rolling my eyes. "Plus, my plan wouldn't have been possible without you."

"Your plan was genius. How did you even manage to trick that guard in the first place? I tried everything I could think of with mine, but they were stubborn as hell."

Now it was my turn to smirk. "It was pretty coincidental. I overheard him talking about me with one of the other guards and pretended to be interested in him until his gun was in my hand. Worked better than I thought."

"Genius," he repeated. "My parents would be impressed. You should have seen their faces when I told them about what you did with the Griffin's wings. Shock and amazement mixed into one." He leaned back. "They'd love to meet you. Would that be alright with you? It wouldn't be proper not to introduce them to you after I've met your mother."

"I'd like to meet them too," I said. He was sitting so close to me, I could feel the warmth radiating off his body. It made my skin tingle.

Mathias smiled, and I felt his arm sliding around my back, wrapping gently around my side. "Tomorrow," he said. "You can meet them tomorrow. Promise."

I just nodded slowly, afraid to move from my spot. Afraid to do anything that might remove his arm from my side. We simply sat in silence, gazing at the spiraling galaxies above us, his wings shielding me from the cool evening wind. An overwhelming feeling of happiness washed over me. The more I thought about it, the more absurd it seemed—me sitting on the balcony of a palace, leaning against the shoulder of a boy with wings. And yet it felt so right… as if it was all I wanted for the rest of eternity. I sighed, shifting my legs closer to Mathias. My mother had been right.

He wasn't just a friend.

262

Epilogue

Two weeks after my return from Earth, the queen threw a ball in my honor. It was one of those events I had dreamt of throughout my childhood— ballgowns, ballrooms, fancy dances among royalty. Those dreams didn't make me very special. Every girl could dream of attending a ball.

Except, in most cases, those dreams didn't turn into reality.

But that wasn't the main reason why I was looking forward to the event. The ball served as a distraction, not only for me but for numerous others. Mathias, Huma, Adelaine and Zarah, all of whom had been grieving just over five days ago, were now cheerfully preparing themselves for what would likely be one of the most memorable events of their lives.

Adelaine, having made a nearly complete recovery in a little over a week, spent most of her time searching for a ballgown. After a long three days of being dragged around boutiques and shops, I stumbled upon a gown she deemed suitable for the ball. It was emerald green and made entirely of satin, with a stunning pearl-beaded corset to match. It also cost a thousand plets. That was a price she would not have been able to pay, had Sorina not lent her cash.

My own ballgown, which had been made by Sorina's personal tailor, was crimson red. Adelaine had said the color complimented my hair, and that she approved of its quality. The corset it came with was embedded with diamonds and felt kind of tight against my ribs, but Adelaine assured me that was normal. It wasn't anything I couldn't withstand.

Since I was the reason the whole event was taking place, I spent the last two hours before the ball being "prepared" for my grand entrance. Those preparations involved me sitting in a room crowded with stylists and makeup artists, who put my hair through all sorts of experiments. Thankfully, they decided to go for a natural look when applying the make-up, so I didn't wind up looking five years older.

Everyone who could afford formal clothing could attend. Sorina allowed me to invite ten of my own guests, who, regardless of their financial state, would receive enough cash from her to purchase their own clothing. Most of those guests were my classmates, with the exceptions of Huma and my mother.

"When the music starts, the doors will open," Cornelia told me. We were standing right outside the dark mahogany doors that led to the ballroom. "Smile and wave at the crowd, and do a little bow, and then go stand next to the Queen. She'll do a short speech, and you know the rest."

I nodded. We had gone over this before, and by now the plan was drilled into my head. Go out, stand next to Sorina, go down the stairs, and dance. Mathias would be my partner. We had devoted hours to practicing our dance and perfecting every move. Neither of us were talented dancers, but the dance we would be doing was pretty simple. I doubted any of us would mess up.

The orchestra began to play and the doors were thrown open before me, revealing a marble balcony. Stairs led down to the floor below, on which I could see hundreds of guests, all of them dressed in formal attire. My heart thudded steadily against my constricted ribs. I did a curt bow, lifting the edges of my skirt as I smiled at the crowd. There were half-bloods and Soratians, young and old, all gathered in the queen's palace to celebrate our victory.

My victory.

I made my way towards Sorina, who politely inclined her head in my direction. Then she began her speech. It started off with a greeting, as all speeches do, and soon moved on to congratulating me and the others that had gone to the Qroes' headquarters. I stopped listening when she began listing the names of the victims. Instead, I focused on Mathias, who was standing at the foot of the stairs, dressed in a black tuxedo. He saw me and smiled. I smiled back.

"-thank you," Sorina concluded her speech, and the orchestra began to play once more. I walked to the staircase. I hadn't practiced this part in my ballgown (it had been reserved for the ball), so my descent was pretty slow. Looking at the crowd was out of the question. My eyes were fixed on the stairs, or at least the sliver of the stairs that I *could* see, making sure I didn't miss a step.

Mathias took my arm the moment my heels stepped on the floor. The music slowed. I could feel the eyes of every guest in the room trailing after me as I made my way to the center of the room. Mathias's hand was planted firmly against my lower back, guiding me through the crowd.

The crimson skirt of my gown flared as he twirled me around. Layers upon layers of cloth, all different shades of red, whirled around me like a ravenous fire eager to consume my body. I smiled. Our waltz had begun to play.

But even the orchestra could not take my mind off of the palace's dungeons still flooded with men, just a few meters below my feet. Some of these men would be executed upon sunrise. Others would have to wait until they had been questioned. They were murderers, these men. Their deaths were well-deserved.

And what most of the guests didn't know, was that I was a murderer, too.

The End

Acknowledgements

Writing a book is not an easy task, so I owe thanks to many for guiding me through the process. None of this would have been possible without my parents, who stood by me during every struggle, never failing to show their support. A huge thank you to Cassandra Rein for her incredibly helpful criticism. Your keen eye has caught errors that many others did not, and for that, I am tremendously grateful. To Isabelle Townley and Kiera A., thank you so much for your suggestions on improving my novel. The feedback you provided me with shaped my story into something worth reading. Thank you to Karlie Mitchell and Poppy Dyer for always being reliable and ready to help. You have made my writing experience so much more enjoyable! Thank you to Alyssa Goddard, for dedicating your time to scrolling through my manuscript and pointing out both the good and the bad in my story. A special thank you to Haajar Yamani, for being there whenever I needed you, and always putting a smile on my face. You are truly an amazing friend.

And lastly, thank you to my supporters, for giving me the confidence to share my work with the world. This book would not exist without you.

About the Author

Dominika Pindor is a teenage author. She was coming up with stories before she could even write and was only fourteen years of age when she published her first novel. She was born in Poland in 2006, and currently resides in Illinois with her parents, sister, and dog. Her writing career has just begun, and she hopes to continue publishing books as she enters high school.